ALEX KAVA

ONE FALSE MOVE

MIRA

MIRA®

ISBN 0-7783-2189-4

ONE FALSE MOVE

Copyright © 2004 by S. M. Kava.

www.MIRABooks.com

Printed in U.S.A.

To
Deborah Groh Carlin

I couldn't have gotten through this one without your steady reassurance, your barrage of questions, your constant challenges, the occasional swift kick in the pants and, oh yes, your unwavering enthusiasm, love and support.

Thank you.

ACKNOWLEDGMENTS

I am constantly amazed at how willing and patient people are in sharing their experiences and expertise with me. They contribute not only interesting tidbits to my novels, but a wealth of flavor and color and knowledge and credibility that could never come from any other source. Special thanks to:

Amy Moore-Benson, my editor and friend, for once again getting me through my own twists and turns and helping me make sense of it all. Your contribution, your dedication and your expertise constantly challenge me and always improve my books.

Patricia Sierra—fellow author, friend extraordinaire and Emily Dickinson scholar—for being my sounding board, my bearer of logic and my peace of mind. And for this particular novel, thank you for providing an inspiring interpretation of Emily's "'Hope' is the thing with feathers."

Leigh Ann Retelsdorf, Deputy County Attorney and friend, for sharing your stories and experiences with me. You are amazing and a true inspiration.

Detective Sergeant Bill Jadlowski of the Omaha Police Department for showing me that a homicide detective is so much more than the literary caricature we suspense writers tend to portray.

C. L. Retelsdorf, Douglas County Crime Scene Investigator, for describing piece by piece the painstaking process a crime scene investigator goes through. Also for taking me through the Norfolk bank robbery crime scene.

Tammy Partsch, now a reporter for KNCY-radio in Nebraska City, for giving me a reporter's account of what it was like to cover the Norfolk bank robbery for KUSO-radio in Norfolk, Nebraska.

John Keenan, *Omaha World Herald* columnist, for sharing your personal trials and tribulations of dealing with a broken collarbone.

The fantastic crew at MIRA Books: Dianne Moggy, Craig Swinwood, Stacy Widdrington, Tania Charzewski, Loriana Sacilotto and Krystyna de Duleba, along with your amazing teams. Special thanks to Christine Langone, Pat Muir-Rand and Mike Smith and his incredible staff for rearranging your busy schedules to accommodate my book. And once again, a humble thank-you to Alex Osuszek and the best sales force in the publishing business.

Maureen Stead, at MIRA Books, for your amazing patience and for always taking such good care of me.

Megan Underwood and Goldberg McDuffie Communications, Inc., for your continued enthusiasm and dedication.

Patricia Kava, my mom, for being one of my biggest fans despite my use of blood and violence (and the "F-word") in my books.

Sharon Car, fellow writer and friend, for always encouraging and listening.

Mary Means and Tammy Hall for taking care of my two most valuable possessions while I'm on the road.

Walter, Emilie and Patti Carlin for all the delicious meals and for taking such good care of me while I hid out to write a chunk of this novel in the comfortable confines of your beautiful home.

Also very special thanks to Kenny and Connie Kava, Patti El-Kachouti, Marlene Haney, Sandy Rockwood, Jeanie Shoemaker Mezger and John Mezger, Annie Belatti, Nicole and Tony Friend, Gene Egnoski and Rich Kava for your love and support, your friendship and your patience in putting up with my long absences.

Once again a humble and sincere thank-you to:

The many book buyers, booksellers and librarians for selling and recommending my books.

And to the readers—you inspire and challenge me, and I thank all of you for allowing me to continue doing what I love.

Lastly, this past year my books have managed to make the bestseller lists not only here in the United States but in Australia, the United Kingdom, Italy, Germany and Poland. I want to thank the publishing teams in each of these countries for doing such a fantastic job and for literally taking me places I never dreamed of going.

PART 1
Blind Man's Bluff

Friday, August 27

1:13 p.m.
Nebraska State Penitentiary—Lincoln, Nebraska

Max Kramer wore his lucky red tie with his blue power suit. While he waited for the guard to unlock the door, he admired his reflection in the glass security window behind them. That Grecian hair formula really worked. He could barely see any of the gray. His wife kept telling him the salt and pepper made him look more distinguished. Of course she would say that. She always said stuff like that when she was suspicious, when she knew he was hunting for someone new. God, she knew him well, better than she realized.

"Big day," the hulk of a guard said to him. But he was scowling instead of smiling.

Max had heard the nicknames the guards had given him in the last several weeks. He knew he

wasn't a popular guy here on death row. But that was
to the guards. To the inmates he had reached hero
status. And they were the ones he cared about; they
were the ones who counted. They needed him to
right their wrongs, to tell their stories, or rather *their*
versions of their stories. Yes, they were the ones
who mattered, but not because he was a bleeding-
heart liberal like the *Omaha World Herald* or the
Lincoln Journal Star seemed pleased to label him.
It was nothing quite as admirable as all that. Quite
simply, all his hard work, all his efforts were for a
day like today. A day when he could watch a client
of his walk out of this concrete hellhole. A day when
he could save his client from the electric chair and
walk alongside him out the front doors and into the
sunlight. The sunlight *and* the spotlight of about two
dozen TV cameras from across the country. CNN's
Larry King had already booked Max and Jared on
his show for tomorrow night. And his red tie would
show up wonderfully tonight when NBC aired his
interview with Brian Williams.

Yes, this was what he had waited for his entire career. All the shitty pay and long hours would be
worth it, and the local media attacks would come to
an end.

He stopped at the doorway to the holding room, pretending to show some respect for his client's privacy.
Pretending. He didn't want to spend any more time
alone with Jared Barnett than necessary. So he watched
from the doorway. Barnett was wearing the same faded

jeans and red T-shirt he had surrendered that first day at the penitentiary five years ago, only now the T-shirt bulged from the muscles Barnett had built up during his days of incarceration. Since Barnett had traded in his orange jumpsuit for street clothes, Max couldn't help thinking how ordinary the man looked. Even his short dark hair had that disheveled but cool look, that just-got-out-of-bed look that Max could never pull off, but that Barnett would probably make trendy after his media appearances.

Max had already made his client out to be the poor misunderstood bad boy who had been framed and then abused by a justice system that had stolen five years of his life. Now Barnett just needed to play the role. He certainly looked it.

The guard at the door stepped aside.

"Paperwork's coming," he said. "You want, you can wait inside."

Max nodded as if grateful for the invitation—for what the guard seemed to consider a courtesy—even though Max preferred that the asshole let him wait in the hall. Too late. Jared saw him and waved him into the holding room. He stood up when Max entered, another courtesy. Jesus! What was this world coming to when convicted murderers started being courteous?

"Relax. Take a load off." Max shoved one of the metal folding chairs in Barnett's direction, scraping it against the floor, the noise grating on his nerves. Only now did he realize he was nervous, nervous that Barnett would screw this up for him.

"Man, I never thought you'd actually be able to pull this off," Barnett said, taking the seat, seemingly not bothered that Max remained standing. It was a trick Max had learned long ago in his early years as a defense attorney. Get the client to sit down while you stand over him, instant authority. At five feet seven inches Max Kramer had to use every trick he could.

"So how does this work?" Barnett asked, even though Max had explained it several times during the appeal. His client sounded as if he believed there was still a catch. "I'm really free to go?"

"Without Danny Ramerez as a witness the prosecution has no case. The rest of the evidence was all circumstantial. As long as there's no eyewitness testimony from Ramerez, there's nothing to connect you to Rebecca Moore." Max watched Barnett, measuring his response, or rather his lack of one. "It was quite admirable of Mr. Ramerez to come forward and finally tell the truth, that he wasn't even there that afternoon."

Barnett smiled up at him, but there was something about his smile that creeped Max out. Never once during the appeal process had he asked how Barnett had managed to get Ramerez to recant his original testimony, but he suspected Barnett had, indeed, made it happen, despite being locked up.

"What about the others?" Barnett asked.

"Excuse me?"

Max waited, but Barnett sat cleaning his fingernails, using his teeth to scrape them out and then bite off the cuticles. He had seen him do this in court—a nervous habit, probably an unconscious one. And now Max wondered if he had heard him correctly. Jesus! What others was he talking about?

Max hadn't handled Barnett's original case, only the appeal. But he wasn't stupid. He knew there had been others. Other women, all murdered with the same M.O. and the signature gunshot wound up through the jaw as if the killer had hoped to remove the victim's identity by shattering her teeth. It didn't matter. Barnett had only been charged with Rebecca Moore's murder. Why the hell would Barnett even be asking about the others?

"What others?" Max finally asked, though he didn't want to know.

"Never mind," Barnett said as he spat out a piece of fingernail then crossed his arms, tucking his hands under his armpits. "You know I don't have a fucking dime to my name, man," he said, changing the subject. "I know you said I don't have to pay you anything, but I feel like I owe you."

Max almost let out a sigh of relief. This was a much safer topic. If there *had* been others, he didn't want to know about them. As far as Max was concerned there had been only one case, one eyewitness. And now there was no eyewitness and no case. If Barnett wanted to get something off his chest he could find a fucking priest. Yes, he preferred that Barnett worry, instead, about paying his debt.

Max knew Jared Barnett was the kind of man who wouldn't like feeling that he owed anyone. He also knew it was a big deal for Barnett to even admit that he might owe him. And that's what he wanted his client to focus on. Max had heard rumors that, after Barnett had been read his sentence of death by the electric chair, he turned to his court-appointed attorney, poor James Pritchard, and told him that it appeared he didn't owe him anything more for his help than a hole in the head. Max liked the idea that Barnett thought he might feel indebted to him. In fact, he was counting on it. "I think we can work something out," he said.

"Sure. Whatever you decide."

"But first I have to warn you. There's a media circus outside waiting for us."

"Cool," Barnett said, standing up. And that's exactly what he looked like—cool and collected, that same lack of emotion that had carried him through the trial and sentencing and every aspect of the appeal process. "So what's the going rate?"

"Excuse me?"

"What are these media blood-suckers willing to pay for an interview?"

Max scratched his head, his own nervous habit which he immediately caught and turned into a smoothing of his hair. Though he wanted to rip his hair out, instead. Christ! He couldn't believe this. The son of a bitch was going to fuck everything up. Money? He expected to be paid for being interviewed?

Max had to watch his temper. He couldn't make it sound as if he even cared whether or not they did the interviews. He couldn't make it seem as though Barnett was doing him a favor. He didn't want Barnett thinking these interviews would be his payback. He needed to think quickly. He needed to appeal to Barnett's core values, to those few essentials that made him tick. One of which, certainly, was not money.

"You're going to be a celebrity overnight, my friend," Max told him, smiling and shaking his head as if he could hardly believe it. "I've got messages from *NBC News, 60 Minutes, Larry King* and even Bill O'Reilly's *The Factor.* You're going to have something money can't buy. But I can understand if you'd rather tell them all to go screw themselves. Whatever you want to do. It's entirely up to you."

He watched as Barnett thought it over, forcing himself to keep quiet, to pretend it didn't matter. He concentrated on breathing, on not thinking about how much he wanted this, how much he *needed* this. He tried to keep his fists from balling up. And in his mind he couldn't stop repeating, almost like a mantra, "Don't you dare fuck it up."

"Bill O'Reilly actually wants me on his show?"

Max swallowed another sigh and calmly managed to say, "Yep, tomorrow night. It's up to you, though. I can tell him…hell, I can tell them all you don't want to put up with the whole lot of them. Whatever you want to do."

"That O'Reilly guy always thinks he's so tough." And now Barnett was smiling again. "I wouldn't mind telling a few of those assholes what I think."

This time Max smiled, too. Perhaps he could control Barnett, after all, but he'd need some sort of insurance. For the first time since he'd met Jared Barnett, Max allowed himself to look deep into those dark, vacant eyes, and now he allowed himself to admit the truth. He knew Jared Barnett had, indeed, killed that poor girl seven years ago. Not only did Max know it, he was counting on it.

Tuesday, September 7

CHAPTER 1

10:30 a.m.
Hall of Justice—Omaha, Nebraska

Grace Wenninghoff hated waiting. The air in courtroom number five felt like a hot, wet towel wrapped around her neck. There were too many people, jammed inside, generating too much heat. The squeaking of chairs as people shifted in their seats and an occasional cough interrupted the silence, but that was all. Judge Fielding's presence kept the crowd agitated but quiet as he looked over the papers in front of him, taking his time, not a hint of sweat or discomfort on his face.

Grace reached for her water bottle, took a careful sip. Come on, let's get this over with, she wanted to yell, but instead tapped her pen against her blank legal pad to keep her foot from doing the same. The judge scowled at her without raising his head, his eyes looking at her through his bushy gray eyebrows and over the wire-rim glasses hanging at the tip of his nose. Her pen stopped in midair. He went back to examining the papers.

Rumor was that the maintenance crew had shut off the air-conditioning in the whole building over the long Labor Day weekend, not expecting the return of ninety-degree weather. Yet, Grace couldn't help wondering if Judge Fielding had purposely shut it off in his own courtroom, hoping to make them all sweat. It wouldn't be the first time. Fielding loved to make attorneys sweat…sweat and wait. That combination today couldn't be a good sign, though Grace tried to remain optimistic. As optimistic as a prosecutor could be with the humidity threatening to turn her usually straight, short hair into something worthy of a Chia Pet. She knew she'd need more than optimism today.

She glanced across the aisle at Warren Penn from the high-priced law firm of Branigan, Turner, Cross and Penn. No sweat visible there, either. How did he manage it in that three-piece suit? She had hoped to see his client, the defendant, Jonathon Richey, in shackles and an orange jumpsuit, reducing the city councilman to the cold-blooded murderer he really was. Instead, Richey wore a steel-blue suit and crisp white shirt with red-and-blue tie. The slick politician didn't look affected in the least by his arrest or the allegations against him. In fact, he looked rather smug, and Grace worried that some old-boy network had already taken care of the outcome of this case. Judge Fielding had a reputation of protecting his inner circle. Could he do it in front of a crowd of spectators and under the scrutiny of the media?

Beneath her own jacket Grace could feel her silk blouse sticking to her skin. She glanced down at it to make sure it didn't look as bad as it felt. What a day to wear silk. The blouse had been a birthday gift from Grandma Wenny, who had been trying to dress Grace in pink since she was six years old, although her grandmother had reassured her that this was fuchsia, her German accent making it sound like some erotic, slightly naughty color. Thinking about that made Grace smile.

She watched Judge Fielding, looking for signs that they'd be proceeding soon. He flipped over another page and started at the top with his index finger. Geez. This was only the bail hearing. At this rate, she couldn't imagine how long the trial would take.

She reached to rub the knot still gathered at the base of her neck. The three-day weekend had been too short. Her husband, Vince, insisted they could live with the stacked boxes everywhere. Easy for him to say, he was leaving for Switzerland tomorrow morning. Sure it was business—a new client insisting on meeting his American account rep face-to-face. Grace and Emily would be left to live with the chaos. But the boxes weren't the cause of the knot at the back of her neck.

She loved their new house, although it was far

from new, a century-old Victorian with plenty of character and enough space for them to convert part of it into a mother-in-law suite—or in this case a grandmother suite—for Grandma Wenny. The renovations were a pain in the neck—yes, maybe even a partial cause for the very real pain in her neck. There'd been workers tramping in and out of their house, leaving mud and sawdust and holes where walls once were. Still, Grace knew all of this was the easy part. The real work, the real challenge, would be in convincing Grandma Wenny to leave her South Omaha home, the small drafty two-bedroom, mouse-infested bungalow where she had lived for over sixty years, where she had raised three children and one granddaughter, a granddaughter who had pledged—actually pinkie-swore—to take care of the stubborn old woman.

"Ms. Wenninghoff," Judge Fielding bellowed, grabbing her attention.

"Yes, Your Honor." She stood up casually, resisting the urge to wipe her damp forehead.

"Please continue," he told her as if they'd been waiting only a few minutes and as if *she* had been the one holding them up.

"As I was saying and as you can see from the arrest warrant, Mr. Richey was arrested at Eppley Airport. Mr. Richey is a flight risk and, therefore, should be denied bail."

"Judge, this is preposterous." Warren Penn drew the word out so slowly it sounded like four words instead of one. He also took his time standing up, then moved out from behind the defense table as if he required additional room to make his statement. Grace guessed it was more for the benefit of towering over her.

"Mr. Richey," he continued in the same drawn-out manner, "is a businessman. He was simply making a business trip. This trip has been on his calendar for months. I have his appointment calendar and phone logs available for Your Honor." He waved a hand at the pile on the defense table but made no effort to get them. "Jonathon Richey," he went on, "not only owns a local business here in Omaha, but he's a city councilman. He's a deacon at his church and president of the downtown Rotary Club. His wife, two of his three children and all five of his grandchildren live within this community. Mr. Richey certainly does not pose a flight risk. Taking all this into consideration, Your Honor, I'm sure you'll agree that Mr. Richey should be released on his own recognizance."

Grace watched Judge Fielding nod and start flipping through the papers again. This was ridiculous. He couldn't possibly be buying any of this crap. Not unless he was looking for an excuse. She glanced over at Richey. Was there some under-the-table deal already set up? He still looked too calm, too cool for this sauna. Grace rubbed her neck again and was disappointed to find it damp.

"Your Honor." She waited until she had his attention, then she pulled out an envelope from her file folders and stepped out from behind the prosecution table. "If I understand correctly, Mr. Richey owns a business that specializes in commercial and residential computerized heating units." She looked over at Warren Penn, waiting for his nod of confirmation. "I have his United airline ticket that was confiscated at the time of his arrest." She made her way forward to hand over the envelope with the ticket inside. "I'm just wondering, Your Honor, what kind of heating business Mr. Richey might have in the Cayman Islands."

She heard the crowd behind her hum and whisper and shift in their seats.

"Mr. Penn?" Judge Fielding was now looking over his glasses and down his nose at the defense attorney. To Grace's disappointment, Warren Penn didn't flinch.

"Mr. Richey meets with his clients, often in a designated place that the client requests."

Grace wanted to roll her eyes. That Fielding was even considering this was crazy. But here he was again, flipping over papers as if he had missed something in the documents he had already examined.

She turned back to her table and noticed Detective Tommy Pakula sitting two rows down, shifting in his seat, impatient and ready. He was dressed for court, a collared shirt and tie, jacket and trousers, just in case she needed to call him today. Instead of calling him, she reached down behind her chair and pulled up the duffel bag.

"Your Honor," she said, bringing the bag out in full view of Judge Fielding, but more importantly in full view of the courtroom, "there is one more thing Mr. Richey had in his possession when Detectives Pakula and Hertz arrested him at Eppley Airport. He had this travel bag with him. If he was not fleeing the country, perhaps Mr. Penn might explain this." Grace unzipped the bag and turned it upside down, allowing the stacks of hundred-dollar bills to fall out onto the table.

This time the room erupted. Several reporters clamored out the door. Warren Penn shook his head as if, of course, he had an explanation for this, too. Grace scanned the room, and now she noticed that Jonathon Richey's smug look was gone.

"Okay, okay," Judge Fielding yelled, ignoring the gavel. He seemed pleased that his voice could still silence a room.

"Your Honor," Warren Penn began, but was interrupted when Fielding put up a hand.

"Bail denied." He stood even as he added, "Court is adjourned," and then escaped, not giving Warren Penn the opportunity to explain or argue.

Grace ignored the defense table as she repacked the duffel bag. The crowd had already turned into a crescendo of voices, shuffling feet and creaking chairs. She wouldn't need to worry about being accosted by reporters. They'd spend their energies on Richey, the price of being such an upstanding member of the community.

"Better make sure it's all there." She looked up to find Detective Pakula.

"Thanks for being here," she told him. He nodded, and she knew Pakula well enough to leave it at that, not to make a big deal of it.

"I found a witness who might be willing to testify against Richey."

"Might?"

"He needs some convincing. Doesn't wanna open his mouth if there's a chance he'll walk."

"He won't be walking," Grace said, finally shoving the last of the money into the bag. She knew where Pakula was going with this, and she didn't want to hear it.

"You know that and I know that. And that's what I'm trying to tell him." Pakula looked around, making sure no one was within earshot. "Our credibility's not riding too high right now with that asshole Barnett on every fucking talk show claiming the OPD framed him."

"Let him talk. Sooner or later he's going to screw up, and when he does I'll be there to nail his ass. Only next time it'll be for good."

"You and me both."

Grace knew the Barnett appeal had been eating at Pakula as much as it had been at her. In the last several months she had gone over and over the case against Barnett, hoping there was something, *any-thing* they might use. Five years ago, she had put her heart and soul into prosecuting Barnett, convinced that it was, indeed, Jared Barnett who had coerced seventeen-year-old Rebecca Moore into his pickup that cold afternoon in the dead of winter, probably promising her a warm ride home from school. But instead he drove her to a remote place where he raped and stabbed her repeatedly before shooting her through the jaw, shattering her teeth.

There were others. Four women, killed in the same manner, all within two years. Grace and Pakula were still convinced that Jared Barnett was the killer in each case. But other than circumstantial evidence, Rebecca's case was the only one they could actually connect to Barnett. That connection was Danny Ramerez and his eyewitness testimony, testimony that he saw Rebecca getting into a black pickup being driven by Jared Barnett the afternoon she disappeared. It had been testimony so convincing, so descriptive, that the jury hadn't hesitated to convict him. Then suddenly, after five years, Danny Ramerez confessed he hadn't even been out that afternoon. Without his testimony, Barnett was free. It was as simple as that.

What wasn't simple was the amount of criticism leveled at the police department and the prosecutor's office. So much so that even a recent string of convenience-store robberies had the media impatient for a resolution.

Grace glanced at the defense table, noticing that Penn and Richey had started to make their way out the door, taking a good portion of the crowd with them. That's when she saw him.

Jared Barnett stood in the back row, waiting his turn to get out the door—standing and waiting as if he were just one of the spectators.

"Speak of the devil," she said to Pakula and he followed her gaze.

"Son of a bitch," he muttered. "I saw him outside on the steps one day last week, too. Just can't stay away, can he?"

Grace had seen him, too, only it was in the coffee shop across the street from the courthouse, and then again right outside her dry cleaner's. She tried to convince herself it was Jared Barnett's way of thumbing his nose at them, at them all. Not that he had singled her out. But just as he got to the door he looked over at her, and he smiled.

CHAPTER 2

7:30 p.m.
Logan Hotel—Omaha, Nebraska

Jared Barnett listened for the elevator, waiting for the grind and scrape of metal, the whine of the hydraulics. Where the hell was he?

He stayed in the shadows and leaned against the wall, ignoring the avalanche of plaster his shoulder set loose. No one had seen him enter the building. No one except the skinny crack whore with dirty-blond hair and eyes so glazed over she'd never remember what day it was, let alone his face.

At the end of the hall someone was cooking spinach. God! He hated that smell. It reminded him of his stepfather who'd forced him to eat everything off his plate, and if he didn't, the bastard shoved his face into the green glob of shit. He couldn't help thinking the stench belonged here. It was a perfect addition to the

dog piss on the carpet and the cockroaches skittering in and out of cracks and under doors. It also
seemed the perfect place for Danny Ramerez to call
home.

He shifted his weight from his left foot to his right
then switched the sacks of takeout to his other hand.
The food would be cold, though it didn't matter
much. He was hungry and he loved Chinese food,
even cold Chinese food. Although he was getting
tired of holding the bags. He had thought about setting them down, but the fucking roaches would be
all over them in seconds.

Jared checked his wristwatch, needing to squint
to make out the time in the dim light. Ramerez was
late. Why the fuck was he late? He had followed him
three nights in a row and could probably set his watch
to him. Now, all of a sudden, the bastard was late. But
then he heard the elevator, the screech and then the
whine. He was on his way up.

Jared stayed in the shadows, waiting. Reaching
the sixth floor took forever, a noisy journey of
squeaky pulleys and wobbling metal. He was glad he
had taken the stairs up. Finally the doors opened.

Danny Ramerez looked smaller in this crappy
light. Jared watched him walk down the hallway,
one of those jerky walks with quick little steps.
Ramerez was at his door with the key in the lock before Jared started down the hall after him.

"Hey, man," he said and Ramerez nodded without looking up. "How ya doing, Danny?"

This time Ramerez did a double take, his eyes getting wide as he recognized Jared.

"I brought us some takeout," he told him, wanting to calm his worries and holding up the bags. "Chinese."

"What are you doing here?"

"What are you talking about? You didn't think I'd come by and say hey?"

Ramerez finally got the door opened, but now he hesitated.

"You did me a big favor," Jared said, this time with a smile. "I just wanted to buy you dinner and say thanks."

Ramerez was studying him, meeting his eyes as if looking for the truth there. Then suddenly he looked away and shrugged. "You don't owe me anything. Your redheaded friend already paid me. Even threw in a laptop computer."

Jared smiled again; it didn't take much to buy off someone like Danny Ramerez. He understood him all too well. That's why he couldn't trust him. "Hey man, it's just some kung pao chicken and chow mein. A few egg rolls. It's no big deal."

He let Ramerez think about it while he stood there pretending it *was* no big deal, still not making any attempt to leave. Finally Ramerez shrugged again and waved him into the small apartment that looked like a cross between a rummage sale and a garbage dump. A pile of clothes covered a threadbare recliner, and Jared could smell what had to be dirty socks or rotten eggs. Magazines and comic books were stacked on the floor. A collection of beer bottles and cans shared the shelves with discarded take-out wrappers and foam containers. A cardboard pizza box lay open on the coffee table with two pieces left, the toppings suddenly skittering out of the box.

Ramerez started shoving things aside as if to tidy up for his guest. While he moved stacks and collected trash, Jared pulled out an oversize, black trash bag from one of the take-out bags and began laying it over the scuffed linoleum floor in the middle of the room. Ramerez glanced at him a couple of times before he stopped.

"What are you doing?"

"I don't want to make a mess," Jared told him.

Ramerez laughed. "You're kidding, right?"

He came over to take a closer look, examining the plastic and even walking onto it, stepping carefully as if looking for a trap. But, of course, he didn't see it. He was still looking down at the black plastic under his feet when Jared whipped the knife out from the same take-out bag. All it took was one slash up under and across the throat, so quick that Ramerez saw his own blood splatter the plastic. He grabbed at the wound, his fingers slipping into the gaping flesh as if attempting to hold it together. His wide eyes met Jared's, shock and realization contorting his entire face before he finally crumpled onto the plastic.

Jared looked around the room and decided on the

recliner. He shoved the clothes off, checked for cock-roaches, then grabbed the other take-out bag and sat down. Danny Ramerez wasn't going anywhere. There was no big hurry to take out the trash. Jared Barnett pulled out a plastic fork and the container of kung pao chicken and began to eat.

Wednesday, September 8

CHAPTER 3

7:00 a.m.
Omaha, Nebraska

Melanie Starks quickened her pace. The sun peeked over the bell towers of St. Cecelia's Cathedral. The days were already growing shorter. Summer was almost over but was making one last grand stand. It was only the beginning of her walk, and already Melanie could feel her breathing becoming labored. The air was thick and heavy with moisture.

She studied the horizon in the opposite direction. Having cursed sunrises for years she almost hated to admit how much she enjoyed them now. But this morning's sunrise gave her a bad feeling, even a sudden chill as a trickle of sweat made its way down her back. The sun was barely able to squeeze through the storm clouds that were gathering, a gravestone-gray sky streaked bloodred. It was an eerie combination, and she could hear her mother repeating one of her silly superstitions:

> "Red sky in morning,
> Sailors take warning.
> Red sky at night,
> Sailors delight."

The weather only seemed to fuel her restlessness, to ignite her disappointment, her frustration… Oh, hell, she should call it what it was—her anger. Yeah, that's right. She was angry, pissed off. Jared hadn't been back two weeks and already things were changing.

She resented having to cut short her morning walk. What was it about *his* sudden freedom that took precedence over her own? That's what it felt like when he called last night and left the message to meet him for breakfast. Summoning her as if he could still boss her around just like when they were kids. He used that brief yet demanding tone of his, "Meet me at that place we talked about. It's time."

"It's time," she mimicked under her breath. She had no idea what the hell he was talking about. It was as if he was talking in code. As if they were kids again, plotting one of their childhood conspiracies. Ever since he had gotten back he *had* been planning something, something big or so he kept saying. But, of course, he couldn't tell her until it was time. That was Jared, so secretive and always calling the shots. He expected complete loyalty with no questions and no hesitation. It had always been that way. Like the Rebecca Moore thing. Jared didn't even bother explaining, instead he insisted the police got it wrong. Melanie knew that could happen. She'd seen it happen years before.

She pumped her arms, keeping her pace and not letting her anger slow her down. She hated that Jared made her feel like she still owed him. It didn't help that she wasn't there for him during the trial.

It was as if nothing had changed in the five years he had been away. And yet everything had changed. *She* had changed, or at least, she thought she had. Although it couldn't have been very much. Why else would she be rushing to meet him, rushing once again to do whatever her big brother told her to do? Like cutting short what had become her daily ritual, her daily gospel and the replacement for a quick fix of nicotine and later still, for four cups of hot scorching coffee. The coffee had helped her get through the initial withdrawal from the cigarettes. Now this new addiction, a three-mile morning walk, replaced the caffeine.

She didn't need Dr. Phil to see she had simply transferred compulsions. She took the same walk every day at the same time. Even walked at the same pace. Only today she had to quicken the pace if she intended to meet Jared. Quicken, she decided, but not cut short. She pushed back her shoulders as if this one defiant thought was the same as standing up to her big brother. Something she had never been able to do in the past. But that was the past. Maybe Jared needed to see that she wasn't that same little girl he could boss around. She was an adult, a grown woman with her own son. She had been forced to grow up while Jared seemed to live in the past, even moving back in with their mother when he was released from jail.

That was a mistake. Their mother was crazy with all her black magic and superstitions. Certifiably crazy or so she and Jared liked to claim, making up any kind of excuse for why she kept picking loser husbands like both their dads. Saying their mother was crazy seemed better than admitting she was simply stupid. Maybe that was Jared's problem. Melanie thought about teasing him that maybe he had inherited Mom's crazy gene, though she knew full well that she would never dare to tease Jared. He would see it as a betrayal, and he would remind her, again, that all they had were each other because of the past they had survived and the secrets they continued to share.

Melanie turned left at Fifty-Second and Nicholas Streets and headed into the Memorial Park neighborhood, a stretch of huge brick homes with carefully manicured lawns. Not a ceramic gnome in sight. That made her smile, thinking of her son, Charlie's, newest obsession of stealing lawn ornaments, even though it annoyed her as much as it amused her. She couldn't help thinking that maybe it was another example of like mother, like son. After all, she had taught him well, making a game early on of their escapades. It may have started as a game, but it bugged her that Charlie still treated stealing as a game, completely unaware of the risks and dangers. Yes, she had taught him well, maybe too well.

She'd brought him in when he was only eight. They stole packs of ground beef—quickly graduating to T-bone steaks—from the HyVee on Center Street, stuffing them into his school backpack. Charlie became so good at it she didn't even notice him steal the Hostess Twinkies and Bazooka bubble gum until they appeared later on their kitchen table, alongside the packs of meat. He was a natural, and now, nine years later, with that baby face and lopsided grin, he could still get away with almost anything.

Their game had started as a matter of survival, a way to supplement Melanie's string of shitty jobs. So what if Charlie swiped a few silly lawn ornaments as long as he brought home a leather jacket or enough CD players to pay the rent? What did it matter that he still considered hot-wiring Saturns a game? Maybe it was that carefree attitude that kept him from getting caught, though Melanie worried that it had more to do with luck than attitude. They had had a long string of good luck, and lately she found herself not trusting it to hold up. But she didn't dare tell Charlie that.

Luck and a little bit of opportunity. That had been her ticket out of the stink hole she grew up in. For the last ten years she had provided a nice home for herself and Charlie in the middle of Dundee, a respectable Omaha neighborhood. A good family neighborhood, though not quite like this one, she thought as she looked around. She kept to the sidewalks, wondering if anyone behind these huge, decorative doors would understand. How could they with their polished black BMWs and Lexus SUVs in their driveways, not a missing hubcap or spot of rust in sight, let alone a homemade In-Transit sign Scotch-taped to the rear window?

She walked past the only pickup parked in the street, a white Chevy, and she knew before she saw the attached beat-up trailer that the truck belonged to a lawn service. Then she saw two young men, shirtless and glistening with sweat, down on their knees on the front lawn of the house. They both had what looked like oversize scissors, and they were cutting blades of grass from in between the pristine white picket fence, obviously unable to use the array of machinery on their trailer for fear of scarring the white wood.

Melanie resisted the urge to laugh. Jesus! What did it cost to have something like that done? She wanted to roll her eyes and make some sympathetic gesture in recognition of their plight, but then they would have known. They would have realized that she didn't belong here, either, that she was an outsider, too. So instead she just smiled and continued walking.

She checked her wristwatch, a sleek, black-faced

Movado with a single diamond that Charlie had given her on Mother's Day. She didn't bother asking him anymore how he got things or from where. She couldn't help thinking the watch belonged in this neighborhood even if she did not. It was then that she saw the eight-by-ten piece of cardboard nailed to the tree. She remembered noticing the tree soon after it was ravaged by last week's thunderstorms. The wounded maple managed to keep only its trunk intact, the branches ripped off, leaving behind what now looked like two severed arms, still reaching in surrender to the sky. This morning someone had added a hand-printed sign, a sort of public epistle that read, "Hope is the thing with feathers." In small print below was written "Emily Dickinson."

Melanie glanced at the house the tree belonged to, but didn't slow her pace. She repeated the phrase to herself, "Hope is the thing with feathers." She snorted under her breath. What the hell was that supposed to mean? And, besides, what did people with brick mansions and BMWs need to know about hope? What problems could they possibly have that couldn't be solved with their money?

She remembered what Jared always said. That people who had money didn't have a clue about people who didn't have money.

Melanie looked back at the tree. Even from almost a block up the street that poor, ugly thing stood out in the middle of this picture-perfect neighborhood. It didn't need a stupid quote from some dead poet tacked onto its pathetic remains to remind it that it didn't belong.

"Hope is the thing with feathers?" she repeated, but still didn't understand. Was somebody poking fun? Or maybe pointing out that they were above having an ugly tree in their front yard? Surely they didn't think hope was going to save it, so it had to be a joke or some highbrow message. It didn't matter. Why was she even wasting her time with it? One thing she knew for certain, hope was something only people in brick mansions could afford to count on. People like herself and Charlie and Jared counted on luck. A little bit of luck could make things happen. She and Jared had crawled up from the same stinking hole. That was the one thing they understood about each other.

She glanced at her watch again. Maybe things hadn't changed as much as she thought, and she picked up her pace. No sense in pissing off Jared.

CHAPTER 4

7:15 a.m.

Jared Barnett watched from across the street, three houses down, in a car he knew she'd never recognize. He had been here once before, but it had been at night, just to scope out the place. He had been pleased to discover no dog or even a trace of one in the backyard, only a shitload of mud and piles of some fucking pebbles that hadn't set properly in the new walkways. He remembered because he'd worried that the sound of him walking over them would wake up the neighbors.

Now sitting here, he wondered why in the world she had chosen a huge, old two-story in the middle of Omaha when she could easily afford a new house out in some ritzy West Omaha suburb? But this was better for him. More traffic; it wouldn't be unusual to have cars parked along the street. Anyone who saw him would simply think he was waiting for a girlfriend in one of the apartments across from her house.

He pulled out the cell phone and flipped it open, stopping to admire it. He might have to hang on to this one. Technology stuff amazed him. He didn't have a clue how it all worked, but he loved having it, owning it. Like a new toy. He'd had fun in the last week taking pictures—sometimes without anyone knowing since the miniature camera was almost hidden in the back panel of the phone. He could take a person's picture then program it into the phone with that person's phone number. It still amused him that, when he dialed a number, the person's photo came up on the tiny video panel inside. And it blew him away when his phone rang, bringing up the caller's photo as a caller ID. Totally cool.

He'd filled up the queue in just a few days. The only problem was he didn't know how to erase them. That was one disadvantage—stolen cell phones didn't come with instruction manuals, and he hadn't been able to figure out the erasing part on his own yet.

He punched in the number, watching the small video panel then almost laughing out loud when the photo appeared. He'd taken the picture as he ate, catching him between bites, his mouth full of cheeseburger. He liked catching him off guard, sort of keeping him in his place, if only for a second or two and if only inside this high-tech contraption.

"Yeah?" Jared heard him say in place of a greeting, trying his best to sound like a tough guy.

Jared held the sliver of metal to his ear and said, "You almost finished?"

"I told you I'd take care of it." But there was no urgency in his voice.

"When you finish, you know where to meet me, right?"

"I remember."

"Good." Jared pushed End. He hadn't even had time to shut off the phone when it began ringing. Jared thought perhaps he had hung up too soon. Was there something he forgot? But one quick glance at the caller's picture, and he groaned out loud. "What?"

"It has to be today."

Instead of answering immediately, Jared gave him a heavy sigh, his best "don't fuck with me" sigh. Then finally he said, "I told you I'd take care of it."

"That's what you said last week."

"Last week didn't work."

"I'm getting pretty fucking tired of waiting. The set-up is perfect for today. It has to be today."

"I already know all that. I'm taking care of it. Now don't fucking call me anymore."

He snapped the phone shut, this time shutting it off.

Jared Barnett was sick and tired of people wanting things from him. Tired of cleaning up messes. This time there would be no mess. He was making sure of that with his own insurance policy. He pulled the cassette tape out of the pocket of his overalls, flipping it around in his fingers, pleased with the power this little flimsy piece of plastic gave him. The cell phone picture hadn't been the only thing he had taken without the motherfucker realizing it. He had their entire conversation on tape, down to the last instruction.

Just then he noticed the front door to the house open. He pulled down the baseball cap and put the cell phone to his ear again. To anyone watching him, he was just some guy parked along the street to make a few phone calls while he waited for someone.

Her big, Italian husband came out with a briefcase in one hand and a huge Pullman in the other. Excellent—a trip for hubby. So he did have the day right, after all. Following close behind was the little girl. The two were packed and in the car by the time she finally came out, stopping to lock the front door.

Yes, it was perfect timing. Jared zipped up the coveralls, despite the fabric sticking to his body. He wished he had worn underwear, now feeling the in-seams scrape against his sweaty thighs. By the time the SUV backed out of the driveway and headed up the street he had his shoes and socks off. He wasn't going to take any chances this time.

CHAPTER 5

8:30 a.m.
Eppley Airport

Grace Wenninghoff hugged the leather portfolio to her chest as she watched her husband and four-year-old daughter say their goodbyes. It was a little like watching an Abbott and Costello routine. Vince was on one knee, still slouching in an attempt to be eye level with his daughter, completely oblivious to the extra creases he was adding to his expensive trousers.

"I'll see you in ten days," he told Emily.

"Not if I see you first," she quipped back, trying to contain the smile but bursting into a giggle even before his eyebrow rose and his hands went to his waist in his pretend look of surprise.

They did this routine before every trip, which was becoming more frequent in the last year, and yet both played their parts with genuine pleasure and surprise. Sometimes Grace wished she was part of their fun and games until she remembered that this exchange wasn't exactly motivated by fun. Instead it was the product of sadness and perhaps a bit of fear.

Vince rose to his feet, stretching his six-foot frame with a slight touch to his lower back, a subtle gesture no one but a nagging wife might notice.

"You remembered your Advil gelcaps?" she asked when he came over for his goodbye kiss, which she planted on his cheek despite his disgruntled look.

"That's your idea of a send-off?" He was joking again or trying to, looking to Emily for his audience and rolling his eyes to get her giggling again.

"It's an eleven-hour flight," she said without a smile, refusing to be pulled into the duo's game of pretend, or what Grandma Wenny might call "denial."

But before Grace could remind him that she was the keeper of logic in this family, that she was the grown-up, he surprised her by pulling her in for a hug, crushing the leather portfolio between them. In her ear he whispered, "You sure you're okay?"

And then she realized it was all still part of the charade, his constant attempt to protect Emily, who Vince either didn't realize or truly didn't want to see had become a precocious, tough tomboy. In fact, Grace wouldn't mind planting a little fear in Emily if it kept her from catching backyard snakes and crickets and dumping them into her kiddie pool to see if they could swim. Sometimes Grace wondered who her husband was really protecting from the cold, hard facts that came with growing up, his daughter or himself.

"I'm fine." She pulled away to meet his eyes so he could see that she meant it. "What's a few boxes? I'll have them unpacked and the house looking like home before you get back."

"That's not what I meant." He frowned at her, his brown eyes no longer playful but clouded with concern.

"What? I'm not allowed to joke? Okay, so it might take longer than ten days to get unpacked."

But, of course, she knew he wasn't talking about the mess of their new home, a huge old Victorian, all the packed boxes still stacked and left exactly where the movers had set them over two weeks ago. No, Vince didn't mean that mess. She knew what mess he meant. He meant Jared Barnett. She had made the mistake of telling him about seeing the bastard at the coffee shop and in the courtroom. Luckily she left out the dry cleaner's. He worried too much, always concerned that some criminal she had sent to prison would someday come back for revenge. Unfortunately, an occasional threat came with the job, an occupational hazard. Most of the time they were empty threats.

"I just don't want you constantly watching for the man in every shadow," Vince said then held out his hand to Emily, closing the subject of serious adult talk. It didn't matter. Grace knew that as soon as she and Emily got into the car Emily would be grilling her.

And, unlike her husband, Grace tried not to lie to their daughter. But she was also guilty of protecting her. She hoped Emily never had to be faced with the realities of her job as a deputy prosecutor. Now that Emily was in preschool the girl's questions became more difficult. Last week she wanted to know why Grace's last name was different than hers and Daddy's. Grace couldn't remember exactly what she told her, but it certainly had not been the truth. How could she tell her four-year-old that the reason she used her own name was that, if any bad people who Mommy pissed off came looking to hurt her, they wouldn't find Emily and her father?

"Don't worry," Grace said, squeezing her husband's hand. "I'll be okay. I always am, right?"

He smiled down at her, apparently satisfied and unaware that her mind had already become preoccupied as she scanned the airport terminal, looking through groups of people coming and going. Making sure that Jared Barnett was nowhere in sight.

CHAPTER 6

9:50 a.m.
Interstate 80

Andrew Kane discovered a hole in the traffic and gunned the engine, easing into a space in the fast lane. He was getting good at driving with his left hand. Still, he kept an eye on the speedometer. No need—the fast lane was doing a whopping forty-five miles per hour. Checking the speedometer had already become instinctive, an annoying new habit. Not that he could afford another reason to take his eyes off the road now that he was relegated to using only one hand. He had enough problems without adding another speeding ticket.

Almost since the moment he drove the torch-red Saab 9-3 off the dealer's lot, it had attracted police radar as if it contained some secret, invisible force. He wondered if it was punishment for buying what had been a magnificent splurge, so much so that he had added vanity plates that read, "A WHIM," as if he needed to explain. Would he ever consider this car the well-deserved reward he intended it to be? After six years of playing the starving novelist and living off one credit card advance after another, he was finally reaping the financial awards, the fruits of his labor, so to speak. In other words, the royalty checks for his five novels were finally adding up. This car was supposed to symbolize his success. It was supposed to represent an end to the struggle and a new beginning, a promise of what was yet to come. Maybe all that was too much to ask of a car, any car.

He checked the rearview mirror. Traffic had slowed enough for him to adjust the canvas shoulder harness that threatened to strangle him and itched like crazy, especially in this sweaty heat. After three long weeks it still bugged the hell out of him. The doctor kept insisting Andrew wouldn't notice it "after a while." He was beginning to think his doctor's measure of "after a while" wasn't the same as his own.

Yet it wasn't the shoulder strap that Andrew wanted to rip from his chest. That hatred he reserved for the blood-sucking contraption that practically glued his arm to his chest. His doctor had also told him that he would learn quickly to make do with his left arm as if his right no longer existed. His doctor obviously had never broken his collarbone or been without use of his dominant hand and arm…hell, practically that entire side of his body.

It didn't help matters that this injury—what Andrew wished he could have chalked up to a simple biking accident—had unleashed the reminder that Andrew's forty-three-year-old body wasn't what it used to be. It was as if his reward for all the hard work and struggles, for his newly acquired success, was high blood pressure and broken bones. His doctor called it "a wake-up call," then smiled when he added, "Who knew writing novels could be so stressful, huh?" Andrew shook his head. Maybe he needed a new doctor.

He glanced at the worn leather briefcase on the passenger seat. It had been with him through the writing of every one of his novels, a gift from Nora back in the days when she said she believed in him and wanted him to follow his dreams. Back before she realized following his dream might include going into debt and having to sacrifice by putting some things off. Things like commitment and marriage and kids. She accused him of using his dream as an excuse to avoid commitment. He told her that was ridiculous, and she couldn't possibly understand what he was going through. It wasn't until after she was gone from his life that he realized maybe she was right. Maybe he had a tendency to drive people away to avoid commitment. Sometimes it was just easier that way. He was better on his own, anyway.

Andrew looked back at the briefcase. Ordinarily it was bulging at the seams with notebooks, the pages filled, sometimes bleeding red from self-edits, the corners creased, stains in the margins from late-night coffee or too much wine. But today the case slouched, thin and frail, with hardly enough inside to keep it upright in the seat. The spiral notebooks were empty, white blue-lined pages ready to stare back at him, taunting instead of coaxing him. When had it become so difficult? When had writing gone from fun to hard work? When had he begun looking at his dream with dread instead of anticipation? Dread, accompanied by this tightness in his chest.

"This is the stuff of early heart attacks," his doctor had cautioned, "especially with a family history. What was your father? Sixty-eight? Sixty-nine?"

Andrew had only nodded, not bothering to correct him. His father had been sixty-three when he died of a heart attack. Only twenty years older than Andrew. Yeah, he definitely needed a new doctor.

He tried to concentrate on the interstate lanes in front of him now that he was approaching yet another construction area. Lines of blinking taillights like little red dots lined up for as far as he could see. Another slowdown. At this rate he'd never get out to Platte River State Park. Though, what was the hurry? He had reserved the cabin for two weeks. Why hurry only to sit and stare out at the glistening lake and find that, perhaps, it could no longer inspire him? He hoped that wasn't the case. In fact, he was counting on this retreat to turn things around. It was his last hope.

Why was the fast lane now the stop lane? Andrew

cocked his head to the left, swerving the car as he did so to compensate for the harness around his neck. He couldn't see any end to the backed-up traffic. What he *could* see were thunderheads, sagging in the west. Just his luck. He had hoped he and Tommy would have time before lunch to do some fishing. He still couldn't believe his hot-shot detective friend had never been fishing before. Finally, something *he* could teach him. It was usually the other way around with Tommy sharing details and experiences of being a cop, teaching Andrew how to give his suspense novels some real-life credibility.

The Saab's engine wanted to race and Andrew considered cutting the A/C to relieve it. Instead, he blasted two of the vents directly in his face and sat back. He needed to relax. His shoulder ached. It constantly ached. And today the back of his head felt as if it would explode at any second. Probably the high blood pressure.

He glanced in the rearview mirror again, this time taking note of the blue eyes staring back from behind the wire-rim glasses. The glasses were new, yet another sign of the toll his newfound success had taken. The result of too many hours spent in front of a computer screen. Recently, his eyes had begun to remind him of his father's, almost the exact blue, chameleon—quick to change with his mood or the color of his shirt.

Andrew remembered that his father's eyes had grown hard and cold in response to the betrayal, pain and disappointment he felt he had been dealt. There was always some reason he wasn't able to succeed, something or someone who kept him from getting what he deserved. Life wasn't fair. That seemed to be his father's motto. He believed that just when you got a taste of success, a sample of happiness, it could all be ripped away.

Andrew had always promised himself he'd never be like that, and yet when Nora left he'd felt a sense of betrayal. She left when he was most vulnerable, before he had even gotten a publishing contract, before he had anything concrete in hand that he could promise or offer her. But he couldn't be angry with Nora. He couldn't blame her. It was his fault. Andrew wondered if he was destined to sabotage any success and happiness that came his way. Because like his father, he worried that all of it could be taken away as quickly as it had come. Is that what his writer's block was about? Was it just another way to sabotage the success he was amassing as a novelist?

"Be careful what you wish for," his father would often warn, usually after several whiskeys, "you might get it, only it won't look anything like you thought it should."

Andrew shook his head and stole one more glance in the mirror. He was not his father. He had spent a lifetime making sure of that, and yet here were his father's eyes, staring at him, warning him again.

CHAPTER 7

10:03 a.m.

He was waiting when Melanie drove into the parking lot. Her stomach took a slow nosedive when she saw him. She knew how much Jared hated to wait. He sat in one of the wooden rocking chairs, the last in a row that lined the restaurant's deck.

She glanced at her wristwatch. She was on time. Okay, maybe a minute late, but only a minute at the most. And even though he sat slouched, feet propped on the handrail, as though content enough to catch a nap, Melanie knew he would be pissed. Pissed that she wasn't the one waiting for him. That she hadn't been anxious and excited, ready to jump when he told her to. In other words, that she wasn't the same little girl who looked up to her big brother, constantly wanting to please him. That girl would have been here on time. No, that girl would have been here early.

He nodded at her without really looking at her. There was something different about him. Something Melanie wasn't prepared for. He was smiling, almost a grin, which made things worse. Jared smiled only for a couple of reasons, none of them because he was happy. This smile was his "I have something over you now" smile. If Melanie had had any appetite left—which she didn't—it would be gone for sure.

He dropped his feet one by one as if he was in no big hurry, each an exaggerated plop against the deck's wood floor. Then he pushed himself out of the rocking chair, scooping up the backpack that Melanie only now noticed.

"That's Charlie's," she said in place of a greeting, pointing to the worn purple backpack, its corners scarred with black-and-white marks. She'd recognize that ratty old thing anywhere. Charlie could lift a new one—hell, he could lift a dozen new ones—and, yet, the boy carried this thing around like that pathetic Charlie Brown character with his worn-out security blanket. Because that's what it was to Charlie. Her son, who wasn't scared of anything or anyone, carried around this pathetic old canvas bag like it was his Superman cape, drawing strength from its simple presence. "Is he here?" she asked, looking around, but not seeing Charlie's pickup in the parking lot.

"No," Jared told her, the smile already gone as though he didn't feel the need to explain. "But he will be."

Melanie watched him sling the backpack over his shoulder with exaggerated purpose, as if to reinforce the fact that Charlie would eventually show up. Sort of like a ransom. Ransom? That was silly. Why in the world would she even think such a thing? Charlie was crazy about his uncle Jared. He looked up to him like a father figure. Even during Jared's five years in prison, it was Charlie who visited when Melanie couldn't make herself go to the prison. Instead she had kept in touch via phone calls and letters. Melanie didn't mind that Charlie wanted to visit. She knew he needed a man in his life to learn how to be a man. And his uncle Jared, despite what their mother called his "unfortunate incarceration," was a better mentor for Charlie than Charlie's own deadbeat father. There was a bond between Charlie and Jared that sometimes drove her crazy.

"He doesn't go anywhere without that thing," she said, not taking Jared's hint and letting the subject drop. It bothered her. She couldn't believe Charlie would have left it willingly, not even with Jared. It contained an odd assortment of what Charlie called his "valuables." "Did he say where he was going?"

"He's running an errand for me."

Jared walked into the restaurant ahead of her, not bothering to hold the door open. A gray-haired man on his way out with his hunched-over wife shot Jared a nasty look. It was a wasted effort. Jared didn't even notice. Melanie ignored them, too. Actually, it didn't bother her. She didn't need any man holding a door open for her.

No, what bothered her more was that Jared wasn't telling her something. He was shutting her out again. He had been like this since he came back, quiet, almost secretive, as if he was holding something back.

The hostess led them to a table in the middle, but Jared continued on to a booth in the corner by the window. Before the woman even noticed, he was tossing the backpack against the wall and sliding in after it.

"This one's not taken, is it?" He was already unwrapping the paper napkin and setting out his silverware while the poor hostess simply stared at him.

"No, that one's not taken, but we—"

"Great. Could we have some menus?" He squinted at her name tag. "Annette?" Then he held out his hand for the menus. Annette immediately complied, a rush of crimson crawling up her neck from her white lace collar, coloring her cheeks.

"I'll send your waitress over to get your order."

"That'd be just fantastic, Annette."

Melanie slid into the other side of the booth, giving the woman only a glance while examining Jared's smirk. What she once considered to be her brother's charm now seemed like sarcasm. Ever since they were kids, Jared would call strangers by their names, catching them off guard by reading their name tags that Melanie never noticed. It had always seemed so cool, so adult, even polite and friendly.

Maybe she was only imagining that he sounded sarcastic.

What was her problem? Why was she doing this, second-guessing things? She and Jared were blood. They were family. They had a bond, held together by promises and secrets. They had vowed long ago to always be there for each other, and Melanie had broken that promise. Not only that, she had let him down when he needed her most. If she had only been able to provide him with an alibi he would never have had to waste five years of his life in prison. She owed him. That's exactly what she told herself as Jared closed his menu, ready to order, waiting once again. He grabbed his fork and began cleaning his fingernails with the prongs. At least she wasn't the one keeping him waiting this time.

Suddenly Jared broke out in a grin. Not at Melanie, but at someone over her shoulder. She turned, expecting to see a waitress, but instead saw Charlie making his way through the maze of tables. He bumped into someone and excused himself, but then turned and rolled his eyes at Jared as if the elderly man had been in Charlie's way and it was his own fault for getting bumped.

Somehow her son seemed to lose his manners in Jared's company, eager to please his mentor and instinctively knowing just how to do that. He annoyed her when he acted like some bumbling idiot, a puppy doing tricks for its owner. He was above that. Or he should be. Melanie would never call Charlie brilliant but the boy was smart, sometimes too smart, learning with ease the trade of manipulation. That red hair, spiked in all directions, along with those irresistible freckles and that boyish grin allowed him to get away with just about anything. Now if only someone could teach him how to dress. She certainly had not succeeded, because here he was wearing those baggy jeans she wished he would throw out and the black T-shirt that read, What if the hokeypokey is really what it's all about?

Melanie hadn't even noticed that he had something tucked under his arm until he got to their table. She might not have noticed it at all except that Charlie stood it in front of them on the table, grinning from ear to ear.

"Here you go," Charlie said, presenting the object to Jared as if he were Indiana Jones delivering some gold treasure he had seized by outrunning violent tribesmen and Nazi henchmen. "You said you needed one more. Whadya do with the one I gave you yesterday?"

Melanie couldn't believe it. Was this the important errand Jared had sent Charlie on? What the hell were the two of them up to? Was it Jared's way of testing Charlie's loyalty? What stupid, immature game were they playing? Because why else would Jared encourage her son's obsession with stealing ugly ceramic gnomes from people's front yards?

CHAPTER 8

10:24 a.m.
Logan Hotel

Max Kramer stopped to catch his breath at the fourth-floor landing of the Logan. Sweat poured down his forehead, dripping off his chin. The son-of-a-bitching apartment building had no air-conditioning. What did he expect of a place that had a security door held open with a trash can? The elevator didn't work. No surprise. And if that wasn't enough, Carrie Ann Comstock lived on the sixth floor.

He took off his suit jacket, threw it over his arm and loosened his tie. He had just put on the crisply pressed suit and already it felt like a wrinkled wet rag. He swatted at a swarm of flies that had followed him in from the street. Maybe he was getting too old to be meeting clients at their houses. He pulled himself up the narrow flight of stairs and stopped again. This time he took a deep breath and almost started gagging.

"Good God!"

Someone on the fifth floor had burned their breakfast. It smelled like scorched milk mixed with something sour, something that reminded him of vomit. He held his breath and hurried up the last flight, pushing through the filthy, heavy door and letting it slam behind him.

He tried wiping the sweat from his face with the sleeve of his shirt and slapped at the persistent flies. He hated feeling damp and sticky, unclean. He prided himself in looking pressed and polished. He kept remembering how good he looked on those videotapes he had made of his recent interviews. Thanks to Jared Barnett he had a whole library of videotapes.

He buttoned his collar and straightened his tie. He took one more swat at the flies then knocked on the door of apartment 615. The number six clung by a loose nail and had swung upside down so that it looked like apartment 915.

A grumble came from the other side of the door. He stepped back and waited for the succession of clicks as the locks were undone. The door opened a couple of inches, limited by the chain that held it. Max wanted to shake his head and restrained himself from rolling his eyes. In this building a door chain was about as worthless as a flyswatter.

"Whadya want?"

Max recognized the woman's raspy voice and knew that it was, no doubt, the result of her prolonged usage of crack cocaine, not cigarettes.

"I'm Max Kramer. Are you Carrie Ann Comstock?"

"Yeah, so whadya want?"

"Actually, Carrie Ann, you called me."

"I did?" She shoved one eye to the crack and gave him a once-over.

"You said your friend Heather Fischer recommended me to represent you."

"She did?"

"I just spoke to you on the phone last week. I told you I'd stop by on Wednesday. Today's Wednesday."

"Oh, right. You're the lawyer guy. Geez! Where's my fuckin' brain today?" She slammed the door. He heard the rattle of the chain, then she opened the door. "Come on in."

Max stepped in slowly, but the apartment wasn't bad. If he hadn't had to endure the hot, smelly, fly-infested climb, he might have called it cozy.

She offered him a seat in what had to be her favorite chair. It faced the TV set and had a small fan blowing directly on it. He declined, insisting she sit, letting her think that he was being polite when he simply liked the feeling of control standing gave him.

"I checked all the charges, Ms. Comstock. With the crack cocaine charge alone you're in some pretty serious trouble."

Her head went down as though she was ready to be punished. He tried to determine how old she was. Sometimes with crack whores it was difficult to tell. If the crack didn't whither their skin, their horrendous nutritional habits did. He decided she might actually be pretty if she cleaned up and put on ten pounds. As for her age, he guessed that Carrie Ann was maybe twenty-five or twenty-six. Her rap sheet had only estimated it. He wondered if Carrie Ann even remembered how old she was.

"I can help you, but we need something you can bargain with. You understand what I'm saying?"

He knew if she was a friend of Heather's she would understand. She looked up at him, and yes, there was already a look of recognition and relief in her bloodshot eyes. That was one thing he liked about his clientele. They could be very grateful to anyone who offered help. They were so used to everyone giving up on them—family, friends, even the justice system.

"When the time comes you'll need to listen and pay close attention to what I tell you. And you'll need to stay clean through the end of the week. If you want to stay out of jail, you'll need to do exactly as I say. Do you understand?"

She nodded, sitting on the edge of the chair as if ready to do whatever was necessary right now. "I know I'm in big trouble. If I just could have one more chance. That's all I need."

"I know. That's why I'm going to help you." Max

wiped his forehead again. God! It was hot in the small apartment and yet Carrie Ann didn't seem at all affected by the heat. She didn't even have any of the windows opened. He wondered again why the hell he bothered to come to his clients' homes. This was ridiculous.

"I really appreciate this, Mr. Kramer. I don't know what I'd do if you couldn't help me. I really can't go to jail."

"And you shouldn't have to. But like I said you'll have to be able to do and say what I tell you. Okay?"

Another nod.

"I know you'll want partial payment today," she said as she slid off the chair onto her knees. "Right?" Without looking up at him she reached up and began pulling down his zipper.

In a matter of seconds Max Kramer remembered exactly why he came to his clients' homes.

CHAPTER 9

10:45 a.m.

Melanie watched the waitress's frustration grow. It wasn't her fault the cook kept getting Jared's order wrong. But the woman shouldn't be taking it out on Jared, either. How could she expect him to eat runny eggs when he'd ordered them fried and well done? Okay, maybe not the first time. Melanie thought she had heard him say sunny side up, too, although she didn't dare say so. Besides, Jared insisted he hadn't, and Charlie backed him up, saying Jared should know how he ordered his own eggs. Here they were, arguing with the waitress for the third time, the entire Cracker Barrel dining room watching them.

Melanie wanted to squirm her way out of the booth. Instead she looked out the window, wishing they weren't the center of attention. She had spent a lifetime trying to blend in, trying to be like everyone else. That's how she had survived her childhood, and as an adult that's how she had become so good at lifting the things she did. She strived to be seen as ordinary as she possibly could, never drawing unnecessary attention to herself. It allowed her to blend in whether she was shoplifting at Lowe's or Dillard's or even Borsheim's.

Jared, however, seemed to want everyone to notice him, to see what injustices had been done to him. Had he always been like this? Or had his time in prison changed him? He usually didn't waste so much time with the small crap. Mostly he just focused on the things or people who pissed him off. Why get so pissed about some fucking eggs and whether they were firm enough? Or was it really about eggs? Hard to tell with Jared these days.

"I'm beginning to think you don't like me, Rita," Jared was saying in that same tone Melanie had thought earlier was sarcasm.

"No, not at all," the waitress said. "I'm just wondering why it took you several bites to figure out they still weren't to your liking."

Melanie's eyes went back to the window and the parking lot outside. This waitress was only making matters worse.

"I guess I was just in shock, Rita. I couldn't believe that you could screw it up for a third time."

Jared's voice had that singsong tone that made Melanie cringe. Outside in the parking lot she concentrated on a KKAR-news station wagon whose driver had a map spread out on the hood, holding it down with the palms of his hands to keep the wind from blowing it away. But he wasn't looking at the map. Instead, he was scanning the sky, and that's when Melanie noticed how dark the clouds had grown. Several pole lights that lined the lot had automatically started blinking, as if trying to decide whether or not to come on. Up on Interstate 80 she could see headlights.

"Forget about it, Rita." Jared was responding to something Melanie had missed. "I don't want any more eggs. What might make me happy—"

"Let me guess," Rita interrupted him. "You'd like me to not charge you for the eggs."

"Actually, considering how many times you and your friend back in the kitchen screwed up…" He lifted his hands, palms up in a hopeless gesture, allowing her to fill in the blanks.

"You'd like me not to charge you for your entire breakfast. Is that it?"

"If you insist."

"Jesus," Rita muttered, scratching out a new ticket. "It's no skin off my nose. I get paid this afternoon, cash my check, pick up my daughter, and we're off for a whole week in Vegas."

"Really? Vegas?" Jared sounded so interested that Melanie glanced at him from her perch at the window. Was he finally cutting the poor waitress some slack? "Well, you have a good time, Rita."

"I'll pick this up whenever you're ready. No hurry, of course."

Melanie wondered if the poor waitress would be back. She stared at Jared, trying to decide whether he meant what he said. Did he respect that the woman stood up to him? Hard to tell. He sat back in the booth, grabbing his fork, wiping off leftover eggs with the napkin and then finishing his manicure.

"You said in your message that today is the day," Melanie said, trying to keep the impatience from her voice. But when Jared's eyes found hers, she knew she hadn't been successful.

"Rita threw me off track," he said, putting his thumbnail in between his teeth to reach what the fork's prong could not.

"But we're still doing it, right?" Charlie jerked forward, knocking the table and sending Melanie's untouched coffee splashing over the cup's lip. "You haven't changed your mind?"

Before Jared could answer, a mechanical symphony started playing in his shirt pocket. He grabbed the cell phone, looking for the on button. Melanie knew the phone wasn't his. In the last week she had seen him using what seemed to be a different cell phone every time.

"What?"

Melanie glanced at Charlie. His outburst suggested he knew more about what they were doing here than she did. But Charlie seemed as impatient as she felt. She could see a slight twitch to the left side of his body and knew, though she couldn't see it, that his left foot was pumping up and down a mile a minute under the table.

"I already told you, I'm handling it," Jared said into the phone, sounding neither angry nor particularly urgent. "It'll be taken care of today."

Whoever was on the other end must not have been convinced because Jared sat listening, his eyes scanning the parking lot. She couldn't measure his expression, but his silence bothered her. Who could possibly have commanded Jared's respect to be allowed such a long audience? Finally Jared said, "I told you, I've got it taken care of." Then he flipped the phone shut, slipping it back into his shirt pocket.

"What's going on, Jared?" Melanie asked. "When are you gonna let us in on this job that you've been planning?" Out of the corner of her eye she could see the look exchanged between Jared and Charlie, and then she knew. She knew for certain what she had already suspected. She was the only one at the table who wasn't in on the plan. "What the hell's going on?"

"Okay, keep it cool," Jared said. "Don't get your panties all in a twist."

She heard her son snicker beside her, and she shot him a look that immediately silenced him like only a mother could.

Jared sat forward, elbows on the table, his hands together in a fist at his lips as if to protect his words. Melanie followed his eyes as he swept them across the restaurant's dining room. Oh, sure, now he was suddenly concerned about not drawing attention to himself?

"I told you before there's a big job I want to do. When the time's right. Well, the time's right."

"Why today?"

He readjusted himself, sighing into his fists as if he shouldn't need to explain himself to her. If he said the time was right, she should just believe him. Five years ago, that's all he would have needed to tell her.

"There's a bank branch about a half mile up the road to the left," he began in a hushed tone. Melanie and Charlie, almost in unison, scooted closer to the table. "On an ordinary Monday there's usually a stash of cash that comes through. Area businesses depositing their weekend takes. But Monday was Labor Day. Huge weekend. Families eating out, shopping. Extra travelers on I-80. Should be a nice chunk of change that came in those doors yesterday and today. Wells Fargo won't get to this location to pick it up until after closing today."

"You can't be serious." Melanie didn't even bother to disguise her disbelief. "You can't possibly be thinking of knocking off an armored car?"

"Keep it down, Mel." But he wasn't angry with her. Ever since he got out of prison, he seemed so calm. Almost too calm. "Not the car. The bank. I figure we do it right before closing time."

Then he sat back, finished, picking up the fork again.

Charlie seemed satisfied, also sitting back and chugging some ice from his glass, crunching it. His jerking left foot was now quiet. Melanie looked from one to the other. They couldn't be serious. A bank? That was totally out of their league, and yet neither of them looked to be joking. Neither of them looked the least bit concerned or anxious.

"Let's get out of here," Jared said, suddenly tossing the fork aside, pulling out his wallet and tugging loose a couple of ones and a folded ten-dollar bill. "Forget the stock market. This is my way of doubling my money." As they watched, he carefully placed the ten in the middle of the table before flipping it over a couple of times. Melanie could see the bill had been cut in half. Jared folded the two ones and slid the ten in between, letting it peek out just enough. Then he put the money on top of the ticket, set his water glass on a corner and was ready to go.

Melanie had to admit she was impressed. And when Jared casually tossed the cellular phone into a corner trash can in the parking lot, she found herself thinking they might actually be able to knock off a bank.

CHAPTER 10

11:30 a.m.
Platte River State Park

Andrew struggled with the bag of MatchLight charcoal, tugging it with his one good hand to try to get it out of the trunk of his car. He was disappointed to see it was only a ten-pound bag. It felt like a twenty-five-pounder. As if to compensate for his pathetic weakness he tucked the bag under his arm and grabbed the six-pack of Bud Light, ignoring the pinpricks of pain that crawled up his good shoulder, across the back of his neck and over his wounded arm.

He was tired of making the trips back and forth to the cabin, though it was less than fifty yards. Actually, *tired* wasn't the appropriate word. He was irritated. Even now, with his good arm and hand full and a pain dancing from one shoulder to the other, he considered grabbing the fishing rod and tackle box. But the approaching thunderheads convinced him to leave the fishing gear for now. It was just as well. It would only be one more disappointment if he realized he couldn't cast left-handed.

He noticed a slice of color moving through the trees, a car making its way up the road. With no free hands available, Andrew raised his chin in an effort to wave to the driver of the Ford Explorer. He waited, wishing he hadn't been so stubborn in thinking he could carry both the charcoal and the beer, feeling the pull in his wounded shoulder even though it wasn't bearing the weight. Again, he tried ignoring the pain, refusing to put anything down, especially not now. Not in front of his friend.

He watched Tommy Pakula pull up beside him. Before he got out of the Explorer he was shaking his finger at Andrew.

"You sure you should be carrying all that, Murderman?" Tommy asked, but he didn't embarrass Andrew by attempting to relieve him of his burden. An ex-fullback, Tommy stood about three inches shorter than Andrew but with broad shoulders and biceps that stretched his T-shirt sleeves. He grabbed his own cooler and Bag-N-Save sack from the back seat. "I brought some filets since it looks like we won't get any fish."

"Don't sound so relieved."

"Hey, don't get me wrong. I was looking forward to the fishing part. I just don't particularly like *eat-*

ing fish. My idea of a cookout is tailgating in the parking lot before a Huskers game. You know, with a nice thick slab of real meat, fresh out of the cooler. Not fishing all afternoon and only catching some puny six-inch thing that needs to be cleaned before you cook it."

"I told you we wouldn't be eating it. This is a catch-and-release lake. Besides, you're missing the point. Fishing isn't necessarily about catching fish."

"Right, sure." Tommy set the cooler on top of the Explorer just long enough to swipe sweat from his forehead, his hand continued over the top of his head, a habit he had developed since he began shaving his head. Andrew wondered if Tommy needed to remind himself that he no longer had hair or if he simply liked the feel of it. "I didn't realize you were like the Zen master of fishing."

"You'd see what I mean if you'd just give fishing a chance."

"Yeah, right."

Tommy picked up the cooler, and Andrew led the way to the cabin, trying not to flinch from the pain, though his back was to his best friend and he wouldn't notice.

"So, what did the doctor have to say? How many more weeks you stuck in that fucking slingshot?" Tommy asked.

"At least three," he managed to say without sounding out of breath.

"Holy crap, that's a bitch. How can you even write?"

"Very slowly." He put down the load outside the cabin so he could open the screen door for Tommy. That courtesy, Tommy allowed, and he squeezed in past him.

"That's partly why I'm so far behind deadline," Andrew found himself repeating anytime someone mentioned his writing, the subject tripping some kind of automatic guilt response. Truth was, his injury was only a small part of the manuscript's delay. He didn't want to admit the real reason, as if the simple admission would seal his fate. Andrew Kane didn't believe in fate or luck. Then he realized that Tommy didn't care, probably hadn't even heard Andrew's lame excuse. Instead, he was checking out the four-room cabin.

"This place is pretty cool," he said before ducking into one of the back bedrooms.

"Yeah, I love it." And he did. It wasn't as rustic as it looked. Though the walls were lined in knotty pine and the ceiling made up of rafters, there was also a skylight of small paneled windows, a modern bathroom and shower, a furnace and A/C unit. The kitchenette featured a full-size refrigerator, an electric range and a microwave that had been added since Andrew's last visit. The screened-in porch that overlooked the lake and the treetops was where he'd be spending the majority of his time, hopefully working late into the night as he had in the past, writing by the flame of a lantern.

This had been his retreat, his sanctuary, and it had

never failed him…yet. He had penned his first book here, but he hadn't been back for several years, too busy to afford himself the luxury of its solitude, its isolation. Instead, he usually ended up writing bits and pieces in airports, waiting for his next flight, or in hotel rooms over cold, mediocre room service. Who would have thought being a writer would include so many hours on the road and in the air? In a strange way the broken collarbone had been a godsend, a painful sign for him to slow down and reassess his priorities. A reminder of why he had wanted to do this in the first place.

"Where's the TV?" Tommy was back after an inspection of the bathroom.

"There is none."

"No TV?"

"Nope. No TV, no radio, no phone, no Internet. Can't even get good reception for my cell phone."

"Holy crap. How long did you say you're staying out here?"

"Two weeks."

"This is why you have no life, buddy. How can you handle being out here by yourself for two fucking weeks?"

"I need to get away from the day-to-day distractions. Besides, I brought a nine-inch portable TV— if that makes you feel better. You know I can't be away from the news for too long."

"Day-to-day distractions? I hate to tell you, but that's just life." Tommy picked up the case of Bud

Light and started putting the bottles carefully in the refrigerator. "So it sounds like you have the same philosophy about writing as you do about fishing," he said from behind the refrigerator door.

"How's that?"

"Fishing isn't about catching fish, right? Sounds to me like writing about life isn't about living life."

"Very funny," Andrew said. But he was annoyed enough to realize that Tommy could be right.

CHAPTER 11

2:30 p.m.

Melanie shoved the overstuffed laundry basket into the closet. She'd get to it tomorrow when things returned to normal. Though somewhere in the back of her mind she knew, she just *knew* that after today, things would never be normal again. It was only a feeling, the kind of feeling that gnaws at your gut. Something about this job of Jared's didn't feel right. Maybe she was simply disappointed that Jared and Charlie had been planning this without her. Maybe it was nothing, too much coffee at the restaurant when she had been trying so hard to do without. How had she ever expected to give up coffee and her smokes at the same time? Too much, too soon. Who did she think she was? Her gut instinct, she realized, had never been wrong before. In the past it had stopped her from doing some pretty stupid things.

She reached for the Pepto-Bismol, screwed off the child-protective cap and took a swig from the bottle.

She loaded her own backpack with a change of clothes and some other necessities. She stopped at the mirror, tucking a strand of hair up under the baseball cap. It had been an effort to contain her thick, shoulder-length hair, first making a ponytail and then stacking it on top of her head. If she had had more warning she would have had it cut. More warning—how much trouble would that have been? There it was again, her anger. Wow! When had she decided it was anger instead of disappointment?

Melanie turned away from the mirror and added a couple of granola bars to the backpack. Jared promised they'd be home before nightfall, and he would say the backpack wasn't necessary. He was probably right. Maybe, like Charlie, she needed her own security blanket this time.

She heard a car pull in to the driveway and glanced at her wristwatch. Right on time. But when she looked out the window, she didn't recognize the dark blue sedan. She did, however, recognize the car's emblem. Another fucking Saturn. What was it with that boy and Saturns?

She opened the front door, holding it for Charlie while she stood on the porch scanning the surrounding houses, catching a glimpse of curtains swinging back into place in the brick bungalow across the street. Old Mrs. Clancy noticed everything in the neighborhood, but thankfully, she kept her mouth shut, whether out of respect or fear Melanie didn't much care. She didn't need some busybody reporting her every time a strange car appeared in her driveway. But, as Melanie watched Charlie, she couldn't help wondering what old Mrs. Clancy was thinking, because she knew the woman was watching from somewhere in her house.

Charlie's usual T-shirt and baggy jeans had been replaced by dark coveralls, the zip-up kind with long sleeves. The coveralls looked out of place in the ninety-degree heat. What looked odder was his bright white high-top Nikes peeking out from under the pant cuffs. That boy took better care of his shoes than his hygiene, which didn't matter much today. He'd be a sweaty mess within a few hours of wearing those coveralls. He had a red bandana tied around his neck, the knot loose and hanging into the collar of the coveralls. Melanie wanted to laugh. Jesus! They weren't seriously thinking of pulling the kerchiefs around their faces like some Wild West bank robbers, were they?

Already she could see lines of sweat running down Charlie's forehead, trailing along his jawline, white lines through the instant-suntan cream he must have applied just before coming over. She wondered, if and when his head started sweating, would the black hair dye leave streaks of red down his neck? His entire disguise could be ruined by perspiration. But Charlie seemed totally unaware of any possible problems.

He walked up the sidewalk with his usual easy stroll, whistling. It wasn't until he was on the porch that she recognized the tune from "Green Acres," the old TV show. The boy could be a walking commercial for "Nick at Nite" programming.

She waited until he was inside the house, the door closed behind them before she said, "That's your idea of a getaway car?"

"What? It's a 2004. Has less than five thousand miles on it. And the windows are tinted. Ain't nobody gonna see inside that son of a bitch unless they have their eyes plastered up against the window."

She had to admit it looked brand new. Probably taken from another dealers' lot, although it didn't have dealer plates. She didn't need to ask. She knew he had already taken care of them, switching the stolen car's license plates with a pair he would have taken from the airport's long-term parking or from one of the apartment complexes in West Omaha. Someplace where the switch wouldn't be noticed for a few days, maybe even weeks. How many people would recognize their license plates were different? The boy was good. Fast. Efficient. But predictable. She tried to drill into his thick skull that it was the common, small mistakes that usually tripped up the best of the best. A speeding ticket, an unpaid tax bill or one too many stolen Saturns.

"Where's Jared?" she asked. "I thought you were picking him up."

"He had an errand. We'll pick him up on our way.

You're supposed to be wearing your coveralls." Charlie had his hands on his hips, assessing her blue jeans and T-shirt.

"It's too fucking hot for coveralls. Besides, I'm gonna be in the car. You already said nobody'll even see me behind those tinted windows."

He didn't look convinced. She pulled the baseball cap down over her forehead and put on a pair of dark sunglasses. "This is all the disguise I'm agreeing to."

"Okay," he said, giving in too easily. "Do we have anything good to eat that I can take with me?" And he headed to the kitchen, not waiting for an answer. He opened the fridge, pulling out the makings for a sandwich.

"Jesus, Charlie! We're on our way to rob a bank and you're packing a picnic?"

"Just a sandwich." He swiped gobs of Miracle Whip on the bread and began building a pile of deli meat and cheese, layering one after another. "Unless you got some chips, too?" He looked up at her and grinned, that stupid, lopsided grin.

She hesitated but only for a second. It had always been hard to deny him anything. Almost six feet tall, but he was still her baby. She began rummaging through the pantry, pulling out an unopened bag of Ruffles. She tossed it on the counter where he already had a Ziploc bag waiting and another grin to get her to fill it for him. She opened the bag, wondering if there were any cold sodas for them to take, too.

CHAPTER 12

3:15 p.m.
Peony Park HyVee

Grace Wenninghoff wrinkled her nose as Emily dropped the Hostess Cupcakes into their shopping cart.

"Emily…"

"They're so yummy. And you said—"

"I *said* you could have them as long as you picked out some fruit, too."

She pointed to the produce section, expecting a protest. The truth was, Grace probably would have given in without her daughter's compliance. She was feeling enough guilt to let Emily have a whole carton of Hostess Cupcakes. In the last month Emily had been a trouper, adjusting to their crosstown move better than either Grace or Vince. And now her dad was gone for over a week.

Grace had left work early and picked up Emily from Grandma Wenny's in the hopes that the two of them could spend some girl time together. Something they hadn't done much of since the move. Maybe Grace needed a break from their routine, an escape from the stress, more than Emily did. In fact, Emily had taken everything all in stride. She had made a fort out of the boxes in her room and decorated the antique dresser and mirror left by the previous owner with pictures of Disney characters. She had even created a new imaginary friend to share the adventure with.

"Bitsy likes Hostess Cupcakes, too," Emily said, mentioning her imaginary friend as though she had read Grace's mind.

At first Grace hadn't liked the idea of her daughter spending so much time and effort with someone who didn't exist. It seemed a bit odd. She worried Emily wouldn't be able to relate to real kids after spending so much time with one who did and said anything she wanted. However, Vince insisted that make-believe friends for four-year-olds were just a normal part of growing up. It had certainly not been a part of Grace's childhood. She tried to imagine what her logical and practical Grandma Wenny would have said had Grace dared to introduce an invisible friend. She probably would have blamed it on Grace's addiction to Nancy Drew novels and Batman comic books.

Vince, on the other hand, claimed to have spent a

good portion of kindergarten with an imaginary friend named Rocco. It still made Grace smile just thinking about it. Leave it to the scrawny Italian kid to invent some little mafioso to protect him. Sometimes she looked at pictures of him as a child and saw Emily, tiny and so vulnerable looking but with a spirit as tough as nails.

"What are these, Mommy?" Emily had picked up a kiwi in each of her small hands and was trying to hold them carefully without squeezing.

"They're called kiwi. They're sweet and good. You wanna try 'em?"

Emily looked them over, turning them first one way then another, gently rubbing her fingers over their fuzzy surface. Then, with a serious, furrowed look, she shook her head.

"No, I don't think so. They look like monkey heads."

"Monkey heads?" Grace laughed.

"Little green monkey heads." And Emily began giggling, too. She was soon laughing so hard that, when she went to put the two kiwis back on top of the stack, she set off an avalanche. "Oh, no, there go all the monkey heads."

Emily stood still, watching helplessly, her lower lip starting to pucker in what Grace recognized as a four-year-old's fine line of not knowing whether to laugh or cry.

"Come on, Em. Help me pick up these monkey heads before we both get into trouble."

The two of them began scrambling to pick up the rolling fruit. Soon Emily was giggling again. Grace's arms were full of kiwi when she noticed Emily on her hands and knees, staring at the last kiwi captured under the toe of a scuffed tennis shoe.

Grace looked up and almost dropped the fruit in her arms. Jared Barnett smiled down at her, his dark eyes like hollow-point bullets, empty but dangerous. He stood there with his toe holding the last piece of fruit hostage, as if there was nothing unusual about him being here, as if it were a mere coincidence.

"I didn't know you had such a beautiful little girl, Counselor," he said casually, but his tone injected ice-cold liquid into her veins.

"Emily, come here." Grace kept her own voice calm, trying not to alarm her daughter, yet unable to move. Somehow her knees had decided to go spongy. Emily, however, was focused on retrieving the last kiwi, waiting with fingers ready to grab it when the shoe was lifted.

"Emily." This time it sounded like a scold and she regretted it even before Barnett grinned. He stooped down and retrieved the fruit himself, handing it to Emily.

Grace held her breath, wanting to tell her child not to take it, not to touch it. As if to do so would contaminate her, would burn her with his evil. But, instead, she waited while Emily took the last kiwi and put it on the pile. Then Grace grabbed Emily's hand and shoved the shopping cart forward, moving them away from Jared Barnett as quickly as she could, feeling his stare like pinpricks on the back of her neck.

"Who is that man, Mommy? Do I know him?"

"No. He's nobody." She pushed the cart to a free checkout counter. "Why don't you watch the man bag our groceries. You like doing that, right?" Grace helped her squeeze past the cart to the end of the conveyor belt, and immediately Emily's attention transferred to the boy carelessly tossing items into the plastic bags.

Grace glanced around the store, checking to see where he might be, then pulled out her cell phone and punched in the number, needing to redo it because her fingers kept hitting the wrong numbers.

"Pakula here."

"I just ran into him again." She tried to whisper but the anger made her sound a little like Elmer Fudd.

"Is he still hanging around the courthouse?"

"No, the produce department here at HyVee."

The elderly woman in line behind Grace perused the tabloid magazines, but Grace knew from the woman's frown and sideway glances that she was listening to her conversation. Grace turned her back to her and kept an eye on Emily, who was now instructing the teenage boy how to bag groceries.

"Could it be a coincidence?"

"You think he just happens to shop at the same fucking store I do?"

Grace ignored the cashier's admonishing look. She didn't care what some twenty-year-old college kid thought. She had more important things to worry about. Like the fact that a man she had prosecuted five years ago for murder, a man who she had argued should be sentenced to death, was now free. Free and shopping at the grocery store she just happened to frequent.

Grace scanned the store again, startled when she heard Pakula. She'd forgotten she was still on her cell phone. "Grace, you okay? You want I can send a black and white to follow you home."

"What good would that do? I can't have a black and white with me everywhere I go. Besides, Barnett's not the first asshole to think he can scare me. And I'm not about to give him the pleasure of thinking he can."

"Barnett's not any old asshole," Pakula reminded her.

She saw Barnett, two check-out lanes over. He looked up, and as their eyes met, instead of looking away, he smiled again. That's when she heard Pakula say, "He's just gotten away with murder. Don't think for a minute that son of a bitch isn't thinking he's invincible right about now."

PART 2
Dead Man's Curve

CHAPTER 13

4:00 p.m.
Interstate 80

Melanie followed every one of Jared's directions. She wasn't about to tell him to save his breath; she knew where she was going. She didn't say anything. There was something about his mood, something about his eyes, that made her keep her mouth shut and just drive.

She kept the A/C on high, drowning out Charlie's rendition of "Gilligan's Island." Charlie had snarfed down his sandwich before they exited Interstate 80. Now he was working on the chips and downing a second Coke.

She glanced at Jared in the rearview mirror. He had insisted on sitting in the back seat by himself. At first she thought it was so he could sit directly behind her and boss her around, issuing directions. But he had already shown them where the bank was this morning. There was no need for directions.

His eyes met hers in the mirror and she quickly looked away, trying to cover her reaction by checking the car coming up alongside her. He was too calm, she decided. The sky had continued to grow darker. In the distance she could see a hint of lightning. The pole lights along the highway had begun to come on again as they had earlier in the day when they were sitting in the Cracker Barrel. Now she wished they were back there, talking big and pretending this was just a job they'd tackle someday. Pretending. That's all.

Jared sat in the back seat, cool and calm like it was a game of pretend, while Melanie's palms were slick with sweat. Her T-shirt stuck to her back, even with the A/C blowing at her. She couldn't keep her eyes from darting back and forth. Her fingers fidgeted. A couple times she caught herself biting down on her lower lip.

Even Charlie's eating, she knew, was a nervous response, an attempt to keep his brain and stomach distracted. But Jared didn't seem the least bit nervous. He watched out the window, not a bead of sweat on his upper lip or forehead. Whatever his secret was for staying so composed, Melanie knew he wouldn't be sharing it anytime soon.

She pulled off Highway 50 and turned into the bank's parking lot.

"Park up there alongside the west end of the lot,

away from the building," Jared said, now sitting so far forward she could feel his hot breath on the back of her bare neck.

There were no cars on this side of the building and the lot backed onto an empty area of overgrown grass. Across the street was a car dealership, a line of brand-new Ford pickups with shiny headlights staring at them. In the distance Melanie could see McDonald's golden arches. She could still hear the hum of the interstate traffic. Yet, as she parked the car, she noticed she could no longer see the cars on Highway 50. Although it hardly mattered. The bank's windows were tinted. She was only fifty yards away and she couldn't see inside.

Jared had certainly done his homework. This morning she had been impressed when he pointed out that the bank was less than a mile inside Douglas County. They would head south and immediately cross into Sarpy County. He seemed convinced that law enforcement officials would squabble over jurisdiction, if and when they came after them. That was one of the reasons he said he chose this particular bank. And it was reason enough for Melanie to believe that Jared might actually be able to pull this off.

Jared was now fiddling with his wristwatch. Melanie wiped the palms of her hands on her jeans, trying to be casual, trying not to draw Charlie's or Jared's attention. She kept the car engine idling with the vents blasting cold air, and she felt a chill. She examined the other cars in the lot. The bank's drive-through lane was empty. The access road was empty. Even across the street at the dealership there was no activity. It almost seemed too quiet. Too perfect. She glanced up and in the rearview mirror saw Jared pull two guns out of his duffel bag.

CHAPTER 14

4:15 p.m.

"Jesus, Jared. Where the hell did you get those?"

"Where do you think?"

"You know how I feel about guns."

"That was a long time ago, Mel. Get over it. Besides, what did you think we'd do? Slip them a note and they'd simply hand over a bag of cash?"

Melanie gripped the steering wheel, keeping herself from spinning around to get a better look. Out of the corner of her eye she could see that Charlie sat sideways, his arm slung over the seat back, watching Jared and smiling. He seemed excited to get his hands on one of those guns. Melanie tried to catch his eye, hoping he'd notice her disapproval. But at the moment the boy couldn't notice anything other than the shiny metal Jared was sneaking forward to him over the middle front console.

Charlie took the gun, keeping it low and out of sight but turning it over and over as if it were a new toy.

Melanie wanted to grab it away from him. She wanted to tell Jared to forget it. She wanted to speed away and not give him a choice. Instead, she sat there frozen, continuing to grip the wheel, trying to ignore the trickle of sweat that slid down her back.

"We've never had to use a gun before." She finally found her voice, though it sounded like someone else's, small and weak. But it was something she was proud of. Charlie and she had never used any kind of weapon. Unless you counted the wire clothes hanger Charlie used to pop the locks of Saturn doors.

She checked the rearview mirror. Jared was transferring the contents of his duffel bag to the pockets of his coverall. "We've never had to use a gun before," she repeated, this time a little louder.

"I heard you the first time," her brother said without looking up. "You don't need a gun when you're pulling off piddly little shit jobs."

She wanted to tell him that those piddly little shit jobs had kept her and Charlie off the streets and living quite comfortably for almost ten years. But there was no way she could stand up to Jared with her cheeks burning and her voice shaky. He didn't seem to think they were piddly shit jobs five years ago. She met his eyes again in the rearview mirror, calm, dark eyes. How could he be so calm?

"Remember everything I told you, Charlie?" His eyes never left Melanie's.

"Yup," her son answered so quickly, so confidently that Melanie jerked around to look at him, shocked to find the red kerchief up over the lower part of his face and a black stocking cap pulled down over his forehead. All she could see were his eyes. She stared at him as he shoved the gun into one of the coverall's oversize pockets, treating it as if it were something he handled every day.

"Leave the car running." Jared lifted his kerchief over his nose and mouth.

Melanie looked from one to the other. Didn't they realize how ridiculous they looked? Then suddenly she decided she wanted this over with, the sooner, the better. Of course, she'd leave the car running, and she reached to turn off the A/C.

"We don't need the engine overheating at a time like this."

"Good idea, Mel," Jared muttered through the cloth, and his rare compliment actually seemed to soothe her a little.

Jared hesitated, checking out the parking lot, craning his neck and looking in all directions. They were out of sight from the traffic and no one had gone in or out of the bank since they had parked. But how much time had that been? Melanie tried to remember.

"Let's go," Jared said, and Charlie didn't hesitate at all.

She watched them in the rearview mirror cross the short distance to the front entrance. Her fingers drummed the steering wheel. Her right foot tapped uncontrollably. Maybe Charlie had gotten that habit from her. She looked away from the bank's entrance for five or ten seconds. Glancing into the rearview mirror, she noticed that her lower lip was red and bruised from biting down on it. She tucked a strand of hair back up into the cap. And that's when she heard the first blast, muffled but loud enough to make her jump. She sat forward, searching the surroundings, hoping to see a car backfiring. The next shots came fast, one after another, three, maybe four. She hadn't counted. She couldn't breathe, how could she count? Before she could react, she saw Charlie and Jared racing out of the bank's entrance, their figures filling the rearview mirror. She sat paralyzed, unable or unwilling to turn around and watch them out the back window. Instead, she stared at the mirror, pieces of them rushing closer.

Jared jumped in beside her. "Go. Go now. Get the fuck going."

"What happened? I heard shots."

"Just get the fuck out of here."

Charlie flew into the back seat as she shifted into drive and floored it, not even noticing the back door was still open until she saw in her side mirror that Charlie was hanging out, struggling to close it. She automatically slowed the car.

"What the fuck are you doing?" Jared slid across the front seat and slammed his foot on top of hers, pushing the accelerator and sending the car fishtailing around the access road. She swung wide to miss a semitrailer as she ran a stop sign, garnering a blast of his horn. The noise startled her and she jerked the car to the other side, throwing Jared up against his door. It took his foot off the accelerator.

"Up ahead." Jared pointed. "Back behind Sapp Brothers. I left a car for us, so we can dump this one." But before Melanie could get to the intersection, she heard a siren. And before she saw the black and white in the rearview mirror, she knew it was coming for them.

CHAPTER 15

4:33 p.m.

Melanie wished she could wake herself up. This had to be a fucking nightmare. Things couldn't possibly have gone so wrong, so fast. Even her vision seemed blurred, the buildings and landscape a swirl of concrete and green speeding past the car windows. Only the buildings and landscape weren't moving. She was. Fast. She was overwhelmed by a sensation of slipping and sliding as if out of control on black ice.

Jared's voice came to her in a muffled monotone. She could make out one or two words: "faster," "turn." It was difficult to hear over the whining sound that filled her head. Difficult, and yet she could hear Charlie retching in the back seat. He must still be on the floor. She couldn't see him in the rearview mirror. All she could see were red and blue flashing lights and the cruiser's grill so close that it looked like shark's teeth ready to bite and swallow them whole.

But through all the chaos she could still hear Charlie, her poor Charlie, retching and gagging. The sour smell of vomit filled the car, and Melanie felt her own stomach lurch. It wasn't the smell of vomit that nauseated her. It was something else…warm and rancid yet almost sweet.

"Get back on 50," Jared yelled at her. "Get the hell out of this maze."

She took a sharp left only to realize it was another parking-lot entrance and not an intersection.

"Fuck," Jared screamed at her. "There. Turn there!"

Where he was pointing looked like another parking lot. She missed the turn, jumped the curb and heard the sickening crunch of metal as the bottom of the car scraped the concrete. But the sound wasn't as awful as Jared's continued commands. He kept yelling at her to get back on Highway 50. She had no idea which way that was. She had lost all sense of direction. All she could see were buildings and parking lots and access roads. She twisted the steering wheel until the screech of tires told her to stop. The force spun the car around, almost a U-turn. And there on the other side of the cruiser barreling down on her was the traffic of Highway 50.

"Jesus Christ," Jared muttered, but he no longer dared to reach for the steering wheel or attempt to step on the accelerator.

Melanie held her breath. She wanted to close her eyes. She wanted to become invisible. She wanted to get the fuck out of here and go home. The black and white began to skid, avoiding hitting her by mere inches, the cars so close she could see the officer's face under the wide-brimmed hat. He was young. That much she could tell. And she thought he looked more surprised than angry. She heard another crunch of metal and squeezed her eyes shut, expecting to feel some impact, some repercussions. When she opened them again, Jared was twisted in his seat, staring out the back window.

"You did it, Mel. You fucking did it."

She didn't turn around. She didn't look in the mirror. She didn't want to know what she had done. Instead, she stepped on the accelerator and headed for the intersection. At the stoplight she hesitated.

"South," Jared told her. "Turn right. We want to leave Douglas County, remember?"

She glanced at him and only then did she notice the front of his coverall was wet and stained. That was when she recognized the smell that filled the car. It wasn't just Charlie's vomit. It was blood.

CHAPTER 16

4:46 p.m.
Platte River State Park

"So you think I have no life?" Andrew revived the subject as he shoved aside his plate and drained his second bottle of Bud Light. He rarely finished one.

Tommy sliced another chunk off his filet and stuffed it in his mouth. He had left his cell phone out on the table after losing the connection and trying to call back whoever had called him. He had pretended the phone call had been no big deal. Yeah, right. That's why he kept glancing at it as if expecting it to ring. "I'm just calling it like I see it, Murderman."

"Murderman." Andrew still smiled at the nickname Tommy and the other Omaha detectives had given him. Actually he liked it enough to use it for his e-mail address. That they had even bothered to give him a nickname had been a sign—an odd one, but still a good one—that the group approved of him.

He sat back in the wrought-iron chair, part of the bistro set on the screened-in porch. They had chosen to eat out here despite the stifling humidity. Andrew glanced at the sky. If only it would just rain and get it over with, but the thunderheads kept their distance, preferring just to threaten. The wind, however, had picked up, and the breeze was refreshing. It brought with it the scent of pine needles and the lulling sound of cicadas.

Andrew watched his friend devour a forkful of deli potato salad, following it with a bite of the garlic bread he had grilled alongside the filets. One thing Andrew had learned through his friendship with Tommy was that cops could eat no matter what the circumstances or surroundings were. He had watched Tommy chow down on a blood-rare porterhouse steak while showing Andrew Polaroids of a dismembered corpse.

Watching his friend, he realized, not for the first time, how very different the two of them were.

"You know, we probably wouldn't have even liked each other as kids?" The beer was starting to give him a buzz.

"I don't know about that," Tommy said. "You want that last piece of garlic bread?"

Andrew shook his head. "Seriously, though. You played tackle football in the middle of the streets during the summertime. I hid between chores on the farm just so I could read."

"We didn't play in the streets," Tommy corrected him, getting up from the table. "We played in the parking lot behind Al's Bar and Grill," he added now from inside the cabin as he pulled the last two beers from the fridge.

"You and your friends would have picked on me. You probably would have called me a sissy or a wuss."

Tommy handed him one of the bottles before sitting back down. "Kids do stupid stuff."

"Even now, you have to admit we're pretty different. You're South Omaha Polish dogs with kraut. You're an usher or some fricking thing at Saint Stanislaus. You coach Little League for your four daughters."

"I see what you're saying," Tommy said. "You're saying we reversed roles or something, right? You saying I'm the wuss now?"

Andrew laughed. He knew Tommy was humoring him, indulging his buzz. The beer seemed to have had no effect on Detective Pakula.

"You investigate murders. You step over corpses, collect maggots, poke around entrance and exit wounds. I just write about it."

"And you do a hell of a job." Tommy held up another forkful of potato salad in a salute.

"You deal in real life. I deal in make-believe."

"So what's your point?" But there was no impatience in his friend's tone, only curiosity.

"I guess I understand why you think I have no life."

"Oh, I see." This time Tommy sat back, finally realizing Andrew was serious and not joking around. "I didn't mean your work. I meant your personal life. When was the last time you were in a relationship? Or wait, I'll make it easier for you—when was the last time you got laid?"

"I told you there was someone I was interested in."

"Oh, that's right. A woman who's already sort of involved in a long-term relationship. The one who lives about a thousand miles away."

"See, why do I tell you personal stuff if you're just gonna make fun?"

"I'm not making fun. Hey, I can see where it might be safe to want somebody who doesn't want you back."

"Safe? Sure you don't mean stupid?"

"No, I mean safe. Especially safe for a guy like you."

"A guy like me?"

"Okay, now don't go getting postal with me." Tommy held up his hands in mock surrender.

"I'm not. Go on. Explain yourself." Andrew grabbed his third Bud Light by the bottle's neck and took a sip.

"You keep saying you don't do commitment, right? As soon as a woman starts showing any signs of getting serious you start running in the opposite direction. So, who do you choose to fall in love with? A woman who ain't ever gonna get serious on you."

"So, if your theory is correct, I'm a real schmuck."

"Oh, yeah, big-time."

"Thanks a lot."

"Actually, you're not a schmuck. It's evidently your method of survival."

"You're saying I don't really have feelings for this woman?"

"I'm saying it's safe to have feelings for her. You said she told you she's in with this guy for the long haul."

"Maybe she's confused."

"Maybe she enjoys jerking you around. You don't think she gets off having someone like you pining for her?"

Andrew sat back again, rubbing his jaw as if Tommy had just sucker punched him. The woman in question, an attractive redhead named Erin Cartlan, owned a small bookshop in lower Manhattan. They had met two years before when she introduced herself at Book Expo America and invited him to schedule a book signing at her store. She was attractive and witty, and he could still swear that she had been flirting with him that weekend though she denied it later, pretending not to know what he was even talking about. Since then they had maintained a sort of friendship, more professional than personal, although Andrew had to admit he constantly found himself hoping it would turn into something more.

Tommy was staring at him, shaking his head.

"Crap, now I've got you thinking about her. You won't get any writing done."

"I think you just like to see me miserable."

"That's my whole point. I *don't* like seeing you miserable. You're missing what I'm saying here. You seem content to pine for a woman you can't have. You write about crime scenes and autopsies but pass up opportunities to see them firsthand. You don't even want to eat the fish you catch." He shook his head. "From where I sit, that's not exactly living life to its fullest."

Andrew felt the heat crawl up his neck, but he kept the anger from his voice when he said, "I didn't bring enough beers for this conversation."

"You know I'm saying what I'm saying 'cause I care about you. You know that, right? Oh, fuck." Tommy grabbed for his belt, twisting the electronic pager attached so he could read the LED. "Sorry, buddy, something's going on. I'm gonna need to take off."

Tommy grabbed his cell phone and started to leave but stopped at the porch door. "You sure you're gonna be okay out here?"

Andrew shrugged with his good shoulder then nodded. "Yeah, of course." But he was still thinking about Erin and wondering how he'd ever fill those blank notebook pages now.

CHAPTER 17

5:15 p.m.
Highway 50

Melanie stabbed at the button on the car's door, locking and unlocking it, then finally bringing down her window. She needed to breathe. She needed some fresh air, some relief from the smell of vomit and blood. She gulped down the warm, damp wind then, grabbing her baseball hat before it blew away, she punched the button for the window to close.

"We need to backtrack," Jared told her, sitting sideways in his seat and watching out the back window.

She saw the gun in his lap, his finger still on the trigger. In the rearview mirror she watched for Charlie. The gags and awful retching had stopped. Occasionally she saw his head bob up into view.

"I said we need to turn around." Jared's voice had

returned to calm and demanding. "We need to dump this car."

He reached into the back seat, and Melanie thought he was checking on Charlie. Instead, he grabbed Charlie's gun by its nose, holding it as though it was contaminated. He opened his window and tossed the gun, flinging it into the grassy ditch. He kept his own gun in his lap while he reached into the back seat and pulled up his duffel bag.

"Turn around up here," he told her again without looking at her or the road.

She heard the duffel bag's zipper, but she kept her eyes on the highway, glancing in the rearview and side mirrors, watching, expecting at any minute to see them fill with blue and red flashing lights. The highway divided up ahead—he must mean the next intersection. She could see the road sign indicating the turnoff for Springfield. Oncoming traffic had tapered to a few cars. She could do a U-ie without much fuss. She started to slow down, watching the line of traffic behind her, some cars already moving over to the temporary passing lane to pass by them. She felt relief that none of the cars looked like police cruisers, yet the uneasiness in the pit of her stomach warned her it was pushing their luck to head back into the line of fire. But she had to trust that Jared knew what he was doing.

"Forget about it," Jared said suddenly. "Just keep going."

"There's not that much traffic. I can do it."

"Fuck it. Keep going."

And then, as they got closer, she saw it. On their left at the Phillip 66 Station was a black and white, Sarpy County Sheriff's Department in bold print on its side. She hadn't noticed it before because it had been partially hidden by the gas pumps. Now, as they drove by, there it was.

"Don't speed," Jared instructed. "Don't make any stupid moves."

Melanie wanted to tell him it wasn't any of *her* stupid moves that had gotten them into this mess. She wanted to tell him if it hadn't been for her quick—not stupid—moves they'd already be sitting in the back of a police cruiser. Instead, she simply flipped on her turn signal and eased back into traffic, trying to ignore her sweaty palms, fists gripping the steering wheel. Her teeth were clenched again, her lower lip between them. Her eyes darted back and forth as she tried to keep her head from moving, from looking in the direction of the cruiser. It was like roadkill in the middle of the highway and that annoying instinct to look even though you knew you shouldn't.

"Stay calm," Jared was saying, suddenly smooth and comforting.

Melanie recognized his seductive tone, the one he used like hypnosis usually to take the sting out of one of his cutting insults.

"No sudden moves," he said. "Just be cool."

She caught a glimpse of Charlie, now huddled on the seat in a ball, hugging his backpack, face white, eyes glazed. She didn't have time to worry about him, not now when it took all her concentration to keep the car in the right lane of the two-lane highway and watch the cruiser in her side mirror.

Jared was watching the highway, too, while digging in the duffel bag. Soon she heard a rhythmic *click-click* and her stomach pitched when she saw him reloading the gun.

She wanted to tell him his gun had already gotten them into enough trouble, to remind him that she and Charlie had never had to use guns before. Instead, she said nothing.

Both she and Jared were so focused on the black and white at the gas station that neither noticed the one in the oncoming traffic. Melanie gasped out loud when it passed by.

"Be cool," Jared said as he turned his entire body to watch out the back window.

Melanie forced her eyes forward. She couldn't, wouldn't look in the car mirrors. She held her breath and kept the car steady despite her shaking hands and pounding heart.

"Fuck, fuck," Jared said. And she knew before he added, "Here he comes."

CHAPTER 18

5:23 p.m.

Grace let Emily wear Vince's William and Mary alumni baseball cap. He had also promised his daughter she could use his favorite travel mug for her juice but Grace couldn't find that box. As Grace passed Emily's bedroom she could hear her daughter telling her friend, Bitsy, about her daddy's favorite cap, his lucky cap.

She checked her watch and decided she had time to unpack one more box before she started their dinner. It was amazing that they had managed these past weeks with all their worldly belongings buried in cardboard boxes, half mislabeled and the other half not labeled at all. This evening she needed to get back to the case files she had brought home. She had a preliminary set for Friday morning. Another crack whore up on drug charges. The only reason she remembered so clearly was because the defendant was being represented by Max Kramer. She thought that perhaps after his media stint with Barnett ole Max wouldn't need to defend any more lowlifes.

Sometimes Grace wondered why men like Max Kramer became lawyers.

For Grace it was easy. When anyone asked— though the question came less frequently these days—why she had chosen to become a lawyer, she always said, without hesitation, that it was because of Atticus Finch. As a little girl Grace had been mesmerized by Harper Lee's character in *To Kill a Mockingbird* who Gregory Peck brought to life on film. In the courtroom scenes, Atticus commanded respect, dressed in that crisply pressed three-piece suit, the shiny chain of his watch dangling when he pushed back his jacket and put his hands in his trouser pockets. Atticus Finch was a strong, quiet hero, the true personification of good in the midst of evil.

Yes, Atticus Finch had inspired Grace to become a lawyer. That's what she told anyone who asked, especially anyone in the media. It was easy, less messy, and for the most part, it was true. However, it was Jimmy Lee Parker who convinced Grace she should be a prosecutor. It was Jimmy Lee Parker who, on a hot, sticky night in July 1964, broke into a police officer's home, sneaked up the narrow staircase to the officer and his wife's bedroom and bashed in their skulls with a baseball bat.

That was the summer Grace turned six. She was spending that night, just three blocks away, at her grandma Wenny's. She didn't remember much about the rest of that summer, the summer she went to live with her grandmother. The summer Jimmy Lee Parker killed Omaha police officer Fritz Wenninghoff and his wife, Emily.

Yes, Jimmy Lee Parker was the reason Grace had become a prosecutor. She doubted that Max Kramer had any Jimmy Lees who had inspired him or surely he never would have believed freeing Jared Barnett to be justice.

Grace ripped open another box using a bit more force than necessary. She didn't like thinking about that summer her father and mother were murdered in their own home, in their own bed. Although she couldn't remember much about it. She dug into the box, shoving aside the flaps. Finally, the bathroom towels. She needed to get her mind back to the present. She loaded up an armful and headed for the bathroom, but this time when she passed Emily's room she heard her daughter say, "You saw the shadow man?"

Grace stopped and listened.

"He was here inside our house?"

"Emily," Grace interrupted, "what shadow man are you talking about?"

"The one Daddy talked about."

Grace remembered Vince telling her to not look for Barnett in the shadows. That had to be what

Emily was referring to. "You mean at the airport?" Emily nodded. She was sitting on the edge of her bed, facing the antique dresser and mirror. "He was only joking, sweetie. There is no shadow man."

"Bitsy says he was here today," Emily said, looking over Grace's shoulder as if her friend was standing there. Only when Grace turned, there was just the dresser and mirror.

"Now, how would Bitsy know?"

"She saw him sneaking around. He took Mr. McDuff."

Grace didn't want to get angry with Emily, but she wasn't sure why she was making all this up. Maybe the idea of a shadow man had really frightened her.

"Are you sure you didn't misplace him?"

Emily shook her head. "He was on my bed where I always leave him."

Grace looked around the room. The rest of the house was a mess but Emily had organized her room. Definitely not a trait she inherited from her mother. The stuffed white dog was nowhere in sight.

"I'm sure he's here somewhere."

"Bitsy said the shadow man took him."

Grace rubbed at the ever-present knot in the back of her neck. She was beginning to get impatient, but kept her voice calm. "Sweetie, you know Daddy and I would never let anyone hurt you. You know that, right?"

Emily nodded again, but she seemed distracted. She glanced over Grace's shoulder again. Maybe it was nothing all. Maybe she really was just playing, just talking.

"Why don't you look around and see if McDuff is downstairs?"

"Okay."

Grace started out the door but Emily said, "Mommy, Bitsy says we should lock the door from the house to the garage whenever we leave from now on."

Grace stared at her daughter, and for a brief second she felt a chill, like a draft from an open door. How in the world did Emily know they didn't lock that door?

Before getting back to the boxes she stopped to check all the locks on the doors and windows. Then she realized how silly she was being. She couldn't let Emily's fear and confusion cloud her judgment or frighten her. And she wouldn't let Jared Barnett make her jump at shadows.

She had unpacked only one box when the phone interrupted her.

"Hello," she answered, distracted and thinking it would be easier to go out and buy new things.

"Grace, glad I found you."

It was Pakula and only then did she remember she hadn't called him back after they'd been disconnected.

"I'm okay. I know I should have called you back after we got cut off."

"What?"

"My damsel-in-distress call."

"Oh, yeah. No, that's okay. That's not why I'm calling. I've got something you're gonna wanna see."

Grace looked around for a pen. She knew if Tommy didn't have time to joke around this was serious.

"What's going on?"

"I'm at the Nebraska Bank of Commerce, that little branch off Highway 50. You know the one? Back behind Sapp Brothers, off I-80."

"You're actually at the bank?" She found a pen and looked for paper, settling instead for the top of a packing box to jot down the directions.

"Yeah, it's a fucking mess."

"Pakula, you're the last one I need to remind, bank robberies are the feds' mess."

"Not when there's a homicide."

She figured as much. "You think it's the convenience-store robber moving up and getting trigger-happy?" There had been three robberies across the city at different convenience stores. It wasn't unusual for a robber to get cocky and think he was ready for a bigger hit.

"A black and white got a good look. We're running the plate number. Hold on," he said and she could hear a muffled conversation. She recognized Pakula's "Holy crap," followed by a "fuck." Then he was back on the line. "This is one fucking mess. You think you can come take a look?"

"I need to take Emily over to my grandmother's. I should be there in about fifteen to twenty."

"I have to warn you, Grace—"

"I know, it's a fucking mess."

"I don't think I've seen this much blood in one place since the Jepperson drug bust in '97."

"So there's more than one homicide?"

"Last count there might be five."

"Christ, Pakula! Why didn't you say that in the beginning?"

"I thought I did. I better go. See you in fifteen."

CHAPTER 19

5:38 p.m.

Melanie laid on the horn but the SUV in front of them didn't budge, adhering to the sixty-five-mile-an-hour speed limit. In the rearview mirror, she could see cars and trucks pulling to the roadside, like waters parting, for the flashing cruiser. He'd be on her tail in seconds. There were hills, inclines, not enough room for passing zones. Yet when Jared yelled, *"Go around the motherfucker,"* Melanie didn't hesitate.

Sure enough, on the other side of the hill was a truck headed straight for them. She'd never make it. In front of the SUV was a blue compact she hadn't anticipated. She jerked back to the right, scraping against the SUV, shocking the driver into pulling to the side of the road. Now in her side mirror she could see him driving through the ditches before smashing into a fence.

"Serves him right," Jared said. "Maybe the others will know to get out of our way."

But even as he said it, Melanie had to weave around the blue compact. A pickup truck with a trailer was up ahead, and Melanie knew she'd never make it around him before the curve. And from what she could see, it looked as if they were coming to another bridge and another town.

"Don't slow down," Jared warned her. "Use the shoulder."

"Are you nuts? It's not wide enough."

"Sure it is. Just do it." He was turned in his seat again with the gun aimed at the back window. *"Do it now, damn it."*

She wanted to close her eyes. The curve was impossible at this speed—eighty-five at her last glance—and she might not be able to keep control.

"You can do it, Mel." His tone was somewhere between soothing and a yell.

She held her breath and twisted the steering wheel to the right. She heard the tire hit the edge and felt the pull. The car bounced, the steering wheel jerking out of her grasp. Before she could maneuver the car back onto the pavement, her hands were slick with sweat. So was her back, the T-shirt fabric stuck to her like a second skin. Her heart pounded loud enough to keep her from hearing Jared's continued instructions. She barely pulled the car back onto the highway before the bridge. A few more yards and they would have been flying into the water.

The bridge slowed down the cruiser. With no place on the sides for cars to pull over, the flashing blue and red lights stayed behind the pickup and trailer. Melanie floored it despite the REDUCE SPEED signs and despite entering the outskirts of Louisville.

More curves. More inclines.

"Turn up ahead," Jared instructed her, and she wouldn't have noticed the turnoff except for a sign with an arrow for Platte River State Park.

She followed his directions, only seeing his wisdom after she took another curve going seventy-five. With all the inclines and curves, the cruiser hadn't been in sight when she turned. He couldn't see her now, either. He would automatically think they'd continued on Highway 50.

"Did we lose him?" She almost didn't want to know.

"Keep going."

"I am. But is he still coming?"

"Up ahead. Off to your right is the state park. Pull in there." He was already pointing but she couldn't see it. "It's a long road into the park. There should be a sign."

"I can't see him." She watched the rearview mirror, her eyes trying to take in all angles. She was tempted to turn around, just for a second or two, to look.

"It's there. It's right there," Jared yelled.

But it was too late. She was going too fast. She

saw the park entrance. Perhaps she felt cocky after all the stunts she had pulled off. She thought she could make it despite not slowing enough. She thought she had judged the distance, the angle. She twisted the steering wheel too much, too quickly, and suddenly the car was airborne, flying over the deep ditch, scraping through the barbed-wire fence—the screech of wire against metal—before slamming hard, the chassis rocking. They skidded through the tall cornstalks, a sound like wind whipping against the glass. The smell of antifreeze and gasoline filled her nostrils along with hot, stale air.

When they finally came to a complete stop all Melanie could see through the windshield were cornstalks and bulging gray thunderheads.

CHAPTER 20

5:51 p.m.

An Omaha police officer waved Grace through the maze of rescue vehicles, cruisers and media vans. She didn't know all the younger officers, including this one, but most of them knew her or at least knew who she was. It wasn't unusual for the police and the district attorney's office to work together, starting at the crime scene. However, it had taken a while—certainly not an overnight victory—for the Omaha Police Department and the Douglas County Sheriff's Department to treat the only woman county prosecutor like an asset instead of a pain in the ass.

At a side door to the brick bank building another officer handed Grace a pair of latex gloves, shoe covers and a face mask. She declined the mask, slipped the paper shoe covers over her leather flats and tugged on the gloves. She followed the narrow hallway past two closed doors, one with a nameplate. Hopefully, Mr. Avery Harmon had taken the day off or left early.

Even before she reached the lobby, she could smell it. It filled her nostrils: sour and rancid, so strong she could almost taste it. She stopped at the doorway, but only because she wanted to examine the scene. She wanted to take it all in, memorize it for later, imagining the lobby without the detectives, without the coroner, without the Douglas County lab technicians.

She counted three bodies. Pakula had said there might be five. One, a woman, lay facedown close to the bank's double glass doors that led to a small entrance. Was she a customer on her way out when the shooting began? From where she stood, Grace couldn't tell where the bullet had entered, though it looked like a back head shot. That's where the blood had pooled. A man in a shirt and tie lay crumpled in the doorway to a side office, his crisply starched white shirt now stained red. At the teller counter lay an old man, flat on his back. He was the closest to Grace, so close she could see his blue eyes staring up at the ceiling, one lens of his wire-rimmed glasses crushed.

"There's another behind the counter," Tommy Pakula said, appearing suddenly beside Grace.

"Tell me," she said, ready to hear his version.

By now the two of them skipped formalities, grateful for the other's direct method or what Tommy liked to call their "no-bullshit approach."

"They left the cameras intact." He pointed out the three various angles. "They're the cheap son-of-a-bitching ones. Three-second delay. That one takes a picture of its piece of the bank, then that one, then the last one. One of the feds took the tapes. We'll take a look in a little bit, but don't expect much."

She glanced at Pakula. He was in jeans and a yellow golf shirt. He always dressed sharp, shirts tucked in, even the jeans creased, but today there were uncharacteristic rings of sweat under his armpits and his head and forehead glistened. It was only then that Grace realized how warm it was inside the lobby. Something must have gone wrong with the A/C. No way would any of these guys have shut it off.

"Not quite sure how this went down." Pakula always said this before he told her exactly how it went down. In the early days she thought he was just another cocky, macho cop until she realized that nine out of ten times he could get it all right: the caliber, the direction and the sequence.

"We think there were two of them. The beat cop who got a look at the car before he crashed his own said there were two of them. Makes sense inside here that there were two. I'm figuring they come in the front. One stays close to the door. The other heads for the counter. The receptionist gets it first." He pointed to the bloody spot under the desk where there was no body. "The guy in the office hears the shot. Comes out to see what's going on, but either he or the teller trips the silent alarm.

He gets blasted. Both customers probably get it next. I'm guessing the teller behind the counter was last."

"Did the receptionist make it?"

"We're crossing our fingers, but she's in bad shape. She slid under the desk after she was hit. May have saved her life. They couldn't see her good enough to know if they'd killed her. It's a head shot, so don't go getting your hopes up for a witness."

"You said the teller was last. Why?"

"Oh, yeah. This you gotta see. Don't have a fucking hemorrhage, though, okay?"

"Why would I have a fucking hemorrhage?"

He led her around the counter, both of them stepping carefully over the old man. Grace noticed his tweed suit, shirt collar buttoned, the tie in a perfect knot. It had to be a hundred degrees out today when you figured in the humidity, and yet this guy had probably dressed up for his regular weekly trip to the bank. She was still thinking about the old man when Pakula knelt down beside the teller, gently lifting her head, the blond hair matted with blood sticking to her face, almost making it impossible for Grace to see the entrance wound. Until Pakula lifted the chin. Then she could see it, a small smudged black hole at the lower left jawline. The shooter would have had to have taken time to shove the gun up under her chin.

Grace met Pakula's eyes and now she understood. They both recognized the wound as a trademark, the signature of a killer who purposely shattered his victims' teeth so it would take longer to identify them.

"It's not possible, is it?" Grace asked.

Pakula just shook his head.

CHAPTER 21

6:05 p.m.

It must have been close to six o'clock when Andrew
first heard it. Out here in the quiet the whirl of the
helicopter blades seemed amplified, the sound echo-
ing off the trees and water. At first he thought it might
be the Life Flight—maybe there had been a car accident, some medical emergency. Except this wasn't
a pass by, or even a low sweep to find a landing. No,
this copter seemed to be circling, flying low over the
treetops.

Andrew saved his file, closed the program and
shut the lid of his laptop. He had been trying to use
the laptop, discouraged and frustrated by the blank
notebook pages, so white, so empty, staring at him.
He left everything on the metal table in the screened-
in porch, then searched for his shoes, sliding them
on without doing up the laces.

It had taken only a few minutes to locate it, but now outside the cabin he could see the helicopter hanging a right to come back over the park. What in the world was it doing? Surely it wasn't checking out the storm? Was it a rescue unit or a pilot in trouble? There was nowhere to land—too many trees and even the pasture that bordered the park was too hilly with ravines and brush. On the other side stretched the Platte River—not much of a choice. If this guy had some sort of emergency, he'd picked a hell of a spot to try to land.

Andrew watched the helicopter almost scrape the trees, and this time it flew low enough that he could see the letters on its side: POLICE.

What the hell was the Omaha police helicopter looking for? Or rather *who* was it looking for? He wondered if this had anything to do with the call that made Tommy take off.

Andrew hurried back into the cabin. He pulled out the nine-inch TV he had brought with him. Rarely did he turn the thing on. Reception was awful out here. If he was lucky he could sometimes get one channel and that was with masterful manipulation of the bunny ears. He plugged in the set, turned it on and began to twist and turn, finally having some luck with Omaha's Channel 7.

He glanced at his wrist—no watch—but it looked as though the six o'clock news was still on. He turned up the volume, a crackled sound track to accompany the rolling lines that blurred the station's anchors. Julie Cornell and Rob McCartney looked a bit purple and outlined in orange but it didn't matter. They were talking about a search for two suspects. Andrew turned up the volume once more.

"Again, that's south on Highway 50. Two male suspects in a late-model sedan," Julie explained as a map graphic showed the route. "The two men allegedly robbed the Nebraska Bank of Commerce late this afternoon. Police chased the suspects south on Highway 50. Details are still sketchy. We'll have more as information continues to come in."

Andrew shut the TV off. A high-speed chase on Highway 50? That was an accident waiting to happen. Maybe that's exactly what *had* happened. He didn't need to hear the media's speculation.

He glanced back out at the laptop and notebooks on the porch's table. Several loose sheets had blown off into the corners, probably gathering spiderwebs. One was stuck up against the screen, having impaled itself on a broken screen wire. The wind had picked up. The storm was getting closer.

Andrew grabbed another Diet Pepsi from the refrigerator and headed back to his work. He shoved aside the laptop. He picked up one of the empty spiral notebooks, opening it and watching the breeze try to flip the pages. In the distance the whirl of the helicopter now competed with the rumble of thunder. Andrew shook out a Uniball pen from the freshly opened box of a dozen, and for the first time in a long time he began to write, adding the scratching sound of pen on paper to those sounds already around him.

CHAPTER 22

6:11 p.m.

Grace took her place beside Pakula in the cramped confines of the van. Special Agent Jimmy Sanchez from the Omaha FBI office and Pakula's partner, Detective Ben Hertz, were also huddled inside.

Darcy Kennedy, one of the Douglas County crime lab techs, slipped one of the bank's videos into a VCR slot. The panel of instruments and equipment didn't look anything like a home entertainment center. The video display screen was a small computer with a keypad.

"I can't do much to it here," Darcy reminded them. "This is the camera shooting the entrance. Keep in mind, there are three cameras in the loop. This one on the entrance, one shooting the teller's counter and another one on the bank's vault. They take turns. Even though it's a video, it's sort of like quick snapshots. Camera number one clicks, then two, then three. It's continuous but there is a three-second delay. Three seconds may not sound like much, but when you consider we only have slices of the big picture, every second counts."

The black-and-white picture barely resembled the bank lobby. No surprise to Grace, especially after a week of viewing crappy convenience-store videos. She put on a pair of reading glasses, but nothing could improve the jerky static.

"I've isolated their entrance. It's coming up."

It seemed to take forever, and Grace finally wedged her way out from between Pakula and Sanchez enough that she could breathe. Despite the cranked-up A/C in the van, it felt like a sauna. And the three men—Pakula's short wrestler's build, Sanchez's tall hunched back and Hertz's pot-belly—took up every possible inch of the mobile crime lab.

Finally two figures appeared on the screen, but they were gone as quickly as they appeared. Darcy Kennedy pushed some buttons to rewind and stop the picture. She tapped the keyboard and the two figures filled the computer screen again. Grace took mental notes but there wasn't much to distinguish them— dark-colored jumpsuits, some sort of mask over their lower faces, handguns held down at their sides.

Darcy tapped again on the keyboard, blowing up a view of their faces.

One man looked off to the side, but the other

stared directly at them, blurred, static-riddled eyes visible between the mask and dark cap.

"He's looking directly at the camera." Pakula said out loud what Grace was thinking. "Almost as if the asshole wanted his picture taken."

"Are those kerchiefs around their faces?" Sanchez asked. "They look like some fucking Wild West bank robbers."

"A modern-day Jesse and Frank James," Hertz laughed.

"We have their exit on tape. It's about as exciting as the entrance. That's all we have on this one." Darcy clicked more buttons then ejected the tape. "The camera on the bank vault has nothing as far as I can tell. The one focused on the teller windows has a few interesting tidbits."

She pushed in the next video. Immediately Grace could make out the long counter, only one person behind it and the old man in front. Already the three-second delay proved annoying, the figures jerking like in an antiquated Charlie Chaplin movie. Then one of the masked men appeared in the corner of the frame. The next frame showed the old man down on his knees with his hands behind his head as if he had been instructed to do so. Suddenly the masked man was on the counter, caught in midjump, bright white tennis shoe clear amidst the grainy static. Three seconds later, and the next frame showed him shoving the gun against the woman teller's chin, this camera's angle catching her wide eyes. By the next frame, she was gone, somewhere down behind the counter, probably under the killer's hunched-over back. Three more seconds later and he was looking over his shoulder, but now the old man was lying on the floor. Another three seconds and the masked man was gone.

"That's it," Darcy said, rewinding and freeze-framing the teller's last seconds of life.

"We don't have anything of the others?" Pakula asked.

"Nothing. The reception desk and that side office are out of view of any of the cameras."

"From what we've got, it's hard to tell what the hell went wrong." Hertz pulled out a cigarette and began tapping the tobacco end against his hand as if he couldn't wait the extra second to take it out when he escaped the van.

"From what we've got," Pakula followed up, "it looks like he fucking meant to kill that teller."

"Jesus, these cameras are shitty," Sanchez said. "The public hears we've caught the robbers on video and they think it's an open-and-shut case. In truth, we have diddly-squat."

"Not quite diddly-squat." Darcy pressed a few buttons and brought up the frame of the masked robber jumping over the counter. "We're taking a shoe print now. With some video enhancement I should be able to read the funny little emblem on the side. By tomorrow morning we'll be able to tell you the make and the shoe size. There was some residue in the grooves, which was left behind on the counter. Mostly dirt but some little blue pebbles with flecks of gray in them. They're actually pretty." She lifted a plastic bag of what appeared to be dirt with tiny bits of colored rock. "I dusted this off the counter earlier. Who knows, I might be able to tell you where he was today before he stopped by."

Pakula took the bag and held it up in front of him, close enough for Grace to get a good look, as well.

"Wait a minute," Grace said. She took the bag and fingered the pebbles through the plastic. Her stomach did a flip despite her attempt to not jump to conclusions.

"What is it?" They were all staring at her now, waiting.

"I think I recognize these. They look exactly like the pebbles I just had put in my backyard walkways."

CHAPTER 23

6:17 p.m.

Melanie's chest ached. It hurt to breathe. And every labored breath tasted of gasoline.

She heard moaning then a rumble. Maybe it was only thunder. Everything else was quiet, even the car's chassis had finally stopped creaking and the engine had stopped hissing. She reached to unbuckle her seat belt, and then realized she didn't have it on. That was why her chest hurt. She vaguely remembered crashing into the steering wheel. The air bag hadn't deployed. She was lucky she hadn't gone through the windshield.

She heard another moan and looked beside her to find Jared gone, his car door wide open. Then suddenly the panic returned and she spun around, climbing over the seat.

"Charlie? Are you okay?"

He lay crouched on the floor, his legs twisted under him, his back facing her.

"Charlie, are you all right?" she asked again, hanging over the front seat and touching his shoulder. No reaction. She tapped, then shoved him before she got a response. Another groan, only this time he pulled himself up off the floor and rolled onto the back seat. That's when Melanie saw the blood on his coveralls, dark splatters as if someone had shaken a Coke bottle before opening it and sprayed it all over. For a minute she worried the blood was his own. When she realized it wasn't, there was little relief. The streaks of yellow vomit, however, were his.

"What happened, Charlie?" she asked, hanging across the front of the seat. "What the hell did you and Jared do?"

He wouldn't meet her eyes. Not a good sign.

"Charlie, I asked you a fucking question."

"We gotta go." Jared startled her, suddenly appearing in the open car doorway. He was out of his coveralls, the stocking cap and kerchief gone, too.

"I wanna know what the hell happened back there," she demanded of the two of them even though it felt as if there were knives poking into her chest whenever she took a deep breath. Her cap was gone, her hair a tangled mess, and she batted it out of her eyes so that she could stare down Jared. Not that it ever worked. "Tell me what the fuck happened. I have a right to know."

"We need to get the fuck out of here, *now.*"

He pulled open the back door and to Charlie said, "I'm sick of this crybaby act. Get the fuck up."

But neither Melanie nor Charlie moved. She had never heard Jared talk that way to her son. Obviously Charlie had never heard it, either. He stared at Jared with glassy eyes, looking as if he had just been awakened from a deep sleep rather than been flung through the air and bounced around the crammed confines of the Saturn's back seat.

"Get those coveralls off, too," Jared told him.

"But you said—"

"Shut the fuck up and get moving."

This time Charlie did as he was told. Melanie stayed still, watching her son wrestle out of the coveralls, ripping the kerchief off and flinging it out the car door. He scrubbed his face with his hands, digging his fingers into his eyes with such force that Melanie wondered if it was an attempt to erase what he had seen.

When he was finished, his face looked striped, the fake suntan rubbed off in streaks. She wanted to wipe his face, a mother's instinct. She also wanted to grab him by the shoulders and shake him—another mother's instinct.

"Hurry up," Jared yelled again. He was on the other side of the car, crouched down, burying something in the dirt between the smashed cornstalks. It was only then that Melanie realized she could see nothing but cornstalks, the rows too tall to look over. Other than the path their car had sliced through the field, they were surrounded by nothing but yellow-green cornstalks and dark gray sky, the bottom ready to drop out at any moment. The rumble of thunder grew closer. The wind had picked up, whistling through the rows, setting the long leaves and tall stalks waving. They were almost ready to harvest, more yellow than green, dry enough that the wind caused them to rustle and crackle.

Beneath the darkening sky, that sound gave Melanie a chill. Maybe it was only the breeze against her damp body. Yet she couldn't help remembering that their mother claimed there were certain sounds and sights that warned of bad luck. Birds were on the top of her list. Melanie listened to the crows, a black cloud of them flew overhead, their caws sounding like scoldings. But then they were gone, quickly replaced by the low growl of the approaching thunder and the increasing whirl of the wind. Except it wasn't the wind Melanie was hearing now.

"Shit!" Jared yelled, making her jump even before she recognized the sound of the helicopter. "We need to get moving. Into the fucking field and stay low."

When Melanie didn't move, he shoved her from behind, almost knocking her to the ground. She saw Charlie disappear ahead, half crawling, half running in the ditch between the rows of stalks. She followed, trying to mimic his moves, Jared prodding her forward. The ache in her chest competed with the pounding in her head and the vibration beneath her feet. And somewhere in the back of her mind she remembered that crows were an omen of misfortune and death.

CHAPTER 24

6:25 p.m.

"It's Barnett." Grace only said out loud what both she and Pakula were thinking. "And he's been in my fucking backyard."

"We don't know that," he insisted.

"Vince special-ordered those pebbles from some landscape place on the West Coast."

"We don't know it's the exact pebbles. They looked like fish-tank rocks to me. Why don't we wait until you get a sample to Darcy and she checks it out?"

"I know it's him."

"There's no reason for him to do this. And there's no reason to try to hide the victim's identity by blasting her teeth to pieces." Pakula leaned against Grace's SUV, his arms crossed. He wasn't buying her theory, or else he was making her work at convincing him.

"Maybe this time it wasn't to destroy evidence or identity. Maybe this time it was simply to thumb his nose at us. You know, let us know it was him."

"He just got out less than two fuckin' weeks ago."

"You said yourself he got away with murder once. Why wouldn't he be feeling invincible?"

"Invincible, maybe, but stupid? I don't think so." He shook his head, but his eyes were still watching the bodies being brought out.

Grace looked at the sky and glanced at her watch. On the drive here she had heard they were in a severe thunderstorm watch. She wanted to pick up Emily before the lightning show. Her little tomboy had recently declared her fear of lightning. And now Grace had created yet another fear…a shadow man.

"So, why even do it?" Pakula asked, bringing her back. "It looks like they didn't even take any cash."

"Start checking out the victims, and I'll bet you'll find some connection."

He looked at her, meeting her eyes and holding them there as if he wasn't pleased with her telling him what to do. Had she nudged him too far? "Isn't that what you're always telling me?" she defended herself.

"It doesn't usually work with random shooting sprees like this."

"Have you been listening to me at all, Pakula? I'm telling you this wasn't random."

"You sure you don't want a black and white checking on you?"

"I'll be fine. Besides, if it is Barnett he's not going to have much time to be following me in the next few days, is he? I'm a little worried about Emily. Vince said something this morning about me looking for a man in the shadows and Emily overheard. Now she's worried about a shadow man watching our house."

"And now you think he might have been watching your house?"

"I don't know. Emily's imaginary friend, Bitsy, saw someone." She meant it as a joke but she could see from Pakula's frown that he didn't get it.

"Her imaginary friend?"

"Oh, yeah, didn't I tell you about that? Ever since we moved in, Emily has had this imaginary friend who seems to be all knowing. You've got four daughters, Pakula, did any of them have imaginary friends?"

"I *wish* their friends were imaginary. Angie's dating a kid who has so many body piercings he looks like a fucking pincushion." He rolled his shoulders, stretched his neck as if reminded of a tension in his muscles. Grace noticed his eyes, though, were still taking everything in. For a brief moment she wondered how a daughter of Pakula's thought she could get anything by him. And just when she thought his mind had wandered back to the crime scene, he said, "Why the hell would anybody wanna put a hole in his tongue? Wouldn't that kill your taste buds?"

"It's supposed to enhance your sex life."

This time he looked at Grace as if this warranted

his full attention. They didn't usually talk about personal stuff, let alone sex. Whatever they knew about each other's family and personal life came in short sound bites and offhanded remarks.

"Thanks a lot," Pakula finally said, but there was no hint of gratitude in his tone, no smile. "That's just what a father wants to hear, that his daughter's new boyfriend is *enhancing* himself for sex."

Grace laughed. She couldn't help it. Detective Tommy Pakula was one of the toughest men she knew, yet she could easily imagine him worried sick about his daughters.

Ben Hertz was walking toward them, waiting for a police cruiser to pass. He tapped its trunk with the palm of his hand. Grace recognized the gesture. Hertz was always patting backs, punching shoulders and even tapping hoods and trunks in place of saying "good job." He waved a piece of paper at Pakula as he joined them.

"You're gonna love this. Plates are registered to a Dr. Leon Matese. But it's not a dark blue Saturn. It's a black BMW. And Dr. Matese has been in L.A. since last Tuesday."

"Let me guess," Pakula interrupted him. "His car's been parked at the airport."

"Yep, long-term parking lot. And the Saturn—"

"Stolen," Pakula finished.

"You got it. These boys did some planning. But a Sarpy County deputy sheriff's in pursuit south on 50."

CHAPTER 25

6:28 p.m.

Razors sliced her skin. At least that's what Melanie thought it felt like as she tried to run. If the cornstalks weren't cutting her they were whipping her face. She held her arms up in front of her but kept losing her balance, her feet stumbling over the mounds of dirt. Jared insisted they not stick to the ditches between the rows but instead run diagonally through the field, so they would stay better hidden. But it was impossible to run, one foot plunging into the indent between the rows while the other foot climbed mounds of dirt.

The stalks were stronger than she expected and closely planted. It was more like trudging through a forest of saplings than a field. She was exhausted, her chest felt as though it would explode, and each gulp of air stabbed as it went in and out of her lungs. Her legs ached now, too, and her arms felt battered and bruised. Her ears were ringing with the sound of the wind, the growing roar of thunder and somewhere the whirl of a helicopter. She expected it to swoop down into the field at any minute. Was it possible that it hadn't discovered the car yet?

She no longer had any sense of direction, and she wasn't sure they'd ever find their way out of the field. It seemed endless. And hopeless. It was difficult to determine what was the wind and what was the helicopter. But the thunder—another rumble sent a vibration through her—continued to grow. So did the lightning. The flashes made the rolling black clouds come to life. In between flashes it had become so dark Melanie could barely see Charlie in front of her. They were in a tunnel; a tunnel with whips lashing out and no end in sight.

Suddenly a gust of wind whirled overhead and Melanie found herself falling. Her knees slammed into the dirt. Her flailing arms couldn't protect her jaw and cheek from scraping down the trunk of a cornstalk, the sharp leaves rubbing her skin raw. Jared fell on top of her, smashing her legs underneath his weight.

"Stay down," she heard him whisper and felt his elbow or knee in the small of her back as if he was making sure she did as he said.

Melanie ached. He didn't have to worry about her wanting to go anywhere. She wanted to crawl into a hole and get away from all of this. She hurt all over.

Then she realized the whirl of wind above them was the helicopter. She tried to quiet her breathing. With Jared on top of her she had no choice but to stay still. She couldn't move beneath his weight. The side of her face pressed against the ground, the soil actually cooling the sting on her cheek.

She lay perfectly still, waiting, waiting for the spotlight, waiting for the cornstalks to be separated and flattened, waiting for the whipping sound of blades to descend on top of them. She listened to Jared's breathing. She could hear his heart banging against her back. She could smell his sweat mixed with the corn and the dirt. Or was it fear she smelled?

Maybe it would be quick. Maybe they would simply riddle their bodies full of bullets. It didn't matter because any second the banging in her chest would surely explode. It seemed as if the helicopter was directly above them. And yet as suddenly as it appeared, it was gone. No spotlight, only the flickers of lightning. No hail of bullets, only thunder.

They laid there for what must have been minutes, but to Melanie it felt like hours. Her face was smashed into the dirt. Her chest ached. She couldn't breathe. And yet she listened. But there was only the ever-approaching thunder. Even the wind had died down. No gusts, no whirls, only a gentle rustling of the stalks.

"They're gone," Jared whispered, shoving himself off her with such force he pushed her deeper into the dirt.

"The lightning," Charlie said. "I bet they can't fly in this weather." He crawled up beside Melanie. She realized he had grabbed his backpack out of the car and was hugging it to his chest, rocking back and forth on his knees. "Do you think they saw us?"

"They had to have seen the car." Jared was trying to look over the tops of the cornstalks. "It shouldn't be much farther."

"Much farther to where?" Melanie wanted to know. "How do you even know where the hell we are?"

"Trust me. And stay close." Her brother started through the rows again. Melanie and Charlie had to scramble to their feet to catch up with him.

The thunder and lightning took turns now almost in rhythm to Jared's steps. When they finally stumbled out of the field all Melanie could see in the flickering dark were trees and brush so thick she couldn't imagine them finding their way in the pitch-black. The field was separated from the forest line by a barbed-wire fence. She could barely see the five strands of wire, but as soon as she reached out she felt a barb prick her finger.

Once again she couldn't help remembering their mother's superstitions. It occurred to her that she wouldn't be surprised at all if hell were sectioned off by barbed wire.

That's when it started to rain.

CHAPTER 26

7:10 p.m.

Andrew ripped another page from his notebook, crumpled and tossed it at a stack of its comrades in the corner. One had gotten caught in a spiderweb, dangling in the wind. The spider didn't seem to mind. It was still there; hardy creature out here in the woods. It would take more than badly written prose to make it evacuate its home.

Andrew sat back, pulled off his glasses and rubbed his eyes. Maybe it was pointless. Here was the perfect setting for a psychological suspense thriller with his very own thunder and lightning. What more did he need to get in the mood to create a masterpiece of murder? Maybe he just couldn't do this anymore. He couldn't even blame it on his injured collarbone. Yeah, it hurt like hell when he gripped a pen, but somehow the pain seemed less annoying than the absence of words.

He stared at the lantern's flame, its light dancing across his page. He had left only a small lamp on in the cabin, not realizing that the storm had brought nightfall much sooner than usual. Actually he had no idea what time it was. But then that was one of the reasons he came here to write. He had always loved the disconnect he felt from the rest of the world.

Below the screened-in porch he could see the lake's surface glittering in the flash of lightning. The storm had swallowed every last shadow, and everything outside the cabin's cozy confines was veiled in darkness. Across the lake a single light at the boat dock glowed yellow.

Andrew knew there had to be a dozen cabins tucked back into the woods around the park's lake. It was just impossible to see any of them at night without their lights on. Up until yesterday they had probably all been occupied, one last getaway. Wasn't that what Labor Day weekend usually signified for everyone? Everyone, it seemed, except Andrew. His getaway began the day after, and he had been counting on the isolation and seclusion. Yet he always forgot how complete and total the darkness could be out here. The storm only seemed to add another thick blanket of dark and quiet.

He loved the quiet when he was writing, but not when the words wouldn't come. Not when he felt as if he had to yank them out one by one. Times like this the quiet, the silence, was too much. It was annoying. It made him hear things that he would never have paid attention to before, like the refrigerator's motor and the gurgle of water in the toilet bowl.

Outside, tree branches creaked and scratched against each other. There had been whippoorwills earlier, calling to each other across the lake, crickets, too, but the steady rumble of thunder had quieted the night creatures. Even the spider stayed put. Andrew realized he couldn't hear the helicopter anymore, either. For a while, it had been a swirling hum in the distance, but now it, too, was gone. He was completely alone. Not such a bad thing. Not at all like Tommy seemed to think.

He had spent plenty of time alone in the past several years since Nora had left. His choice. He had decided to focus on his new career. He told himself he didn't miss feeling obligated and then guilty when he didn't follow through on those obligations. He liked not having to answer to anyone. He needed the freedom to take off and seclude himself for weeks without Nora accusing him of shutting her out. These were the things he told himself.

He had grown up in a house listening to his father and mother argue about anything and everything. He'd shared a bedroom with his older brother, who allowed him two drawers in the dresser they also shared. His younger sister tattled on him whenever she caught him reading in one of his hiding places. He grew up longing for his own space, a piece of privacy. Now he had all he wanted. Why would he ever consider giving that up? And, as much as he missed Nora, he had to admit…God, he hated to admit it but it was true—when she finally left it had been a relief. And he wasn't even sure why.

Who was he kidding? He knew why. He was afraid of commitment, plain and simple. He was afraid of depending on someone other than himself, of counting on someone and then being let down. He had come to believe that maybe he was meant to be alone. And then Erin Cartlan came along, and suddenly he realized what he was missing in his life— what he truly wanted all along—was standing right in front of him. Right in front of him but miles out of his grasp.

He rubbed his shoulder and readjusted the harness. He stared at the blank notebook page, then glanced back into the cabin. The thunder had begun to change from rumble to cracks and came now as a resounding crash. He hadn't noticed that the rain had started until he felt a spray of it coming in through the screen.

He stacked his notebooks and file folders on top his laptop and headed inside. Maybe tomorrow would be more productive. There was always tomorrow.

CHAPTER 27

7:25 p.m.

Grace tried to hold the umbrella over her and Emily. The stupid garage remote refused to work. Maybe it was the batteries. Maybe the lightning. Figures it would go on the blink during a thundershower and one of her first attempts to actually use the garage.

She couldn't keep up with Emily, who raced up the porch steps to the front door as if trying to outrun the next flash of lightning.

"Hurry, Mommy," she called, just as Grace stepped ankle deep into a puddle. More a hole than a puddle and right in the middle of the front yard.

The house was pitch-black and now Grace wondered if the electricity was out. Vince had programmed timers on several lamps, one downstairs, two upstairs. It was his answer to Grace constantly forgetting to use the security system.

As she unlocked the front door, she glanced around at the rest of the neighborhood. All the streetlights were still lit. She could see a couple of porch lights on, and across the street the reflection of the Rasmussens' big-screen TV glowed in their front window.

She reached for the first light switch, the one in the entry, and was relieved when it came on. Relieved enough that she decided not to worry about why Vince's timers hadn't worked. Maybe there had been an interruption in service. It was an old house. She didn't want to think about Jared Barnett sneaking around her backyard. It was bad enough that she already had Emily worried about a shadow man. Besides, if Barnett had tried to pull off this bank heist, it was only a matter of time before they caught him. Maybe they already had.

Emily stayed so close to her that Grace could feel her bumping against her leg. Her tough little tomboy wouldn't admit she was scared, an annoying habit she had picked up from her mother.

"Are you still hungry?" Grace dangled the McDonald's bags to remind her. She had let Emily talk her into fast-food takeout. Not much of an argument. Grace was a fast-food junkie, too. Another habit she seemed to have passed on to her daughter. But they only exercised it when Vince was away. They both were usually able to hold out longer than the first night of his absence, but it was long past dinnertime and Grace was exhausted, especially after spending almost an hour explaining to Grandma Wenny that everything was fine. Emily had told her about the shadow man, and the old woman's vivid imagination had gone into overdrive. She had never liked the idea of Grace pursuing a career in law enforcement, following in her father's footsteps. And so once again she'd lectured Grace to be careful, offering her the Smith & Wesson .38, Grace's father's service revolver, that the old woman still kept in the drawer of her own bedroom nightstand. It wasn't the first time they'd had this conversation. It wasn't the first time the offer had been made and refused. But it was the first time Grace wondered if perhaps she should get a gun of her own.

"Can we eat in the family room?" Emily asked. "On the floor?"

"Yes to the family room, but on trays. No floor."

Emily was already getting out the folding contraptions, half carrying, half dragging them into position. Grace knew better than to suggest helping. Instead, she went into the kitchen and took out two plates, unwrapping and arranging their cheeseburgers and fries. She could still teach Emily the art of enjoying a meal—it didn't count as fast food if you put it on real plates, or so she told herself.

She doused both orders of French fries with ketchup, her contribution to making their meal "homemade."

"Could I have Pepsi, too?" Emily asked, but her eyes were watching out the kitchen window as flickers of lightning illuminated pieces of the backyard. The same backyard that Jared Barnett might have been sneaking around in. Grace needed to stop thinking about it.

"Take our plates to the trays, please, and I'll get the Pepsis from the garage. We'll need a couple of glasses of ice, too." Grace wanted to keep her daughter busy, keep her eyes and mind off the storm. It would soon pass. "One plate at a time, Em," she said over her shoulder as she opened the door to the garage, then flipped on the light.

She almost tripped over the toy on the first step down to the garage. Before she yelled at Emily for leaving her things out, she realized she didn't recognize it. It wasn't a toy at all. She picked it up to get a better look. It had to be one of Vince's practical jokes. Maybe his idea of a housewarming gift for their front lawn.

The ceramic gnome was so ugly, it was almost cute.

Thursday, September 9

CHAPTER 28

2:09 a.m.

Andrew jerked awake. It must have been a clap of thunder that woke him. The lightning outside the bedroom window reminded him of a blinking neon sign, constant but dim. The rain tapped against the glass. But the thunder was gone. No, wait. A flash of lightning lit the room, and Andrew began to count, "One, one thousand, two, one thousand, three, one thousand, four, one thousand—" The crack wasn't quite as loud as when he had gone to bed. The storm seemed to be moving away according to his brother, Mike's, archaic meteorology.

He turned on his side, the wrong side, and the jolt of pain flipped him to his back. He had forgotten what it felt like to sleep in any position he chose. Or to sleep through the entire night.

He adjusted the hard foam pillow, wishing he had

brought his own. Since his accident he had learned to appreciate the value of a soft but firm pillow. He wondered if he'd be able to stay out here for two whole weeks without a decent one. Geez! He was already looking for excuses to leave. What the hell was wrong with him?

He watched the shadows of tree branches dance across the ceiling every time the lightning blinked. It wasn't that long ago that he'd lay awake in bed, unable to sleep and worried about how he would pay his monthly bills, wondering which credit card he would take out a cash advance from this time. He had come such a long way since those sleepless nights. Now he worried that his good fortune—his windfall, as his father would have called it—could all disappear with one severe case of writer's block.

Sometimes he could hear his father's voice in the back of his head telling him, "What makes you think you deserve all this? You think you're something special? You think you're better than the rest of us?"

His father had been gone for almost five years, and yet he lived inside Andrew's head, in a tiny dark corner in the back, just enough of a presence to keep Andrew in line. To warn him when he dared to get too confident. To bring him back to earth when he dared to dream too big.

Andrew closed his eyes and tried to ignore the sudden tightness in his chest. He needed to think of something else. Or perhaps someone else. He tried to conjure up Erin's image and how she made him feel when she smiled at him or laughed. She had a great laugh. He remembered—

A noise startled him and his eyes flew open. He stayed still, holding his breath and listening. It hadn't been thunder. That he was sure of. It sounded as though it had come from inside the cabin.

He waited and listened. Squinted into the dark. He had left a lamp on in the main room, but its dim light didn't reach the hallway to the bedrooms. He waited out the rumble of thunder then listened again.

Nothing.

Maybe his imagination was playing tricks on him. He probably shouldn't have had three beers when he was still taking pain meds. It also didn't help matters to be dreaming up a killer for his novel in the middle of a thunderstorm.

He heard it again. And this time he was almost certain it came from inside the cabin.

He tried to concentrate, tried to explain the sound away. It could simply be one of the open windows or a loose screen banging against the sill with the wind. There had to be a logical explanation.

That's when Andrew saw a shadow move along the wall of the hallway.

Someone was inside the cabin.

CHAPTER 29

2:23 a.m.

Andrew tried to stay calm. He could barely hear over the pounding of his heart. Could it be a park worker? Someone who'd came to warn him about the storm or check up on him? Was it a knock on the door that had wakened him? It made sense. A park worker would have a key.

Damn! Had he even locked the door? Of course he had. He was a city boy. It was instinctive.

Then his stomach did a somersault. He wasn't sure the flimsy screen door to the porch *had* been locked. All the back-and-forth he and Tommy had done to the grill. And he knew he had left the door between the porch and the cabin unlocked. He always left it like that so he wouldn't accidentally lock himself out. He was in the middle of the woods, for God's sake. Why would he need to lock doors?

The intruder had to be a park worker. Someone checking to make sure he was okay. Someone who didn't call out because he didn't want to disturb him. Someone who—

He heard a floorboard creak. His eyes darted around the small bedroom as he tried to lie still, tried not to make a sound. His suitcase sat on a chair in the corner. His mind frantically went through the contents. *Damn it!* Everything was airport security approved. He had even changed to fucking Gillette Super Blue disposable razors.

There was a shuffling sound. He couldn't tell if it was headed in his direction. Andrew slid out of bed and onto the floor. His injured shoulder banged against the bed rail. He bit down on his lip until the pain subsided. He crawled between the bed and wall to the closet. Straining his eyes to see, he waited for a flicker of lightning. Nothing inside the closet. Not even a broom. Then he remembered the wooden rod for hanging clothes. He had noticed it because he thought it was silly to think anyone would bring clothes that required hanging to a cabin in the middle of the woods.

He slid his body up the wall, stopped and listened. He reached into the closet, feeling for the rod. Please, please let it not be secured. His fingers wrapped around the smooth wooden rod. He stopped and listened. There was a soft rustle and then a crackle. He held his breath. *Damn!* He still couldn't hear over the pounding of his heart in his ears.

He leaned his cheek against the paneling and cocked his head toward the door to the bedroom. Another crackle, maybe a slow ripping sound. The intruder was going through his things. He tried to remember where he had left his wallet. Maybe whoever it was would take it and leave. Andrew lifted the rod out of its slots, and quietly, slowly he eased it up and out of the closet. He got a better grip. He raised his good arm, testing to see how high he could lift it before the pain shot across his shoulder and stopped him. Not bad, though he wished he had taken more of the physical therapy his doctor had nagged him about.

He made his way to the door, then hesitated and listened. He thought he saw a blue glow that wasn't lightning. The refrigerator, maybe? A hungry thief?

Andrew tightened his grip on the rod. It felt good in his hand. It felt good enough that maybe this son of a bitch wouldn't be taking his wallet, after all.

CHAPTER 30

2:35 a.m.

Andrew kept his back against the paneling, sliding inch by inch down the hallway. He held the rod down by his side, ready, despite his sweaty palm. The sounds continued from the kitchen area. The blue glow from the refrigerator lit the opposite wall. He could see a partial shadow, and it looked crouched over. Now was his chance, while the asshole was going through the fridge.

He rushed out of the hallway, three long steps, raising the clothes rod and ready to swing. The woman spun around, her eyes wide, and her hands immediately flew up to protect herself from the blow. But Andrew stopped.

"Who are you? And what the hell are you doing?"

She was filthy, her clothes slathered with mud. She batted wet strands of dirty-blond hair out of her eyes. Her face looked bruised, her cheek scraped raw, though it was hard to tell what was bruises and what was dirt.

"I asked, what the hell are you doing?"

He saw her eyes look over his shoulder. He felt the breeze and smelled the rain, and he knew the door between the cabin and the porch was open. He turned slowly, keeping an eye on her. The small lamp he had left on sat in the corner on the floor, its dim yellow glow enough for Andrew to see the two men out on the porch. One sat by the table. The other stood behind him. From what he could smell, they were as filthy and wet as the woman.

"What do you want?" Andrew asked. At some point his fear had transferred to anger. Anger was better, he reminded himself, and tightened his grip once again on the wooden rod.

"We just needed to come in out of the storm," one of the men said as he shifted his weight in the chair.

It was too dark on the porch for Andrew to see either man's eyes or much of their faces. The flickers of lightning were fading, the thunder a distant echo.

"Did your car break down?" Andrew glanced again at the woman. Her eyes kept darting from Andrew to the man, but she avoided Andrew's eyes. There seemed to be a nervous energy to her, yet she stood still, with her hands in the pockets of her jeans, as if she didn't quite trust Andrew.

When she didn't answer he looked over at the other man. The one standing had moved closer to the screen as if there was something down below that had caught his interest.

"Yeah, you might say we had a bit of a car accident."

There was something in the way he said it that made Andrew adjust his grip on the rod. He wondered how hard it would be to move closer to the door that separated the porch. Could he close and lock it before they reacted, before they realized what he was doing? Then he'd still have the woman to deal with. He glanced at her again. She was small, wet and scared. Yeah, she was scared. But was she scared of Andrew or of the two men on the porch?

"It's a hell of a night to be out, that's for sure." Andrew tried to sound sympathetic. He moved into the room, pretending to look out the window. "Looks like the worst of it may be over."

A couple more feet and he could rush to slam the door. *Damn!* He'd need to drop the rod in order to do it. He was thinking like a two-handed man instead of a one-handed one.

"I can drive you to Louisville." He kept talking. He still had the element of surprise on his side. He was about to make his move, when the man stood up. In one slow, easy motion he raised his hand to Andrew as if to offer to shake it. It was such a casual gesture that Andrew loosened his grip on the rod. He didn't even see the gun until it was too late.

Until the blast filled the room.

CHAPTER 31

2:47 a.m.

Melanie couldn't believe it. Jared had meant to kill the man. Just like that. The bullet had grazed his forehead and knocked him off his feet. A half inch to the left and it would have gone through his fucking brain.

Now Jared stood over him, his finger still on the trigger. The man looked as if he was out of it, rubbing his fingertips over the wound and looking at the blood as if he couldn't believe it was his own. Melanie stood back and watched. So did Charlie. She expected Jared to lift the gun and fire another shot. She expected to see the man's head explode this time. She wanted to close her eyes and, yet, she couldn't look away.

Instead of lifting the gun and firing it, Jared turned. He just walked away. Melanie stared at him as he sat down in one of the easy chairs. From the side of the table he grabbed what looked like a leather briefcase and suddenly became interested in its contents. He rifled through the case's pockets, undoing zippers, taking out notepaper, examining it all and shoving it back into the case. He pulled out a couple of books, checked the covers and started to shove them into the briefcase, as well, when he stopped. Jared examined one of the back covers of the books, glanced at the man on the floor then at the cover.

"You're *this* guy," he said, flipping the book over to look at the front again. "You wrote this book, huh? Andrew Kane."

Melanie watched the man—Kane. He looked up at Jared when he said his name, so maybe he was okay. Maybe the bullet hadn't done any damage.

"So you write books," Jared continued.

She couldn't decide if Jared was impressed or if he was making fun. She didn't seem to be very good at reading her brother lately.

"How many books have you written, Andrew Kane?" Jared was flipping through the book, stopping several times, and it looked to Melanie as though he was actually reading parts.

She finally sat down across from Jared on the worn sofa. She couldn't believe how wonderful it felt to sit, and only now did she realize her legs were numb. Her arms felt raw, and even in the dim yellow light she could see all the scratches and cuts. She pulled her legs up under her and wrapped her battered arms around herself in an effort to stop shivering. Her wet, aching, cold muscles seemed secondary to trying to figure out what the hell Jared was up to.

Melanie tried to remember when the last time was that she had seen Jared with a book. Even as a kid he rarely read or did homework, usually getting someone else to do it for him. But here he was, sitting back, apparently fascinated, not just with this book but that he had an author right in front of him. Wounded and bleeding, but right in front of him. Right where Jared liked to have people he wanted to control.

All Melanie could think was, *Poor Andrew Kane.* If only he had simply left his fucking keys inside his car. That was all Jared had wanted. Melanie had offered to slip in, find the keys and slip back out. No one else needed to get hurt, Melanie had said, remembering the blood splatters all over Charlie's coveralls. But no. Jared decided he needed something to eat. Evading the law evidently gave him an appetite.

"Seriously, how many books have you written?" Jared asked again.

Melanie watched as Andrew Kane untangled his legs from underneath himself and leaned against the wall. It seemed to be an effort for him to move. She wondered how he had ever intended to defend himself with only a pole, his right arm practically attached to the side of his body.

"That's my fifth one," he told Jared in a voice that

sounded stronger then he looked. Then he sat there watching Jared, waiting for the next question, as if it was the most normal thing in the world for them to be sitting down having a conversation about writing books right after Jared had tried to blow his head off.

"I write a little poetry," Jared said, and Melanie stared at her brother, trying to keep her jaw from dropping. She glanced at Charlie to see if he was buying any of this bullshit. Charlie, however, had found a bag of cookies and was working his way to the bottom.

"Do you know 'Richard Cory'?" Jared asked the writer.

Now Melanie wanted to laugh. How ridiculous that Jared would think he and Andrew Kane would know any of the same people. Yet to her surprise Kane answered, "'And Richard Cory, one calm summer night, went home and put a bullet through his head.'"

"Yeah, I love that poem." Jared smiled. "Here's this guy, this Richard Cory, and everybody fucking admires him because he's rich and handsome and has it all. Or so it appears, right? And yet, this guy goes home and blows his fucking head off. Goes to show not everything is what it appears to be, right?"

It was a poem, a fucking poem. Melanie couldn't believe she was sitting here wet, cold and filthy while Jared exchanged rhymes with a man he had tried to kill. This had to be the perfect ending to a nightmare she hoped was, indeed, ending soon.

PART 3
Under the Radar

CHAPTER 32

8:05 a.m.
Hall of Justice

When Grace arrived at work, she found Max Kramer in her office, sitting in her visitor's chair, using her phone while he waited. He glanced at her, holding up one finger to indicate that he was almost finished with his call. No apology for using her phone. Finally he said into the receiver, "No, it's white. That's all I can tell you. I gotta go." And he hung up, sitting back in the chair, taking his Starbucks coffee cup from the corner of her desk and sipping it, as if this was his office.

The coffee's aroma filled the small space, reminding Grace that their office brew couldn't possibly be related to this wonderful scent. She tried to focus on that rather than be pissed off by Kramer's presumptuous attitude.

"Forgot my cell phone," he said almost as an afterthought and still no apology.

"You must have heard how bad our coffee is," she said instead of addressing his rudeness. She slipped past him to get behind her desk, putting down the mug of coffee she'd brought in with her.

"I'm addicted to this stuff. In fact, I've started chewing gum in the afternoon to curb my withdrawals."

She pulled out a couple of files from the two stacks on her desk and glanced across at him. That wasn't his only addiction. She could tell that he bit his nails, too. Expensive suit, salon-cut hair, silk tie and yet he paid no attention to his hands. Odd for an attorney, she thought, since her own hands were an integral part of her court presentations. She probably couldn't make a closing argument without using her hands. Of course, Vince would most likely say she couldn't talk without using her hands.

"Your client has several priors," she said, getting down to business. A brief chit-chat about coffee was all the niceties she was willing to grant the man who'd fought for Jared Barnett's release. "What makes you think she has any room to bargain?"

"She may be able to identify who's responsible for the string of convenience-store robberies." He said it like it was an official announcement, then sat back and sipped his coffee, looking pleased with himself, as if he had handed her the thief's name, address and DNA sample.

"What makes…" Grace stopped to check the name, "Carrie Ann Comstock think she might be able to do that?"

"She was in the vicinity of the store on Fiftieth and Ames when it was robbed. She saw the man leave."

"The store was robbed at one-fifteen in the morning. What exactly was she doing in the vicinity at the time of the robbery?"

She watched his hands. His fingers tapped the oversize cup that he held between both hands. His right hand index fingernail had been bitten down to the quick. She decided she didn't trust an attorney who bit his nails and spent more money on his hair than she did.

"It really isn't important what she was doing."

That was exactly what she'd expected him to say. She sat back in her chair with her hands wrapped around her mug, as if ready for a showdown.

"So she thinks she got a good enough look that she might be able to identify him?"

"She got a good enough look that she was able to *recognize* him," Max Kramer said with a smile.

"Why didn't she come forward sooner?"

He shrugged, a practiced gesture that raised his shoulders almost to his earlobes. "Who knows? So do we have a deal?"

"Hey, Grace." Pakula suddenly filled her open doorway. "Oh, sorry. I didn't know you had—" He stopped when he recognized Max Kramer. "I didn't realize you had a pile of trash in here."

Grace had to restrain her smile. Instead, she watched Kramer shake his head and shift his weight in the chair to give Pakula his back. Detective Tommy Pakula had been one of the detectives involved in Barnett's case and his appeal process. Grace knew the detective well enough to know it'd be easier to cut out Pakula's tongue than to get him to refrain from speaking his mind. He leaned against the doorjamb, arms crossed, waiting for Grace to indicate whether or not she wanted to be interrupted, whether or not she needed rescuing.

"Actually, we were just finishing up," she announced, enjoying Kramer's raised eyebrows and his befuddled look, probably another practiced gesture. He obviously didn't think they were close to being finished. "Why don't you send me the details later today, and I'll get back to you," she said, standing now—a practiced gesture of her own—and pushing back her chair as if she had an appointment with Pakula.

Max Kramer reluctantly stood. "Okay, so I'll do that and give you a call this afternoon."

Kramer hesitated at the door, waiting for Pakula to step aside. Grace wished she could get Pakula's attention, just long enough to give him Grandma Wenny's evil eye and warn him to keep his cool, to play nice.

"No hard feelings," Kramer offered when Pakula stepped away just enough to let him pass. Grace cringed. Why didn't Kramer cut and run?

"Oh, sure," Pakula said. "Why would there be any hard feelings? You go on national TV and tell Bill O'Reilly and the whole fucking world the Omaha PD framed Jared Barnett. Why would I have any bad feelings about something like that?"

Kramer shook his head as if he didn't have time to deal with such nonsense. "It's nothing personal."

"No, of course not," Pakula agreed, but Grace knew…she knew that wasn't the end of it.

"If you ever need to dial 911 and nobody shows up—that's nothing personal, either."

Kramer shook his head again. That's when his phone started ringing, and he reached inside his jacket's breast pocket, bringing out a slim cell phone. He was answering it and walking down the hall without even considering that he might owe Grace an explanation. After all, didn't he say he forgot his cell phone?

Pakula stood in the doorway watching Kramer. Grace waited. Finally he looked at her and said, "You had breakfast yet?"

She shook her head.

"How 'bout we pick up a couple of Egg McMuffins on our way to the autopsy?"

CHAPTER 33

8:15 a.m.
Platte River State Park

Andrew no longer noticed the residual pain from his mending collarbone. Who'd have guessed that an instant remedy would be a bullet wound to his head?

Christ! It hurt. It felt as though the entire side of his forehead had been scraped away and left raw and bleeding. He felt as if he was going to vomit as waves of nausea rolled over him. His vision had finally begun to return to normal after seeing triple for a few hours. He wished he could turn off the ringing in his ears, though, and the banging in his skull meant his head would surely explode any minute and simply take him out of his misery.

They were taking turns using his shower and eating his food. Maybe when they finished they'd simply take his car keys and wallet and leave. He still wasn't sure if the guy named Jared had intended to shoot him or just scare him. After getting a good look in his eyes, Andrew thought he recognized the guy, but he couldn't place him. He didn't think this Jared was the type who missed a shot. Maybe that's what Andrew wanted to believe. Maybe that's what he needed to believe.

The younger one, Charlie, had helped Andrew up onto the sofa. Like an idiot, Andrew had thanked him, an automatic response but so inappropriate that even the kid had looked at him as if he had misunderstood. Then he'd grinned and nodded. All cleaned up and with his hair red instead of black, he looked like a kid. He had overheard him call the woman Mom, and Andrew couldn't help thinking that was just great. He was being assaulted and robbed by Ma and Pa Kettle out in the middle of the woods.

It was Charlie's turn to watch over Andrew while the woman showered and Jared took a nap in the back bedroom, probably stretched out where Andrew had been only hours before. He hoped he was finding that damn foam pillow just as uncomfortable as Andrew had.

Charlie had Jared's gun. Andrew noticed the two men handle the gun, but neither allowed the woman to have it. The gun currently sat tucked in the waistband of Charlie's jeans—actually, a pair of Andrew's jeans. He and Jared had helped themselves to Andrew's clothes.

Charlie had chosen one of Andrew's favorite Nebraska Huskers T-shirts. The clothes were too big for him but somehow he made them fit.

Charlie was in the kitchen constructing his second sandwich. His mom had made him the first one. That must have been what she was doing when Andrew had discovered them earlier.

Andrew didn't care. They could eat his food and take his clothes, his wallet, hell, even take his brand-new car. That had to be what they really wanted. He wanted them to leave.

From where he sat he could see out the porch, and he could make out a piece of the sunrise through the trees. Soon it would be completely light and maybe this nightmare would be over.

The woman came out of the bathroom, wrapped in a towel. With her hair wet and her skin pink and clean she looked too young to be Charlie's mom. Actually, dressed in only that towel, it was difficult for Andrew to think of her as anyone's mother.

"Do you think you have anything in your suitcase for me?"

Andrew stared at her, surprised that she'd bother to ask. Not just ask but actually make it sound as if there might be something special in there for her. Or did she simply want him to look at her? Was that *her* game? The menfolk got off by bullying him. Was this her way of *getting off?*

"Help yourself," he told her, waving his hand at the scattered contents of his suitcase. Jared and Charlie had left everything on the kitchen table. They'd shoved the case aside to make their sandwiches, leaving a pair of socks dangling over the edge. She started sorting through his things almost hesitantly, slowly and carefully, even folding some of the mess the guys had made. Maybe Andrew had read her wrong. Maybe she had asked out of politeness, out of respect.

He continued to watch the horizon, preferring the blurred blue and purple hues to the chaos inside his cabin, his retreat.

"Does this work?" Charlie had found the nine-inch TV and was already plugging it in. "Probably no cable out here, huh?" But he searched for it along the walls, anyway. He kept his sandwich in one hand while he turned on the TV and started moving around the rabbit ears with his other hand. The static didn't slow down his bites. However, when he dropped a piece of its precious contents—a slice of tomato, followed by a slice of onion—he stopped everything to pick it up off the carpet, give it a quick inspection and pop it into his mouth. "Seven-second rule," he said to no one in particular.

Finally he found a station that came in. Andrew recognized the orange halos from his own attempt to watch last night. It looked like the morning news.

"No tornado touchdowns reported, though there were several reports in Douglas and Sarpy Counties of funnel clouds being spotted. We'll have more about that later. Now for an update on the bank robbery that took place at the Nebraska Bank of Commerce on south Highway 50. The amount of money that the two masked robbers got away with is still undetermined."

Andrew glanced at Charlie who seemed glued to the TV. The woman had stopped to watch, too. He remembered the report from the night before…two suspects in a high-speed chase, south on Highway 50. The helicopter had been sweeping the park looking for them. How the hell had they missed them? Because they *had* missed them—here they were sitting in his fucking cabin.

He watched the news station display a graphic of where the suspects were last seen. Their car was reportedly found just off Highway 6 and residents in the area were warned to lock their vehicles and be on the lookout. There was no description of the robbers given, and Andrew immediately found himself making a mental list of their characteristics.

"The two are said to be armed and dangerous. As of this morning's report the names of the victims have not been released."

Andrew jerked to attention. *Victims?*

"What we are allowed to tell you is that two bank employees and two customers were killed. One employee remains in critical condition at the University Medical Center. Police have not released any details, however, an anonymous source close to the investigation has said that all four victims were shot at close range. If you have any information…"

But Andrew's mind flew into panic mode. Suddenly he realized why Jared's face looked so familiar. He had seen him on several news shows. His picture had been plastered on the front page of the *Omaha World Herald.* Jared Barnett. Andrew had heard Tommy Pakula curse that name over the last few weeks, insisting Barnett had gotten away with murder. Andrew had done too much research, had spent too many hours listening to cops, knew too many statistics to deny the one thing he now knew for certain. Jared Barnett wouldn't simply be taking his wallet and his car and leaving.

At least not before finishing what he must have tried to do last night—but missed.

CHAPTER 34

8:27 a.m.

Melanie fell back in the chair, her hands wringing the khaki shorts she had pulled from the heap of clothes. All that blood. She had seen it on Jared's and Charlie's coveralls. What did she think it was from? And the gunfire. Of course there were victims. Someone probably got in the way, made a stupid move. That's probably what happened.

But four…shot at close range. There had to be a mistake. The media always blew everything out of proportion, hyped the news for better ratings.

She watched Charlie. He was cleaning his high-tops, rubbing off the mud with a towel from the bathroom, trying to return them to his standard of bright white. It hadn't fazed him one bit to listen to the report, to hear what kind of mess he may have left behind. Instead, he seemed more concerned with the mess his shoes were in. That's when Melanie noticed he was scrubbing two pairs of high-tops. She had forgotten that Jared had borrowed a pair when he first got out of jail. And here Charlie was cleaning his uncle's shoes, too. Taking care of his uncle. It should have been the other way around—Jared should have been taking care of Charlie.

She smoothed the fabric of the shorts with shaking hands, not taking her eyes off Charlie. Her boy couldn't hurt anyone let alone shoot an innocent bystander. And certainly not at close range. Charlie didn't even know how to fire a gun. They had never had to use guns before. She wouldn't allow it. Wouldn't even allow them in her house. Accidents happened with guns, bad accidents. Maybe that was what had happened in the bank. Maybe it *was* an accident.

"We have half an hour." Jared startled her, making her jump. She wondered how long he had been standing there, leaning against the wall. "Fill that cooler." He pointed to a small one in the corner. "Maybe with sandwiches and Pepsis. And why aren't you dressed yet? Forget about fashion statements. Just put something the fuck on."

Her cheeks burned, but she didn't move. She could feel Andrew Kane's eyes on her. Charlie hadn't moved from the TV screen.

"You can't boss me around like when we were kids, Jared. I'm not moving until you tell me what the hell happened." There, she'd said it. It didn't matter that her voice sounded small and whiny.

"You let me worry about things. Do what I tell you to do and everything'll be fine."

She couldn't help thinking that was exactly what he had said all those years ago. The other mess they had gotten into. It was almost twenty-five years ago, when she was ten and he was twelve. There had been so much blood back then, too. Blood splattered on the walls and in the cracks of the kitchen linoleum. And there had been a gun, too. Jared had told her he'd take care of things. Everything would be fine, he had promised. It would be their secret.

"I need to know what happened," she insisted, disappointed that her voice sounded too much like that ten-year-old little girl.

"It's not up for discussion, Mel. We need to get the fuck out of here."

Jared pushed past her, bumping her chair. He started going through Andrew Kane's things. He turned over one of the brown sacks, spilling the food contents all over the counter. He ripped open a box of granola bars and started searching the room.

"This is bad, Jared," Melanie tried again. Maybe it *had* been an accident, she repeated to herself. That's what her mother had told her happened with that Rebecca girl, though Melanie wasn't sure how their mother knew. Jared never talked about it.

Jared ignored her, passing back behind her again. He grabbed two muddy backpacks from under a chair. That was the first time Melanie realized Charlie had remembered to bring her backpack along with his own.

"This yours?" Jared dropped it on the table in front of her. "So you're saved. Probably got a change of clothes and a makeup kit. Right? Go put some clothes on, Melanie."

"On the TV news they said there were victims, Jared."

He swung Charlie's backpack onto the table beside hers and opened it to put the granola bars inside. But instead he started shuffling through the contents, pulling out one of Charlie's comic books, a couple of maps, several Pez dispensers, which he held up for a better look, shook his head then tossed back inside.

He kept one of the maps out and started unfolding it. Then he stopped and with the sweep of his arm, cleared the tabletop of everything—mayonnaise jar, spoons, open loaf of bread, empty Pepsi cans, all crashing to the floor, along with Andrew Kane's suitcase and clothes. The only things to survive his sweep were the two backpacks and the map, which he began filling the table with.

The racket pulled Charlie away from the TV and into the kitchen area. However, Melanie noticed that Andrew Kane didn't flinch.

Charlie stood over Jared's hunched shoulders, not just curious but worried. Melanie recognized that pinched forehead and narrowed eyes. He didn't like anyone messing with the few items he felt were valuable enough to keep in his backpack.

"What the hell are all these red circles?" Jared pointed out several on the map.

"I got a bunch of different state maps." Now Charlie sounded excited, the little kid anxious to impress his mentor. Charlie reached for his backpack and began pulling out a stack of folded road maps. "I circle towns with cool names. You know, someday I'd like to visit them, just to say that I did."

Charlie crouched down closer to the map spread out on the table. "See here—" he put his index finger on one "—Princeton. Bet you didn't know there was a Princeton, Nebraska. I figured it'd be cool to tell people I went to Princeton."

Charlie laughed and Jared actually smiled.

Jared started looking over the map, too. He pointed to a red circle and said, "I see what you mean, kid. Here's Stella, Nebraska. You could tell people you spent the night *in* Stella." He shoved Charlie with his elbow. *"Get it? In Stella?"*

Melanie watched them. She couldn't believe the two of them, laughing and making jokes.

"I'm thinking they'll be looking for us on the interstate," Jared said.

"Actually, they think we stole a red pickup from some farmer," Charlie interrupted with a wide grin. "I heard it on the news."

"Really? That buys us some time. We'll stick to Highway 6 all the way to Colorado. Looks like you'll get to go through some of your red-circled towns, Charlie."

"Cool. I've got the Colorado map, too. I've never been to Colorado."

Melanie picked up her backpack, hugging it to her chest, ignoring the crusted mud flaking off and smearing the towel. She stood up, ready to go change, but waited, watching the two men in her life plot her future. Neither of them had even asked if *she* wanted to go to fucking Colorado. They had gotten her into this mess and yet neither of them seemed to realize how much of a mess it was.

"They said you killed four people, Jared." She didn't mean for her voice to sound so hysterical, but it worked. It got both their attention. "Is that true? Four victims. That's what they said on the news. All shot at close range. Dead."

"Four?" Jared repeated and he looked to Charlie, who nodded his confirmation. "You mean one of those fuckers is still alive?"

CHAPTER 35

8:32 a.m.

Grace took the last bite of her sausage biscuit just as Frank Irwin pulled back the drop sheet from the corpse.

The woman looked smaller now laid out on the stainless-steel table. With all the blood washed away Grace could see that the gunshot wound had sliced open her jaw. The gash started just under the chin and stretched almost to her ear.

"The bullet shattered all her teeth on that side," Frank said, opening the woman's mouth with his gloved fingers. "Entrance was here below the chin. Exit was here, taking out the left tonsil and the side of the neck."

"Pretty strange way to shoot someone, right, Frank?"

"Pakula already told me your theory, Grace."

"And?"

"It was seven years ago. I wasn't here back then, although I heard about it. I pulled the photos and X rays." He walked over to the light box, flipped a switch and propped up two X-ray films side by side.

He didn't need to tell her. Grace knew the other X ray was of Rebecca Moore's shattered jaw. Rebecca's body had been found in a ditch, north of Dodge Park seven years ago. She had been raped, stabbed three times, shot in the mouth and her body stuffed in a huge, black garbage bag before being thrown into a ditch. Another high-school student, Danny Ramerez, thought he saw her get into a pickup outside of Central High School with Jared Barnett. Seven years later Danny Ramerez suddenly said he was mistaken.

"The injuries are similar," Frank said. "I wasn't able to determine the caliber. And it sounds like we don't know for sure what kind of weapon he used here, or do we?"

"We recovered a casing in the wall behind her," Pakula answered. "It's a .38, but that's all I know right now. It looks like there were two guns used. Ballistics report probably won't be back until tomorrow."

"What do we know about her?" Grace was anxious to find out why Jared Barnett may have singled out this young woman, this bank teller.

"Her name is Tina Cervante," Pakula began, not needing a file or notes. "She was twenty-three years old, single, lived with two girlfriends in West Omaha. She's from Texas. All her family's down there. She came up to go to college, dropped out and landed the bank job. I'm gonna talk to one of the roommates later today. But here's something interesting. About a year ago she got busted for DUI, her third offense. Pretty serious stuff. Guess who her fucking attorney was?"

Grace was more interested in the woman's hands. "Hold on a minute." She pulled the sheet back and checked out her toes. "She probably lived with two roommates because she wasn't making enough money to be out on her own. Maybe she even had some college loans to pay, especially if her parents were pissed off that she didn't stick with it. And yet she could afford to have her fingernails and toes professionally manicured? Maybe even on a routine basis."

"She's also had a nose job." Frank pointed to a hairline scar that Grace would never have noticed otherwise. "A very professional job. Not cheap. Probably within the last six to eight months."

"So she had screwed-up financial priorities. It's an epidemic with kids that age." Pakula sounded impatient, as if talking from experience, perhaps reminded of his own daughters. "She could have had someone else helping out or taking care of her. What I wanna know is how an attractive, clean-cut young woman like Tina Cervante ends up with a scum-sucking attorney like Max Kramer."

"Kramer was her attorney on the DUI?" Grace wondered if Pakula was simply fishing for something. Kramer handled all kinds of cases. A DUI wouldn't be anything unusual, especially since the client was an attractive young woman.

"It's not my job to pass judgment," Frank interrupted. "But I'm not sure how clean-cut a young woman with three DUIs could be. Also…" He brought over a stainless-steel basin from the equipment tray and lifted the towel off to show them. "She was about two months pregnant."

CHAPTER 36

9:00 a.m.

The nausea had finally passed, though Andrew's panic had not. While Jared and Charlie prepared for their cross-country trip, Andrew's mind raced. He tried to go over everything he had brought with him and then began visualizing the contents of the cabin. He remembered there were several dull knives in one of the kitchen drawers, a poker for the fireplace—which he couldn't see anywhere—but nothing else. Even as the light crept over the treetops in brilliant oranges and began to illuminate the dark corners of the cabin, it seemed hopeless.

His vision still blurred without warning, going in and out of focus like the TV reception. He hardly noticed his shoulder anymore. What did it matter that he couldn't move his right arm when his entire body had become numb?

He tried to test his feet, but Jared was suddenly there waving the gun at him. He wondered why they didn't just get it over with, just put him out of his misery. His answer came soon enough, and he couldn't help remembering one of his father's favorite sayings, "Be careful what you wish for."

Jared plopped down in the chair opposite him. The gun was tucked inside the waistband of a pair of Andrew's jeans, held there by a leather belt and strange buckle, some kind of carved emblem Andrew didn't recognize. He was staring at the belt buckle, when he realized Jared was talking to him. He caught only the last words.

"…Pretty fucking good. How do you know all this stuff about murder?"

That's when he saw his latest hardcover in Jared's hand, his trigger finger inside the pages, marking his place. He must have taken it with him for his nap in the back bedroom. He was reading Andrew's book. Jesus! And now he wanted to sit and chat about it.

"You must do like lots of research, huh? I mean, I know you make it up, but some of this…man, I'm telling you, it's pretty fucking real. I loved the autopsy scene where they find out the killer took the stiff's thumb. How do you come up with that crap?" He opened the book and started flipping the pages, still keeping his place. "Yeah, it's pretty fucking real." Then suddenly he looked up and smiled. "I think you like your killer."

Andrew leaned his head back against the worn

fabric of the sofa. He wished the throbbing would stop. It skewed his thinking and interrupted his hearing. If he didn't know any better he'd say a murderer had just given him one of his best reviews. He smiled to himself, wondering how his publisher might use it, maybe on the paperback—four-time, no make that five-time murderer says, "It's pretty fucking real."

Jared didn't seem to mind that he wasn't getting any response, any feedback. Maybe the man preferred one-sided conversations. He continued to remark on the realism before he launched into his analysis of the parts Andrew had gotten wrong. Yep, a true book reviewer after all.

Andrew simply rubbed his aching head and listened. Somewhere during Jared's diatribe Andrew realized that Charlie and Melanie had been in and out of the cabin, packing the car. He noticed his belongings being carted off. He jerked forward, sitting up and twisting around. Where the hell were his briefcase, his notebooks and laptop?

"Relax, man," Jared said, but this time he sounded as if he was comforting rather then restraining Andrew. "I'm making sure they get everything you need."

"Everything I need?"

"Yeah, you're coming with us. Consider it research."

CHAPTER 37

9:41 a.m.
Omaha Police Department

"What else do we have?" Grace asked Pakula over really bad cheap coffee at his desk. Maybe it only tasted bad because she kept remembering the smell of Kramer's Starbucks.

"Shoe print is a size twelve Nike Air. Darcy might have the breakdown of those pebbles tomorrow." He met her eyes and held her gaze as he said, "So, what if they match the ones from your backyard?"

"Just one more reason to believe it's Barnett."

"Why would he snoop around your house?"

"Are you kidding? He shows up in the courtroom, outside my dry cleaner's, at the same grocery store I shop? He's trying to freak me out."

"Yeah, but how can he freak you out by sneaking around your backyard if you don't know he's there?"

"Look, Pakula, I'm not making this up."

"Hold on. I'm not saying you are. All I'm saying is if he gets a rush by showing up and having you see him, then why sneak around your backyard? Why not pull in to the driveway or something like that?"

"So what are you saying, Pakula?"

"Are you sure he wasn't inside?"

Grace stared at him. It wasn't possible, was it? She didn't want to think about Jared Barnett walking through her rooms, touching her things.

"We need to catch this bastard," she said. "What about the manhunt? Last I heard on the news they had found the Saturn."

"Yup. Crashed in a field off Highway 6. A farmer had his pickup stolen about the same time. Didn't see it taken. It was gone when he came home. They must have made their way through the storm and the field and took the pickup before the roadblocks got set up. We've got an APB on the pickup. They won't get far."

"Okay. Great. So we'll probably have him by the end of the day. If it is Barnett, he won't be getting out of jail free this time." Grace shoved aside her coffee and stood up to stretch. The mess on Pakula's desk was worse then hers; she couldn't remember having ever seen its surface. "What about the receptionist?"

"Upgraded to critical. She's not conscious. Doctors aren't sure if she'll regain consciousness. Doesn't sound good."

"I need to get back." She crumpled her foam cup and tossed it into Pakula's wastebasket. For once it wasn't overflowing. "Oh, here's something that might cheer you up. Max Kramer wants to plea-bargain a client who just happened to recognize our convenience-store robber."

"Well, isn't that convenient, indeed. Who's his client?"

"Carrie Ann Comstock."

"You gotta be kidding. That crack whore couldn't remember and identify her own mother if she saw her robbing a store."

Grace shrugged. "Probably, but I'm curious to see who she's willing to finger."

Pakula's phone interrupted them, and he held up his hand, a familiar gesture Grace knew meant, "Hold that thought."

"Pakula."

"Yeah," he said and waited, nodding at first then shaking his head. "Holy crap." He tapped a pen against a notepad on his desk, so hard Grace expected it to snap. "No, I'll meet you out there."

He slammed the phone into its cradle.

"That farmer's pickup? Turns out his stepson and a friend took it without his permission. Who knows where the bastards are by now. We're back at square one." He grabbed his jacket from the chair's back and threw it over his arm. "I'll talk to you later." He headed for the door but stopped and came back, standing directly in front of Grace. "I'm gonna have a black and white checking your neighborhood. I'm just telling you so if you happen to see it, you don't go busting my balls about it, okay?"

He headed out the door, without waiting for a response, without letting her thank him.

CHAPTER 38

10:00 a.m.

Melanie didn't think Andrew Kane was in any shape to drive. His eyes didn't look right, even after he put his glasses on. And the baseball cap hid very little of the wound. But Jared had insisted. And quite honestly, Melanie was too relieved to argue, thankful that Jared hadn't decided the writer was a liability better left buried somewhere back in the woods.

This was more like the Jared she knew, making the best of a bad situation. Or as Jared liked to say, "Making chicken salad out of chicken shit." She didn't know the Jared who may have left four people dead at the bank. She didn't even want to think about that Jared. She wanted to put it all out of her mind. The important thing was to go someplace where they'd be safe.

"We're gonna do some zigzagging, Andrew,"

Jared said from his favorite seat, directly behind the driver. He had told Melanie to sit up front, claiming cops wouldn't be looking for a good-looking couple in a red luxury car. He sat in the back with Charlie's map folded open across his legs so he could follow the yellow-highlighted route he had mapped out at the cabin.

"We're gonna go southeast first. Then we'll…hey, turn the fucking radio up."

Melanie found the volume. The news report had already started.

"…learned that the two young men had taken his pickup without permission. Authorities now believe the two alleged robbers had a backup vehicle stashed somewhere. According to an anonymous tip, that vehicle, another stolen Saturn, this one white, was reportably seen traveling south of Rock Port, Missouri, on I-29, heading possibly toward Kansas City. The license plate of this vehicle is Nebraska NKY-403. However, we're told that these two suspects have been known to trade license plates with other vehicles, vehicles sitting in parking lots at malls or at the airport. Also, we're reminded to advise listeners that the men are considered armed and dangerous. If you see this vehicle, call authorities immediately. We'll have another update at the half hour. For news radio KKAR, this is Stanley Bell."

The radio talk-show host came on next.

"It's 10:06. Do you know what your license-plate number is? How do you like that? We can send guided missiles to hit targets hundreds of miles away. We can watch live pictures of Mars. But we can't find a white Saturn. And what is it with these two guys and Saturns—"

"Turn it down," Jared said and Melanie reacted without thinking, even though she wanted to hear more. Or maybe she didn't.

Jared pulled a cell phone out of the writer's brief-case. He punched in a number and waited.

"Hey, it's me. Never mind that." Jared sounded cool and calm even though Melanie could hear the person on the other end yelling. "You called in the tip, right? You're the fucking anonymous source? How the fuck did you know I wasn't in that fucking white Saturn? Huh? How did you know I didn't backtrack and get it? You setting me the fuck up, you son of a bitch? Is that it?"

Melanie wished she could hear the other person's response. Who else knew about this job? Who the hell would Jared trust with details about his backup vehicles? She hadn't even known about it until they were on the road. It had to be someone he had met in prison, she decided. She put her thumbnail be-tween her teeth, a recently developed habit to avoid biting down on her lower lip.

"I left some unfinished business," Jared was telling his friend. "You're gonna need to take care of it for me." More yelling and this time Jared held the phone away from his ear. *"Just do it,"* he yelled, then snapped the phone off and closed.

"Son of a bitch," he muttered to no one in particular. "Can't trust anybody these days."

Melanie saw him slump against the car door, and for a brief moment he reminded her of that twelve-year-old boy, staring out the window at the passing pastures and cornfields, looking betrayed and alone, searching for something better and never satisfied. They had both been cheated out of their childhoods, forced to grow up too soon. Sometimes Melanie couldn't help wondering if things would have been different if only their mother had cared more about her children than the array of colorful pills she washed down with vodka. How could she not see, how could she not stop her own husband—Melanie's asshole father—from beating her children? Shouldn't a mother protect her child above all else? Wasn't it instinctive or something? That was certainly the way Melanie felt about Charlie. And yet, Melanie couldn't bring herself to blame her mother. Neither could Jared. Maybe it was that blood thing, that thing Jared always said about family sticking by each other. And Jared had stuck by Melanie. She owed him.

She stared at the highway ahead, the two winding lanes with little traffic. The rain had washed everything clean, cooled things and left the sky a freshly scrubbed blue. Melanie remembered how she and Charlie talked about going for drives out in the country. This wasn't exactly what she'd had in mind.

"Take the turn for Nebraska City." Suddenly Jared was sitting forward, ready to be Andrew Kane's co-pilot. "We need to look for an ATM." He held up a bank card he must have taken from Kane's briefcase. "You're about to make a little cash withdrawal."

CHAPTER 39

10:46 a.m.
Platte River State Park

Tommy Pakula slowed his Ford Explorer. He could see the mobile crime lab's van and a police cruiser off to the side of the Platte River State Park entrance. His breakfast turned to lead in his stomach. *Holy crap!* He had no idea the crash site was this close to the park. They'd simply said Highway 6 south of Louisville.

The investigators had pulled in as close as they could behind the skid marks and broken barbed-wire fence. The car had plowed through the fence. This morning, after a night of thunderstorms and down-pours, the torn path was filled with water. It looked as if it would take some serious boots just to get to the car.

Pakula waved to Ben Hertz and rolled down his window. "Anybody check the park yet?"

"One of the boys talked to the park superintendent. He lives here on the grounds. Said the park's pretty empty. Only one cabin occupied and everything looked nice and quiet."

"A buddy of mine is the lone occupant. You know Andy Kane, writes suspense-thriller novels?"

"Yeah, sure. Murderman, right?"

"Yep, that's him. He's out here writing. I'm gonna go check on him. I'll be back."

"Helicopter guys said the car was empty when they found it. These two hightailed it outta here pretty fast. It wouldn't surprise me if they did have another car stashed someplace close. Just heard that an anonymous tip was phoned in about a white Saturn. One thing for sure, they didn't stick around here long. They'd have to be stupid to do that."

"Yeah, you're probably right. Like I said, I'll be back." He rolled up the window and turned into the park.

Hertz *was* probably right. So why did Pakula have such a bad feeling in the pit of his stomach? He made his way up and around the winding road, climbing to get to the Owen Cabins on the far side of the lake. Before he pulled around the last curve, he knew Andrew's car was gone. He couldn't see the bright red Saab through the trees and tall grass. He pulled in to the slotted space, parked, opening the car door while shoving the emergency brake on.

Walking down the pathway to the front door he wondered why he didn't think to check on Andrew last night. Maybe Andrew had simply gotten cabin fever and gone out for a drive, or maybe headed into Louisville for breakfast. And then again, maybe Andrew had heard about the wild events of yesterday and decided to pack it up and work from home. Andrew had brought his TV with him, so he wasn't as isolated from the world as Pakula had been making it out.

He knocked on the door but didn't wait long to try the doorknob. It opened easily, and he could feel the hairs on his arm stand to attention.

"Andrew? Hey, you here, buddy?" Pakula called out, hoping to get an answer, but he already knew the place was empty. That bad feeling was crawling upward from his stomach toward his chest.

Clothes were scattered all over the kitchen area with open jars and empty Pepsi cans thrown onto the heap. He cautiously walked from room to room. A pile of wet bath towels and soiled hand towels lay in the middle of the bathroom floor. Toothpaste and shampoo stained the countertop. Mud and dirt lined the drain of the shower and sink. Checking out the bedroom, he realized the bed looked slept in.

Pakula backtracked, taking his time, trying to slow down and examine what evidence was left behind to determine what had happened. Who was he fooling? He knew what had happened here. Andrew had had some unexpected guests last night. Guests who'd helped themselves to his things. Pakula couldn't see Andrew's laptop anywhere, although the TV sat in the middle of the room still plugged in.

He checked the screened-in porch—muddy shoe prints all the way up the back steps. "Andrew, buddy, you didn't lock the fucking back door, did you? And where the hell are you?" He didn't expect an answer.

Maybe he got away, ran into the woods. At this point, Pakula was relieved he hadn't yet found his body, shot execution style like those poor souls in the bank. He stared out at the lake and woods on the other side. Andrew would have the advantage, even stumbling around out there at night. He knew this park.

Pakula headed back into the cabin, whipping out his cell phone to call in a new APB. At least Andrew's car would be easy to find, torch red with vanity plates. Who said these guys weren't stupid. "No service," his phone's digital display read, and he remembered his cell phone going dead yesterday in the middle of his conversation with Grace. He shook his head. Poor Andrew. He wasn't even able to call for help.

No, he had to stop thinking that way. Pakula told himself Andrew was fine. It was actually a good sign that he wasn't lying inside unconscious or dead. He had to have gotten away. Maybe they'd be sipping beers and laughing about this by nightfall.

That's when Pakula saw the blood.

ChAPTER 40

10:53 a.m.
Highway 75

Andrew kept checking his rearview mirror. All the times this red car had tripped the speed traps and set off the radar, why couldn't it now? He pushed it over the speed limit, trying to keep it steady with the flow of traffic so Jared wouldn't notice. Where was the state patrol? Why weren't there Black Hawks looking for these three?

They'd killed four people, maybe five, in a bank robbery and yet, they didn't take any money. Unless they'd stashed it somewhere. Maybe they were afraid of marked bills or recorded serial numbers. But wouldn't they keep enough cash for their getaway? Or did things go so terribly wrong they'd walked away with nothing?

One obvious fact—Jared was pissed that Andrew's daily ATM withdrawal was limited to four hundred dollars. Maybe he thought cleaning out Andrew's bank account would make up for his botched bank robbery. Whatever the reason, Andrew had made sure he pulled up close enough to the ATM drive-through that the small camera peeking from the face of the machine could include a shot of the back seat. Or so he hoped. He'd also thought about jamming his card into the wrong slot, rendering it useless and possibly forcing Jared to allow him to access his account by going into the bank. But Andrew didn't want to risk Jared walking into another bank.

It didn't matter. It was over. Jared had four hundred dollars. They were back on the road, heading south on Highway 75 after leaving Nebraska City. In the rearview mirror Andrew could see Jared listening to the radio—no new information. Charlie stuffed his face, this time with little chocolate doughnuts.

He glanced at Melanie sitting beside him. Her head leaned against the car window. At first he thought she was sleeping, then realized she was staring out at the landscape. Something about Melanie made Andrew believe that her heart wasn't in this. All the signs added up, her nervousness, or outbursts regarding what had gone down in the bank, gave Andrew the impression that maybe she might be the weak link in this threesome.

Now if only he could attract a speeding ticket. Back in Nebraska City he had even made an illegal left turn, hoping someone other than Jared would notice, but the pickup driver he cut off simply stopped and politely waited. Just his luck to be taken hostage and need to depend on people too polite to even imagine anyone in their small picturesque town could be taken hostage.

"Turn it up," Jared yelled, startling both Andrew and Melanie. Without hesitation she grabbed at the radio's volume button.

"…possibly taken from Platte River State Park. Local authorities now say they are looking for a 2004 red Saab 9-3 with Nebraska plates reading A-W-H-I-M, A WHIM. The two suspects may also have taken with them the car's owner. We are told that this is an ordinary citizen and is not connected to the two suspects. Presently this person's name is being withheld until confirmation has been made. Again, local authorities are advising that if you do see this vehicle, a 2004 red Saab 9-3 with vanity plates that read 'A Whim,' please call the special hotline, 800-555-9292, or 911. Do not approach or try to stop them as we are warned the two suspects are considered armed and dangerous. Authorities have released the names of the four victims who were killed in that—"

"Fuck! Fuck! Off! Shut it the fuck off!"

"What the hell are we gonna do now?" Melanie

clicked the radio off, then spun around to face Jared, as if this was the last straw for her.

"Just shut the fuck up, Mel. Shut up and let me think."

"This is crazy, Jared. Charlie and I didn't sign on for this crap."

"I told you I'd handle this, Mel. Now shut the fuck up."

She turned back around. Andrew could see her hands wringing the hem of her shirt. He thought he could see her lower lip tremble but it disappeared between her teeth.

Andrew kept an eye on Jared in the rearview mirror. The cool-and-calm attitude had quickly dissipated. He jerked around in the back seat, clearly agitated. His entire body shifted to look from one window to the next, and he bent down at one point to get a look at the sky as if expecting to see a police helicopter. Charlie followed Jared's lead, watching out the window and focusing on the sky.

"How the fuck did they figure this out?"

Andrew thought he was just blowing off steam, not really expecting an answer to his question. Then he felt the slap on the back of his head, hard enough to make him swerve and unexpected enough to make his stomach lurch.

"How?" Jared yelled again. "What did you do to tip them off?"

"Nothing," Andrew said, and suddenly his heart

was pounding in his ears again. Was there any reasoning with a man who didn't need a reason to do what he was doing? Would he dump the car along with Andrew? "How could I do anything? I've been with you the whole time."

He needed to calm his own panic and not give in to Jared. He needed to think positive. He could use this turn of events to his advantage. He had to try. What did he have to lose? While Jared twisted around to watch out the back window, Andrew slipped his hand down to the bottom of the steering wheel. From there he could reach over and turn on his headlights. He should have thought of that sooner—anything to get someone, *anyone* to notice his car. Maybe the pickup driver back in Nebraska City had already called it in. Maybe they were tracking them or at least sending a cruiser to investigate. If he could buy some time—yes, that's what he needed to do. He needed to think.

"This could work to your advantage," Andrew said, trying with effort to keep his breathing steady. If only he could think. If only he could remember all his research and access it now when he needed it. He knew volumes about criminals and sociopaths. Couldn't he use his knowledge to his advantage? One thing he knew for certain, he had to sound as if he was on Jared's side.

"What are you talking about?" Jared was still twisting around in the back seat.

Andrew could see Melanie turn toward him, looking for the first time interested. Up until now she had barely acknowledged his presence.

"They're looking for this car, right?" Andrew continued. "I could be your decoy. Hell, I could drive all the way down to Kansas, maybe cut across Missouri. In the meantime, you could be headed in the opposite direction."

Silence.

Jared stopped fidgeting. Melanie shifted in her seat to look back at Jared. It took effort for Andrew to keep quiet, to not oversell his plan. He resisted the urge to glance in the rearview mirror. He couldn't look overly anxious. Jared had to think about how the plan benefited him. A true sociopath thought only in terms of "me." Andrew was counting on it.

Finally Jared sat forward, reached across the front seat and pointed. "See that farm up ahead. Pull off and head up there."

CHAPTER 41

11:00 a.m.

Melanie dropped her head back against the soft leather headrest and let out a sigh of relief. Finally Jared was listening to reason. For a brief second she wished she could stay in the car and drive off with Andrew Kane, never mind that it meant certain capture and arrest. She just wanted an end to all this madness.

After following the long driveway, Jared insisted Andrew pull up to the house. The gravel snapped and popped against the bottom of the car despite the Saab slowing to a crawl. Rainwater had filled the tire ruts and the smooth luxury ride turned into a bumpy carnival ride.

Charlie started whistling the theme song from "Green Acres," and Jared actually laughed before he told him to "shut the fuck up."

Melanie tried to ignore them. She admired the farmhouse, a big two-story home. When she was a little girl growing up in a smelly roach-infested apartment, she had dreamed about living in a house like this with a long porch, though she would never have told Jared. He would have laughed at her and told her to stop dreaming. The porch even had a swing, the kind you saw in the movies with people sitting out on summer nights, sipping lemonade. This was a house that said, "Come in, make yourself at home, stay awhile."

"How we gonna do this?" Charlie asked and Melanie could hear him already pulling his backpack from the floor.

"Everybody keep your mouths shut. I'll handle it. That goes for you, too, Mr. Ordinary Citizen."

Jared used the radio guy's term as if it were an insult. Or, Melanie wondered, did he want to remind Andrew that he wasn't a part of Jared's team? Not that it mattered; she couldn't help thinking there didn't seem to be any perks to being on Jared's team.

A farmer appeared from the side of the barn. He must have seen them coming up the driveway. He didn't look at all like Melanie expected. Instead of overalls and a flannel shirt he wore blue jeans and a pale yellow oxford button-down. Instead of a straw hat or feed cap, he had on a red baseball cap.

"Hey, look, Andrew—" Jared pointed "—he has on the same fucking cap you have on."

The farmer waved to them and started toward the car.

"Everybody fucking smile," Jared told them.

Melanie heard a rustling from the back and glanced around just in time to see Jared removing the gun from his waistband. Her stomach lurched. She wanted to scream at the farmer to stop.

"Jared, what the hell are you doing?"

"Just smile, Melanie, and relax. Charlie, you take this." And he slid the gun over to her son who didn't hesitate in slipping it under his leg. "You stay with Andrew in the car. Make sure he doesn't go anywhere. Melanie, you and me need to use this guy's phone."

She didn't have time to figure out Jared's scheme. She was so relieved he wasn't going to use the gun that she didn't care what he asked her to do.

Jared pressed the button and the window slid down silently. It was too late for him to reprimand Andrew when he brought his window down, too.

"Morning," Jared said in a friendly tone that Melanie recognized as fake. "We're a bit lost. We're supposed to help a friend move, but we can't find his place. You mind if we use your phone to call him?"

"What's his name? I know just about everybody around here." The man stopped in between the two car windows, first glancing and nodding his head at Andrew, then turning to Jared.

"Actually, he just bought a place down here. We're helping him move in."

"That's odd. I don't know of any place that was up for sale. Know the name of the person he bought from?"

Melanie started twisting the hem of her blouse. This guy was screwing it all up. *Why didn't he just let them use the fucking phone?*

"Gosh," Jared said, "I really don't know. All I know is we were supposed to be there an hour ago. He's really gonna be pissed at us. You mind? I promise I'll make it short. Your wife won't mind, will she?"

"No, no. She's off having her hair done. Her girlfriend picks her up every Thursday, and they spend the morning in town."

"That's real nice that you let her do that."

"Let her?" The farmer laughed. "Son, if you think you have any control over what women do you're in for a mighty big surprise. They have minds of their own. Isn't that right, ma'am?" He bent down to look in at Melanie, and she smiled back at him, wanting to warn him not to fuck around with Jared.

"Come on in," he finally said, standing up straight and waving a hand for them to follow.

Jared didn't hesitate, opening the door and climbing out, but he turned to nod at Charlie and shoot Melanie a look of warning. She knew that look. It said, "Keep your mouth shut."

Inside the kitchen Melanie took in everything, from the cute little plaques of hand-painted vegetables to the cheery yellow and white-checkered curtains. She found herself wanting to sit down at the table with a cup of coffee. She wanted to stay awhile.

The farmer pointed out the phone on the counter

to Jared. At some point, both Melanie and the farmer had missed seeing Jared grab a butcher knife from the wooden block on the counter. Suddenly he had the man by the collar, the knife to his throat, forcing him into a chair.

"Get something to tie him up, Mel."

She couldn't move. Her knees threatened to give out. She stared at them, recognizing the surprise as well as the panic in the farmer's wide brown eyes. That day so many years ago came back as if it was happening all over again. Jared holding her father from behind, his small arms wrapped around his thick neck, holding on despite the fact that his feet were dangling off the ground and her father's arms were twisting and flailing, trying to grab onto Jared. "Get something to tie him up," he had yelled at her. Only she couldn't move then, either. She couldn't believe they were actually going to do it. They had gone over their plan, again and again, plotting every night after one of the beatings. Sometimes Jared's eyes would be so swollen Melanie would have to do the writing, despite her nose still bleeding, dripping down onto the small notebook where they hid their list of things they'd need. The list had never included the gun and yet somehow it had shown up that night.

"Melanie," Jared yelled again. "Get that extension cord."

Finally she spun around, looking behind her. She almost expected to find her father standing there, bloodied and dirty as if he had crawled his way out of the grave Jared had dug for him. But there were only yellow and white-checked curtains and a daisy suncatcher dangling from the curtain rod.

"Don't make any funny moves, Mr. Farmer," Jared told him. "We just need your car keys. We need to borrow your car."

"Sure. No problem." The man started to point, but stopped when Jared shoved the knife up under his chin. "Keys are hanging by the door. The ones with the Saint Christopher's medallion."

"Melanie." Her brother's voice took on that soothing tone. "Mel, get the keys and bring me that extension cord."

It felt like a dream. A bad dream. Melanie stared at the trickle of blood that stained the farmer's yellow collar. Her stomach started to churn. She tried to keep her mind focused. She tried to stay here, in this sunny kitchen instead of slipping back to that small, dingy kitchen from her past. So much blood—she could see it seeping into the cracks of the linoleum, cockroaches skittering through it.

"Melanie, the keys."

She did what she was told, walking with spongy knees. They'd tie him up. They'd take the keys. She could do this step by step. She could get through this. She had done it before, she could do again. She'd focus and concentrate on what needed to be taken care of. And then she'd leave this warm, cozy kitchen and step back into her nightmare.

CHAPTER 42

11:12 a.m.

Andrew watched Charlie in the rearview mirror. He couldn't help thinking the kid looked like a puppy dog waiting and watching for his master's return. The gun stayed on the seat next to his thigh, exactly where Jared had left it. Charlie's hand, palm flat against the leather seat, was beside it as if he didn't want to touch the gun but wanted to be ready if he needed to.

Andrew tried to size him up, almost like a character profile for one of his books. He was streetwise but otherwise not so smart. There was an innocence, a sort of childlike quality about him that didn't jive with being street-smart. At first Andrew had thought it might be a ploy, a manipulation, part of an act the kid did to get what he wanted. He was a good-looking kid in a geeky sort of way, with an easy, carefree manner, as if he didn't think any of this was wrong. Almost as if he thought it was a game. Or maybe it was all an act.

Charlie met Andrew's gaze in the mirror, but Andrew didn't flinch. Charlie looked away first.

"You and Jared been friends for a long time?" Andrew asked as if making polite conversation.

"Friends?" Charlie looked as if the question required thought. "Jared's my uncle."

So that was the tie. Andrew had wondered if there was a romantic connection between Jared and Melanie, but this made more sense. Now he knew.

He checked the door to the house and then the garage. Nothing. Somewhere in the back of his mind he remembered a tidbit about kidnappers having a difficult time hurting their hostages if they started to think of them as real people. Hopefully that's what was going on inside, but the longer it took Jared to get the keys from the farmer, the more Andrew got nervous about him agreeing to let Andrew just drive off and be his decoy. Whatever Jared ended up doing inside that house could determine Andrew's fate.

"He seems like a nice guy if I had a chance to know him," he said, glancing at Charlie in the mirror again.

"Oh, yeah, Jared's cool." He nodded. "He knows a lot," he added as an afterthought.

"He's kind of hard on your mom sometimes, isn't he?" Andrew tested the water. Where exactly did this kid's loyalty lie?

"Whadya mean?" But the topic wasn't enough to draw his attention away from his vigil out the window.

"I don't know," Andrew said, keeping it casual, as though it were only an observation. "He yells at her a lot."

"Oh, that." Charlie snickered under his breath.

Andrew waited for an explanation, but none came. Evidently, it wasn't something Charlie thought deserved a response.

Suddenly the garage door opened and a blue Chevy Impala backed out. Andrew saw Charlie grab the gun, but his hold loosened when he recognized Jared behind the wheel, Melanie beside him in the passenger seat. They pulled up alongside the Saab so that Andrew wouldn't be able to open his car door. Jared rolled down his window and indicated for Andrew to do the same.

"Charlie, transfer our stuff."

The kid practically jumped out of the car. Andrew popped the trunk and Charlie filled his long arms. The sooner they got this over with, the sooner Andrew could be free of them. He felt Jared staring at him, and he didn't like the prickle at the back of his neck that his scrutiny produced. Was he sizing Andrew up, deciding whether he could trust him? Or was he trying to decide what to do with Andrew's body?

Jared reached out his hand. "Give me the keys, Andrew."

He didn't hesitate, pulling them out of the ignition and handing them over. Okay, so what if Jared wanted to play games? He waited, expecting him to toss them into the gravel, so Andrew would have to search for them on hands and knees, slowing him down and maybe humiliating him one last time. But Jared didn't toss them. Instead, he called Charlie over, said something to him and gave him the keys in exchange for the gun.

Andrew's panic returned, an immediate banging in his chest. Christ! Was this guy crazy? Why had Andrew ever thought Jared would leave him alive? But he'd believed it, and now it was too late for a backup plan. Andrew's eyes darted back to the house, though he knew if the farmer weren't dead, he wouldn't be coming to the rescue. Jared wouldn't have left him without, at least, locking him in a closet or tying him up.

Jared inched the Chevy forward, enough that Jared was free to open his car door but so Andrew's door was still blocked by the bumper of the Chevy. Jared got out and looked at him, his eyes never leaving Andrew's as he came around to the passenger side and opened the door.

"Come on, Andrew."

Terror paralyzed him. Not only was Jared going to kill him but he wanted to humiliate him by making him crawl out of his own car.

"Why don't you just do it right here?" he managed to say.

"What the fuck are you talking about?"

"If you're going to shoot me, just do it. Do it right here. Right now." He couldn't believe the words actually made it over the gathering lump in his throat. He grabbed the steering wheel with his one good hand as if in a last defiant move. Why not here? Why not die in his brand-new car, the fucking car that was to symbolize his success, his new beginning?

"Andrew, get the fuck out of the car. We don't have all day."

When he still didn't move, Jared started to laugh.

"If you don't get out of the fucking car, man, I am gonna shoot you, you asshole. Come on. You're driving. Hell, when you drive this fucking Chevy after being spoiled by your Saab, you'll probably wish I had shot you!"

Slowly, reluctantly, Andrew crawled out of the car, banging his shoulder as he tried to protect his head wound.

In a matter of minutes they were ready to go, waiting while Charlie parked the Saab in the garage. Andrew watched it disappear behind the descending door and with it went any sense of hope he had left.

Andrew was just about to pull out, when Jared suddenly said, "Wait a minute. I forgot something."

Andrew didn't think anything of it until he saw Melanie's face, her wide eyes watching Jared run up the porch steps, her lower lip between her teeth again.

"What do you suppose he forgot?" he asked her.

She didn't look at him. She didn't look as if she even heard him.

Then, just as sudden as her panic had been, so was her relief when she saw Jared come out the front door, jumping off the steps and jogging back to the car, too quickly to have done what she must have feared he would do. Andrew watched her entire body relax into the fabric of the seat and there was a hint of a smile. It had only been the farmer's red baseball cap that Jared had forgotten. He slung it on in an exaggerated gesture, making Charlie laugh.

Andrew, however, felt his entire body stiffen. *It couldn't be.* No, he was being paranoid. In his latest novel Andrew's killer goes back to take a victim's fedora, only it's in the dead of winter and the killer needs it for warmth, thinking to himself why not take it, the dead guy's not gonna need it anymore.

He watched Jared, smiling at the others as he climbed into the back seat. How ridiculous. How could he even be thinking about his stupid book? Except that Jared had commented about it, mentioning specifically about Andrew's fictional killer taking one of his victim's thumbs. Jared had paid attention and seemed fascinated by the book. But he was in and out of the house so quickly. And there hadn't been a gunshot. Christ! Things were bad enough, he didn't need to make them worse in his mind.

"So, Andrew," Jared said as Andrew started back down the long driveway, the gravel sounding like bullets firing against the metal. "We have matching caps now. I thought I'd help myself since I know for a fact that farmer's not gonna need it anymore."

Andrew met Jared's eyes in the rearview mirror, those dark, smiling, hollow eyes, and he knew. And Jared wanted him to know that this was his way of making him a part of all this, a part of his evil.

PART 4
Wrong Turn

CHAPTER 43

11:15 a.m.
Hall of Justice

Grace shoved the second videotape into the VCR. She had decided to review the security tapes from the convenience-store robberies before she talked to Max Kramer again. The investigation was at a standstill, but she didn't like the idea of needing Max Kramer or his so-called witness. Bottom line, she didn't trust the guy.

The tapes had been reviewed over and over again. There wasn't much to see on any of them, anyway. The robber always wore a black mask over the bottom half of his face, a stocking cap, gloves, a dark-colored long-sleeve T-shirt and jeans. The picture wasn't as static riddled as the bank film, but not much better. The cameras in all three stores shot down at an angle from behind the counter and included the cash register and a slice of the store, a couple of aisles and usually the back freezer case.

She had already watched each of them once and was going through them again from the beginning. She hit Play. *Damn!* She'd gone back too far. She kept doing it with the first tape, as well, expecting there to be more. She recognized her mistake because there had been customers in the store each time right before the robberies. But the robber always waited. He had to be outside, watching, anticipating.

Grace reached to fast-forward past the array of customers coming in and out of the camera's view. But she paused it instead.

That was odd. Had she picked up the first tape again by mistake? She stopped and ejected it. No, this was the second one. She pushed it back in, rewound it and hit Play.

She watched the back of the store where a young man—probably a teenager, it was difficult to judge from the grainy picture—walked in front of the freezer case. She hit Pause and left the image frozen with him suspended in midstride. She found the videotape marked #1 and slipped it into the small TV/VCR combo on the shelf below. She rewound it, making sure she went back far enough then she pushed Play and watched and waited.

There he was.

She hit Pause. She stood back and examined the two screens. It had to be the same kid, same spiked hair, same loose gait and baggy jeans and the same bright white high-top tennis shoes. It was the shoes that she'd noticed first. What teenager, especially a boy, was able to keep his shoes so white? Could it be a coincidence that he was in both stores just minutes before the robberies?

She opened her file folder and shuffled through to find the stores' addresses. One was on the north side. The other in West Omaha. The third in the northwest section.

She pulled out the third video. Two could be a coincidence. She replaced one of the others with this one, rewound and hit Play.

Nothing.

She rewound farther back and tried again. The store was busy. This must have been the afternoon robbery. The others had been at night. But this last one the robber must have gotten cocky and struck in the afternoon, in broad daylight.

Grace watched closely. She didn't see him. No walk-through in front of the freezer case. There were others but not him. She rewound the tape again and started from the beginning one more time.

"Grace?"

She hit Pause, turned and looked up at Joyce Ketterson in the doorway to the small conference room.

"It's the call you've been waiting for. Zurich is on line two."

"Thanks, Joyce."

She grabbed the receiver, her eyes staying on the paused TV screen.

"Hey, sweetie," she said. "Sorry I missed your call earlier."

"I've got about five minutes before they begin serving dessert and coffee. How are things?"

Vince sounded tired. She knew without asking that he probably hadn't slept yet, except for a cat-nap on the long flight over.

"Things are going okay." She wouldn't worry him about Barnett. There wasn't a thing he could do about it. "How'd the meeting go?"

"It's still going. So, seriously, I do need to get back in there, but I just wanted to see how you were."

She smiled. He was doing a good job sidestepping the topic of Barnett, too.

"Hey, what's with the ceramic gnome?" she asked. "Are you planning some tacky front-yard landscaping? Actually, it's kind of cute."

"I don't know what you're talking about, Grace."

"The ceramic gnome?"

"Gnome? You mean like dwarf?"

"Yes, silly. The one you left on the steps down to the garage."

"Grace, I swear I don't have any idea what you're talking about. Richard's waving me back in. I gotta go. You sure you're okay?"

"Oh, sure, fine."

"Okay, give Emily a hug for me. Love you."

"Love you, too."

She decided she'd ask Emily about the ceramic creature. Maybe one of the workers had left it. Although they hadn't been back since last week. Then it occurred to her—what if Jared Barnett *had* been in the house? But why leave something like a stupid ceramic gnome?

She shook her head and stared at the TV screen. That was when she saw *him* again, or rather a sliver of him.

She was certain it was the same kid. He had his back to the camera. His right hand reached up over the door to the freezer case—a strange way to hold it open. But then she saw the reason. A little girl stood below him, getting something from the same case. He was holding it open for her, holding his arm way above her head, so as not to touch her. His hand was in a place where no one else probably touched, where there still might be some fingerprints. And, yes, there at the foot of the screen was one of the bright white high-tops.

She picked up the phone again and dialed.

"Darcy, it's Grace. There's something I'd like you to take a look at. Believe it or not, I may have found some fingerprints for us in one of the convenience stores."

CHAPTER 44

11:17 a.m.

Tommy Pakula sat in his Explorer, the door open, his cell phone in his lap. He could see the Sarpy County sheriff's deputies, their wide-brim hats bobbing between the trees as they searched the woods around the cabin. Bloodhounds were on the way, but Pakula didn't think they'd find anything. If it hadn't been for that farmer panicking and calling in his stolen pickup, they would have had the fucking dogs out last night, though he had to admit he wasn't sure they could work in the lightning and rain. Hell, they even had to ground the helicopter. The sons of bitches had lucked out.

Pakula ran the palm of his hand over his head. It was a good sign that they hadn't found a freshly dug grave, and yet the flip side wasn't much better. He had come close to letting the media reveal who the owner of the red Saab was. They'd find out soon enough if they started digging into the registered vanity plate. He had considered plastering the television stations with Andrew's name and photo. Someone may have already seen him. Could have called it in. But if the killers saw it, they might see Andrew as a liability. One thing Pakula was sure about, if that happened, these two psychos wouldn't be letting Andrew catch a ride home.

Pakula left the deputies and drove the short distance to where Hertz and the crime lab techs were still going over the crashed car. He could see they were taking the long way around to avoid sloshing through the tire ruts. Their alternate route didn't look much better. There was more rainwater between the rows of corn, and there was mud everywhere else.

He stepped over the busted barbed-wire fence and noticed a No Trespassing sign still attached, now mud splattered and barely hanging on. That summed it up pretty good. These two guys had no respect for authority, no respect for private property, no respect for anybody but themselves.

"We're getting what we can," Ben yelled to him as Pakula stepped from one mud pile to another, making his way to the car. "Then we'll haul it in and comb the inside." Ben tapped out a cigarette, and when one of the techs scowled at him, he headed back the way Pakula had just come.

Pakula recognized the tall, skinny kid, Wes Howard, and mumbled a hello. He didn't envy these two, crawling around in the mud, trying to do their grid of the scene with latex gloves on and plastic bags in hand. He stayed back about twenty feet, trying to get a sense of what those two assholes went through during their scenic crash in the country. What did they do next? How did they happen to stumble onto the cabin Andrew had rented?

"Air bag deploy?" he asked.

"Nope and thank goodness," Wes said. "Sometimes they make a mess of the evidence."

"Yeah, but sometimes you end up getting some blood or snot for DNA."

"No blood or snot but plenty of vomit in the back seat."

"Really? Isn't that interesting. Anything else?" Pakula asked.

"We'll dust the interior for prints after we haul it in. Footprints around the car are pretty much washed away. Although I think I have a partial on the inside back doorstep."

"Nothing got left behind in the car?" Pakula came close enough to glance inside. It was looking more and more like the assholes didn't get away with any money.

"Couple of pairs of bloody coveralls, one kerchief. No weapon. We'll do a good vacuum job back at the ranch. I did find this in the mud." Wes held up a plastic bag with what looked like a piece of jewelry, some kind of pendant or locket. "It's not tarnished, so I don't think it was here before the car crash. Just dirty. And I don't know too many farmers who'd be wearing something this fancy while plowing the field. Has an engraving on the back." He took a closer look then handed it to Pakula. "TLC and JMK. Mean anything to you?"

"Probably not tender-loving-care, huh? Mind if I hang on to this for a couple days?"

"No problem. You might check with Darcy. I think I remember her saying she found a broken necklace on one of the victims."

"Remember which one?"

"No, sorry."

"Where did you say you found this?"

"Along the side of the car, down in the mud. Kind of deep in the mud, actually. I might not have found it except that I was scraping for a soil sample. If it was dropped accidentally, it was also stepped on hard enough to press it into the dirt."

"You think they might have buried it so it wouldn't be found on them?"

"Who knows. I guess it's possible."

"So we have this and a partial shoe print on the back doorway." Pakula stared at the car as if seeing it for the first time. Something didn't add up. The Saturn's hood was smashed in, the front bumper hanging off. There were scrapes where the barbed wire had tried to hold it back. The radiator was probably busted. No windshield cracks, so no heads were busted. But there was something wrong with this picture.

"Is this exactly the way the car was when you guys got out here?"

"Yup. They probably jumped out and ran. Didn't even take time to close the doors."

That was it, Pakula thought. That was what didn't fit.

"Why are there three doors left open?" he asked. "And you said the partial footprint was where?"

Wes met Pakula's eyes, and he could see the kid was already thinking the same thing.

"Back doorstep," he said.

"Can you tell if it was stepping back into the car as if someone was getting something?"

Without hesitation Wes said, "No, it was definitely on its way out of the car."

CHAPTER 45

11:33 a.m.

"We're headed in the wrong direction." Melanie said. She had spent most of her life within a hundred-mile radius of Omaha, Nebraska, but even so, she still knew that Colorado was west. They were headed south.

She was getting hungry and tired and the sun was blinding her. She pulled down the sun visor only to be face-to-face with a gold-framed Jesus pin-tacked to the inside fabric of the visor.

"Jesus!" she grumbled and flipped it back in place. She'd rather have the sun in her eyes.

"I'm hungry," she said, hoping it sounded pathetic enough for Jared to allow them to drive through at the next fast-food joint. Though out here the miles between towns kept getting longer. She glanced over her shoulder at Charlie, who was sleeping with his head propped against the window. His red hair stuck up in spikes and his right fist was tucked under his chin. No use trying to enlist him in her food dilemma.

"I said I'm—" She was interrupted by a package of granola bars flying over the seat into her lap. "I need some—" The bottle of water missed her head by inches.

"For Christ's sake, be careful. Geez." Melanie glanced at Andrew, embarrassed. She shook her head.

Charlie snickered, stretched and then added, "Yeah, can't we stop? I need to take a piss."

Melanie hid her smile. Finally, she wasn't the only one.

"How we doing on gas?" Jared leaned over the seat to see for himself as if he didn't trust Andrew. "The next town's Auburn. It should have some kind of convenience store. We'll get gas and supplies. Charlie can take a piss and then we'll turn around."

"Whadya mean turn around?" Charlie piped up before Melanie had the chance.

Jared handed him the map, opening it to the right panel. "We'll cut back and head for Colorado."

"I knew it. I knew we were headed in the wrong direction," Melanie said to Andrew, but the writer hadn't said a word since they left the farmer's place. In fact, he'd just been staring straight ahead at the road as he drove, his left hand at the top of the steering wheel, barely moving. His eyes were hidden behind a pair of sunglasses he'd found on top of the visor on his side.

Melanie held off opening the package of granola bars. She could see the town just beyond the next curve. Maybe the place would have slices of pizza or one of those turning roasters with hot dogs. Some of the nicer convenience stores had both. She wanted real food, and only now realized she couldn't remember when she ate last.

Jared hung over the front seat again, getting a better look at the approaching town.

"Can we buy some toothpaste and a toothbrush?" Melanie asked. "How much can we spend?"

"Isn't that just like a woman?" Jared said to Andrew, slapping him on his shoulder as if they were best buddies now.

Melanie cringed, thinking an injured shoulder harnessed up like that must still hurt like hell, but Andrew didn't flinch. He didn't even move. He just stared ahead, like a robot. She hoped he wasn't falling asleep. Her bruised ribs couldn't take another car crash.

"Can we get some Tylenol, too?" she asked Jared.

She figured he owed her big-time for helping him tie up that farmer. She just kept reminding herself that the guy's wife would be home soon, and he'd be put out of his misery.

"That looks good. Pull in over there." He pointed to what looked to be a freshly painted Gas N' Shop. "Melanie, check the fucking glove compartment. I need a pair of sunglasses."

"Yeah, that's what I need, too. Can you pick up a pair for me?"

She dropped open the glove compartment and shoved the contents around—map, tire air gauge, matchbook, a pack of cigarettes and finally a pair of dark-lense glasses. She handed them to her brother as she hesitated in closing the compartment. She'd forgotten how wonderful, almost sensual, the scent of cigarettes could be. Her fingers wanted to grab the pack and tap one out. Just one. *God!* She'd love to have just one.

"Melanie, you fill up. Charlie, go take a piss but don't take forever. *Melanie,* did you hear what I said?"

"Can I go in and get what I need?" She turned and glared at him as though he hadn't heard her before.

"No, you're not going in."

"Oh, come on, Jared. I need some things, and I want some real food."

"I'll take care of things."

She scowled at him. "That's what you always say."

She had to be careful. She didn't want her whining to push him too far, to send him over the edge. He had never gotten angry enough with her to hurt her or Charlie or even their mother. But she had seen what his anger could do. And she found herself wondering if that's what went wrong in the bank. Did someone not listen? Did someone have a smart mouth?

"I'll get everything you fucking need," he told her. "Put the gas in the fucking car, and then you wait."

She saw Jared checking the gun, and suddenly she wasn't hungry anymore. He shoved it into the waistband of his jeans and pulled the T-shirt over it. He patted it, checking to make sure it was secure.

She wanted to tell him to leave the gun. It had already caused enough problems. She wanted to ask how the hell he could rob a bank and not take any money. Instead, she said nothing. So he'd rob a convenience store with a gun instead of a con. It was easy. It was cheap. She'd probably have done it, too, if she didn't hate guns so much.

One thing she did know for certain was that when you stuck a gun in someone's face they'd do just about anything. They'd beg and plead. They'd even cry like a little baby. Her father had. He'd started crying like a little baby when he realized his empty apology for beating the hell out of Jared and Melanie wasn't going to save him. There had been too many beatings, and it had been way too late for apologies.

"Everybody ready?" Jared asked, startling Melanie. Then he tapped Andrew on his harnessed shoulder again. "Ordinary Citizen Kane, *you're* coming with me."

CHAPTER 46

11:41 a.m.
Auburn, Nebraska

Andrew had been trying to block out their voices. The whine of their arguing felt like sandpaper on his brain. He wished he could disconnect, get inside his head and forget about everything around him. Sorta like when he was in a good flow of writing.

Unfortunately, as he had discovered this past year with his writing, it wasn't something he could control, like a switch he could turn on or off. If only it were that simple. If only he could access it right now. Go away for a while in his mind. Pretend. Isn't that what Tommy had told him was his problem? That he lived too much in the world of pretend rather than the real world?

When was that? Was it days ago that he and Tommy had sat on the porch at the cabin? No. Just yesterday. God! That seemed impossible. Then it occurred to him. It was Tommy. It had to be. Tommy must have gone back to check on him. That's how they knew. Of course, how stupid of him. If Tommy was on the case, maybe there was a way he could leave a message for him. But what? How?

"Let's go." Jared punched Andrew's shoulder. The pain shot down to his fingertips. It took all his effort to keep from flinching, but he wouldn't react. He wouldn't give this son of a bitch the satisfaction.

"Keep your cap on and your sunglasses," Jared instructed. "You stay close to me. We'll take our time. Go slow. Don't look like you're in a fucking hurry. When we see that Mel's finished filling up, you pay for everything with a credit card. They'll be tracking your account. It'll look like we're headed south."

Jared handed him his wallet, and it was the first time Andrew realized Jared had taken it. Of course he had his wallet. He had his bank card. Focus. Why the hell couldn't he focus? If only the throbbing in his head would quiet down. He needed to get his mind out of the spiderwebs. That's what it felt like— a lacy mess tangling up his thoughts.

"Did you get that? Hey—"

"Yeah, I got it," Andrew said in time to stop another assault on his wounded shoulder.

"And let me do the talking. You keep your fucking mouth shut."

"I really gotta pee," Charlie said.

"Okay, okay. Let's go then."

All four car doors opened almost in unison. Andrew took his time in an exaggerated stretch. It did feel good to get out and be on his feet. He used the time to examine the area around the convenience store. With the dark sunglasses on he could check out the side streets. His eyes darted all around, taking in as much detail as possible, including the newspaper machines out front. The *Omaha World Herald* headline shouted, Killers on the Loose. The *Lincoln Journal's* was simple and bold, Manhunt.

In the time it took to walk from the car door to the door of the convenience store Andrew contemplated his alternatives. Why not give Jared a quick shove and take off running? He was in good shape, at least up until he broke his collarbone. Andrew stood at least three inches taller, but Jared looked much leaner. Yet even with the throbbing in his head Andrew wanted to take his chances. What did he have to lose?

He took one last look at the side streets lined with houses. That was good, backyards and alleys. The main street was too open. To his back Andrew knew the highway separated them from a parking lot. Not good. And behind the convenience store Andrew guessed the slice of fence he could see probably ran along the whole lot. The houses across the street were his best bet.

Now he just needed to shove him hard enough to push him over. Maybe into the newspaper machines. That might slow him down. Andrew watched from behind his dark glasses. Jared was right beside him. A couple more steps. Already his heart banged against his rib cage in anticipation. One quick shove. He could do this.

That's when the door to the convenience store opened and a woman and her toddler came out. And Andrew realized he'd have to wait.

CHAPTER 47

11:46 a.m.

Detective Tommy Pakula found the house after driving in and out of about a half dozen culs-de-sac. He hated these new housing developments that were built on confusion and sold as privacy. He'd take his South Omaha home any day, where a neighborhood was still a block.

As he walked to the front door, he took a good look at the neighborhood and wondered how Tina Cervante could afford this huge split-timber. Even sharing the expenses with two roommates, the rent had be double what one of the higher-end apartments in the area would cost. He remembered the girl's autopsy, the pricey manicure and pedicure, the nose job. From what he had discovered about her parents—her father was a mechanic for a Dallas trucking company and her mother an assistant manager for a Red Lobster restaurant—he doubted that, although they made decent money, they had any to spare, especially with four more kids still at home.

He knocked on the ornate front door, still trying to figure it out. Maybe one of the other girls had some family money. Maybe this house was a tax write-off for one of the other parents. Maybe it was just Pakula being his suspicious self.

The young woman who answered the door looked like a Britney Spears wannabe, only her midriff hung out of the tight, cropped T-shirt and the dark roots gave away her true hair color.

"Are you Danielle Miller?"

She ran her fingers through her tangled hair and yawned, not bothering to cover her mouth. "Yeah, are you here to fix the air conditioner? You're a bit late. We could have used you two days ago when we called the first time."

Pakula wanted to laugh; he had been worried Tina's roommates would be too distraught to even talk. As it turned out, Danielle was more upset about the fucking A/C being out than her old roommate ending up splattered all over the bank's floor.

"No, Miss Miller, I'm afraid I don't know much about air-conditioning units." Pakula dug in his jacket for his shield as she rolled her eyes at him, and just as she was deciding he was some door-to-door salesman, he flipped the badge for her to take a look. "I'm Detective Pakula with the OPD. I'd like to talk to you about Tina Cervante."

"Oh, you mean about the thing at the bank yesterday."

"Yeah, the thing at the bank," he repeated, trying not to show his impatience. She reminded him too much of his oldest daughter, Angie, although she was a bit younger than Danielle Miller. Same generation, though, and that same lazy use of the English language, same carefree attitude.

"Whadya wanna know?"

"Just some basic stuff. You mind if I come in for a few minutes?"

"Sure, I guess." She walked back into the house, leaving him to follow.

The inside decor matched the outside, all designer pieces, a couple of signed lithographs on the wall and an expensive Oriental rug.

"How did you girls ever find this place?" Pakula asked. "It's very nice. One of you a decorator?"

"Oh, God, no." She laughed as she curled up into the corner of a leather sofa, tucking her bare feet under her. "Tina found it for us." She shrugged as if it were as simple as that. "It's not really my style. A little too much like living in my parents' home, you know what I mean?"

He nodded instead of saying that it was probably too classy for her style. But at least he was getting her to talk. It seemed to be his talent, getting people to confide in him. And sometimes he relied on it too much, thinking he could talk his way out of any situation.

"Tina had a real talent for that kinda stuff, you know?" Finally Pakula could see a hint of moistness in Danielle's eyes. "She could get people to, like, give her things or let her use stuff."

"Really? What kind of stuff?"

"Oh, I don't know. Like cars and stuff."

"You mean like boyfriends?"

Forget the moistness, Danielle was back to rolling her eyes at him. "She goes for guys, like, your age. You know, she likes old guys for some reason. Oh, God! Not like I mean you're old or anything."

"Where does she usually meet these older gentlemen?" He tried not to sound offended.

"Oh, geez. I don't even know where she met this last one. I get the idea he's pretty pissed off at her right now, so they might have broken up."

"What makes you think he's pissed off at her?"

"Just that whenever I answered the phone lately and she, like, didn't want to talk to him, so like, I'd have to make up some excuse and he'd get all postal with me."

"So he called here?"

"Oh, yeah."

"But you don't know his name?"

"Just Jay."

Pakula dug out the plastic bag from his jacket pocket and handed it to Danielle. "Did he give Tina this?"

"Oh, yeah. For her birthday in July. That seemed to be when things started to go downhill, 'cause I think Tina thought it should mean more and yet she didn't see him changing anything."

"A guy gives an expensive, sentimental piece of jewelry like this, I'd say that means something."

"Yeah, you'd think so, but…you know, it's kinda like I keep telling her, or told her…God, I can't believe she's dead."

Pakula waited. This time Danielle seemed genuinely choked up. She had been slipping from present to past tense the whole time. Not unusual in an interview with someone who'd been close to a victim. But now it seemed to hit her. He bowed his head and waited. He'd learned that people really didn't want to hear all that crap like, "It'll be okay." Most of the time they just wanted you to wait until they composed themselves. Waiting was tougher, though.

"So it sounds like you kinda figured out this relationship wouldn't work long before Tina figured it out, huh?"

"It never does work," she said, reaching around to a Kleenex box hidden behind a flower vase. She dabbed at her nose. "That's the problem with dating older men. They always stay with their wives."

CHAPTER 48

11:52 a.m.

Andrew kept trying to catch the eye of the woman behind the store counter, not an easy task with sunglasses on but also because she didn't stay in one place for long. She hustled from one end of the long counter to the next, pausing just long enough to give them a nod when they entered.

Jared loaded up Andrew's free arm, handing him everything from Tylenol, toothpaste and razors to chips, candy bars and comic books. It looked as if they were stocking up for a monthlong road trip.

Andrew continued to watch the woman, hoping, *wishing* she'd glance their way. Was it too much to hope for her to ask a few questions: "Where you boys from?" "Where you headed?" Instead, she kept moving, her gray-haired head down, small body scurrying from the little oven where she replaced mini pizzas with freshly made ones, to the hot-dog roaster, to the counter space where she constructed submarine sandwiches. Andrew was amazed.

She worked here because she had to, Andrew decided. Maybe her social security benefits weren't quite paying the bills. He wondered if her kids or grandkids worried about her working at a convenience store. No, probably not. In Omaha, yes. But out here? It was just another job. Hopefully it would remain just another job. Maybe she'd never know she had waited on a murderer today.

There had been no customers enter the store since the woman with the toddler left. Andrew guessed they were hitting a lull before the anticipated masses for lunch. He checked his options, slowly trailing his eyes over the shelves, searching for a back door. There had to be one, maybe down the small hallway in the corner. But what if they kept it locked during the day? Running out the front posed the risk of running into another customer.

Then it hit Andrew. Jared wanted him to charge all this. He needed to sign the charge slip. If Tommy was on the case, would he think to go through the actual charge slips? He knew they'd be watching his accounts now that they knew he might be with them. Jared was even counting on it.

Could he get a message to Tommy via the charge slip?

Jared grabbed a six-pack of beer from the cooler just as Andrew noticed Melanie getting into the car, this time into the driver's seat. Jared noticed, too, and gave Andrew a shove toward the counter. They piled their bounty in front of the little woman who now was looking them over.

"That pizza smells good," Jared said. "You make them here?"

"Crust's frozen. We add the toppings." She began to ring up each item and place it into a bag before going on to the next.

"We'll take a couple of pizzas and a couple of sandwiches."

She scurried off to wrap them, the pizzas in square containers, the sandwiches in wax paper. She dug out two huge dill pickles from a jar and wrapped those individually to go with the sandwiches. In less than a minute she was back. Still no questions, no conversation. Other than the first once-over, she didn't really look at them.

"With the gas that comes to $43.67."

Andrew handed her his American Express card.

She swiped it through the machine and handed him the copy to sign. Just as she handed him a pen, he said, "Gum, I forgot gum."

Jared looked around, and when he turned to grab a pack off a rack behind him, Andrew flipped the charge slip over and scribbled "CO via 6." By the time Jared tossed the gum onto the counter, Andrew had his name signed and was handing the slip back to her.

She picked up the gum in one hand and charge slip in her other. "You paying for this separately?"

"Yes." Andrew dug the change out of his pockets, hoping his hieroglyphics wouldn't be noticed, at least for now.

Finally finished, Jared gave Andrew one of the two bags, then tucked the six-pack under Andrew's arm, as if purposely weighing him down. Melanie had brought the car right up to the front door. They headed outside, Jared holding the door to the convenience store open while Andrew handed Charlie the beer through the car window. He was getting in the front passenger seat when he noticed Jared hadn't left his post, hand still holding open the store's front door, as if he was waiting for someone else to go in. Andrew looked around the parking lot, only there was no one else there.

"I saw what you did, Andrew," Jared said, waiting for Andrew's eyes to meet his. As Andrew began to understand, Jared slipped back into the convenience store.

Andrew's stomach fell to his feet even before he heard the gunshot.

CHAPTER 49

12:15 p.m.

"*What the hell did you do, Jared?*" Melanie asked for the second time, trying to keep her voice controlled. She had driven with hands shaking, pretending that what she'd heard wasn't a gunshot. Now, as she waited at a stop sign, she glanced at Jared in the rearview mirror. He was stuffing his mouth with a slice of pizza and popping the cap off a beer. Another glance at Andrew made her insides churn. The writer had doubled over, his forehead pressed against his hands, almost as if he was expecting to be sick.

"What did you do, Jared?" she asked again.

"What did *I* do?" he asked through a mouthful of food. "You should ask your buddy what *he* did." This time he flung a piece of paper over the seat. "Take a right."

"We just came from that direction." But she didn't

argue and pulled onto the highway. She grabbed the paper before it slipped off the seat to the floor. It looked like an ordinary credit card receipt with a signature.

"What? He signed the correct name."

"On the back, stupid."

"Don't call me stupid," she said before she could stop herself. Her hands were shaking so bad she couldn't read what was printed on the back. "What's coviale?" she asked, pronouncing it as best she could.

"No, no. It's CO via 6. Don't you get it? He was trying to tip them off. Tell them which way we were headed."

"Oh, I get it," Charlie piped up and Melanie could see him grinning in the rearview mirror like a schoolboy who'd answered a question correctly. "Colorado via Highway 6. That's what it is, right?" He looked to Jared for approval.

"You didn't need to kill her," Andrew said without lifting his head, his voice a quiet muffle.

"The way I see it, buddy, pal, Mr. Ordinary Citizen Kane, you killed her." Jared spat out the words with such exaggerated enunciation that Melanie could feel his angry spittle on her neck and could smell the pepperoni on his breath.

Silence. It was suddenly so quiet Melanie could hear Jared chewing and swallowing. There was some rustling of paper and she saw that Charlie had joined in, unwrapping a sandwich and ripping open a bag of chips. Nothing seemed to spoil either of their appetites.

She knew as far as Jared was concerned the subject was closed. This was crazy. Another person dead? When would it stop? Had Jared lost his mind? This was not the brother she knew. She tried to keep her mind on the road. Every intersection had her checking for police cars. What if someone heard the gunshot? What if someone saw them drive away?

As if he could read her mind, Jared said suddenly, "We need a new car."

"But I just filled this one up," Melanie said, recognizing immediately what a stupid thing it was to say. Stupid, yes. Maybe Jared was right. She was stupid. Stupid to ever trust him, now knowing full well why she wasn't in on "the plan" from the start. The guns, the getaway—she would never have agreed to any of this. Now Jared had them all in such a mess there was no turning back.

"Whadya think, Charlie?"

"I noticed some kind of manufacturing plant a few miles out. Parking lot with a bunch of cars. Should be up here." Charlie sat forward, surveying the area.

Melanie hadn't noticed it, but, of course, Charlie would have. Sure enough she could now see the building back off the highway, partially hidden by trees. Some farm-implement maker or so she guessed something called Val-Farm Manufacturing would be.

She took the turn for the access road without needing Jared's instructions. She noticed Andrew had sat up. He had taken off the sunglasses and was rubbing his eyes and forehead with such force she expected the wound to start bleeding again. What was wrong with him? Did he want to hurt himself? Sure enough, drops of blood fell onto the car seat. She grabbed a napkin she hadn't used earlier and tossed it into his lap. He stared at it, then finally, after glancing at her, picked it up and put it against the wound.

Jared and Charlie looked like two kids in a candy store scoping out the cars as Melanie drove up and down the rows.

"Not another Saturn," Jared said. "And nothing flashy."

"I can do Tauruses pretty good," Charlie said. "How 'bout that one over there? It's kinda dirty. I can't even tell what color it is. I can exchange license plates with that Ford Escort behind it."

"It's perfect. Melanie—"

But she was already pulling in to an empty slot two cars away.

Charlie jumped out and walked up to the car as if it was his and they were dropping him off. It didn't matter. There was no one around. And the building didn't have any windows that looked out over the parking lot.

Charlie grinned as he opened the Taurus's door without jimmying the lock. The owner hadn't even bothered to lock it. Melanie watched him slide into the driver's seat, his head disappearing while he hotwired it. But suddenly his head popped up with a wide grin as he dangled the car's keys for them to see.

"Christ," Jared said. "People are so fucking trusting out here. They deserve to have their cars stolen."

CHAPTER 50

4:10 p.m.

Max Kramer slammed the telephone receiver into its cradle. He couldn't believe it. Grace Wenninghoff had just passed on his offer. Was she recklessly stupid or did she know something?

Rumor was the cops didn't have jackshit as evidence in the string of convenience-store robberies. Nothing except maybe the stores' videos, which they had shown snippets of on the ten o'clock news. Not much to see there. It looked like the same routine, even the same guy in the same getup, but it also looked as if it would be impossible for anyone to ID the guy from those crappy videos.

There went his insurance policy, down the drain. Now he was stuck defending another crack whore who couldn't afford to pay him. Not even two weeks ago he was on the *Larry King Show* and he didn't think life could get any better. Well, he was right, because just when he thought he was on top of the world, he was sliding down shit hill again.

He leaned back in his leather chair and stared out his office window that overlooked the Gene Leahy Mall and downtown Omaha. It was this window and this view that made the small, cramped space prime commercial real estate. He couldn't afford it, but did, because he liked looking out over the city and feeling a sense of power. He had worked long and hard to win this city's respect. He wasn't about to have it taken away from him now.

He could cash in on his national media coupe for only so long. He knew that. It wouldn't take much before his colleagues started to try to knock him down—the bastards.

He sorted through the stack of voice messages. A half-dozen idiots, all wanting something from him. The one idiot he needed to hear from hadn't called. He checked his watch. He had to start thinking about an alternative insurance policy. It shouldn't be this difficult. After all, who better than a defense attorney knew exactly what the cops were looking for?

Max set aside the three messages from his wife. She'd want to know what time he'd be home. Should she keep dinner warm?

He hated that the bitch kept such tabs on him. He was sick and tired of her subtle threats. He had hoped after his national media blitz that he wouldn't need her or her money. What was he thinking? That *Fox*

News would cancel Greta Van Susteren and be calling to offer him his own legal talk show? How likely was that?

Instead, he had a shitload of messages from death-row assholes all across the country, all wanting him to get them off. More assholes who didn't have a fucking dime to pay him. And there weren't any more favors he needed from any of them. Hell, the one bastard who *did* owe him couldn't get things right.

He checked his wristwatch again. He had better be getting a phone call and soon.

CHAPTER 51

5:56 p.m.

Tommy Pakula searched the bleachers, squinting against the sun and finally putting a hand up to his forehead. Claire was on the second row from the top, waving at him and at the same time yelling at their daughter to "use your head." It looked as if he had missed most of the first quarter, but his team was ahead by one goal.

He climbed up the bleachers, and the pack of screaming parents automatically parted, allowing him to get to his designated seat. But because he was late he got only nods as greetings, no time for talk. The game was on.

This was the first year Pakula had sat in the bleachers instead of on the sidelines, wearing his sweat-stained ball cap with the tattered white COACH embroidered across the front. He missed it, but both he and Claire had decided something had to give. He was running himself ragged.

He barely sat down before Claire was pulling out a Pepsi and a sandwich from their beat-up mini-cooler. She handed him the drink while she un-wrapped the sandwich, her eyes never leaving the field. He could already smell the spicy meatballs, last night's leftovers that she'd managed to resurrect with mozzarella cheese, hot mustard and sourdough bread. His mouth started watering before she had it out of the wax paper. It was a running joke between them that he'd never be able to divorce her because he'd never be able to live without her cooking. Of course without it, he probably wouldn't have to spend as much time and sweat every morning in their basement, slamming all those calories off with his punching bag.

"How's she doing?" he asked, his eyes finding their eight-year-old with no problem. Jenna was the smallest one, a skinny little blonde who could dart in between the other players. He found her easily on the field.

"It's so muddy," Claire said. "They've all been sliding into each other. Oh, she did that thing you showed her."

"Yeah? How'd it work?"

"Too hard. The ball flew out of bounds."

"That's okay. She had some power behind it. That's good."

He glanced over at Claire as he took a bite of the

sandwich. She turned and looked at him, smiling. He automatically wiped at his mouth, thinking she must have spotted a wad of mustard. She shook her head, the smile still there when she turned back to the game, but she reached over to pat his knee and that's where her hand stayed.

For some reason the gesture reminded Pakula of Andrew and their conversation out at the cabin. Andrew had given him a hard time about being an old married guy who couldn't possibly advise anyone on romance. But this, watching their daughter on the soccer field on a glorious evening with the sun setting behind them, having a meatball sandwich and his wife's hand on his knee, this was good, really good.

All he had tried to get across to Andrew was that he was missing out. He knew there was something in his friend's past, some miserable breakup, some failed relationship that had happened before the two had become friends. Stuff like that happens. You shake it off. You go on and find someone else. But not Andrew. Andrew seemed to react by closing himself off. There were too many emotional barricades set up with that guy. Even as friends, Andrew had only allowed Pakula to see and know as much about him as he wanted, bits and pieces doled out little by little. From what he did know about Andrew, he guessed the guy's father had really played a number on him, instilling in Andrew that he wasn't worth much. Amazing how easily parents could fuck up their kids.

Claire was watching him again, only this time she looked concerned. "You're worried about him," she said and Pakula did a double take, wondering how the hell she could always do that. How did she always know what was on his mind?

"He's not prepared for something like this."

"My God, who is?"

"I should have checked on him sooner. Especially when I knew they were headed in that direction."

"Tommy." This time she squeezed his knee to get his full attention. "You can't take care of all of us all the time." When she could see he wouldn't let her words exonerate him, she added, "Andrew's going to be all right. He has to be or I'll never forgive him."

That made Pakula smile, as if her ability to inflict motherly guilt could overreach all boundaries. But before he could go back to his sandwich, his cell phone began ringing. Not an unusual occurrence, and yet everyone turned to scowl at him as if he had broken some rule. He had it out before the third ring.

"Pakula," he said, twisting around as much as possible and turning his back to the crowd and the field. Claire reached for his sandwich and drink to free his hands.

"Detective Thomas Pakula?"

"Yeah. Speak up. I'm at a soccer game, so we might…" He was interrupted by the chants and applause before he could get off the warning. He waited then tried again. "Okay, go ahead."

"Sheriff Grant Dawes down here in Nemaha

County. Someone downtown told me I should be talking to you."

"Yeah, okay." Pakula didn't know the sheriff, but he was quickly getting impatient with his slow, polite manner. "What is it you need to tell me, Sheriff?" There were about to be more screams and applause. Out of the corner of his eye he could see his team racing down the sidelines. He turned to watch, not wanting to miss another goal.

"We found…" The rest of the sheriff's words were drowned out.

"What's that?"

"We found the red Saab with the license plate A WHIM."

Pakula froze. The noise erupted again around him, so that he couldn't even ask the one question that came instantly to mind. Claire stopped cheering when she saw his face and met his eyes. He gestured that he couldn't hear as he rose, shoving his way back down the bleachers, everyone too excited about their team scoring to bother being upset with him. He retreated to the parking lot, hoping he hadn't lost the sheriff.

"Are you still with me?" he finally asked when he could hear again.

"Yeah, I'm here."

"You said you found the car?"

"Yep, it's sitting in a farmer's garage. They took his Chevy, but not before slitting his throat."

"Holy crap!"

"There's more."

Pakula leaned against his Explorer, bracing himself for the worst. Had Andrew Kane been left behind, too, with his throat slashed?

"Up the road in Auburn we've got a dead clerk in the Gas N' Shop. Son of a bitch shot her right in the face, ripped her jaw wide open."

Pakula waited. Finally he asked, "Any other victims?"

"Ain't two enough?" ·

"No, it's two too many." Pakula ran his hand over his head, relieved and kicking himself for sounding like it. "Sheriff, how long ago were the bodies found? I'd like to get our mobile crime lab down there asap."

"Actually, that's what I was hoping you'd say. I've got my men isolating both scenes, but I don't have the resources to tackle this kind of thing."

"This a good number to reach you?" Pakula asked as he checked his cell phone to make sure the sheriff's phone number got logged on his phone's memory.

"Yeah, I'll be here."

"Give me a few minutes, and I'll call you back. Hold on. I don't suppose you have a license number for that Chevy?"

"Not yet. The wife's not in much shape to be remembering such things, so I'm having someone look it up. I'll have it when you call back."

"Good." Pakula ended the call, punching in the next number without hesitating. He needed to act and not dwell on Andrew. And he reminded himself of Claire's words only changing them a bit and saying out loud, "Andrew will be all right. He has to be or I'll never forgive myself."

CHAPTER 52

8:20 p.m.

It was easier this way, Grace told herself as she searched for clean linens for the guest room. Easier than arguing with the old woman. When Grace picked up Emily from Grandma Wenny's she had insisted on coming home with them, at least until "Vince returned from the Alps." That was exactly how her grandmother referred to Vince's trip to Switzerland as if he was there on some ski trip.

Grandma Wenny had been concerned ever since Jared Barnett had been released from prison, though Grace hadn't confided anything about him following her. Nor had she shared her suspicions that he was one of the bank robbers now on the run. Yet the old woman seemed to have a sixth sense about these things. Even the night Grace's parents had been murdered, Grandma Wenny had lit a candle in the window for protection from the "bad air" of the approaching thunderstorms, not realizing it was a storm of another kind that would hit her son's house only three blocks away.

Grace had left Emily to show Grandma Wenny the house, knowing her daughter would make the suite they'd renovated for her sound like more of an adventure than a prison sentence. It was one of the reasons Grace had given in so easily to her grandmother coming home with them. It was ridiculous to believe the old woman could somehow protect them, especially since Grace had insisted the .38 stay back at the bungalow. But maybe, just maybe she could convince her grandmother that her presence was wanted and needed in their home.

The bottom line was that Grace wanted Grandma Wenny to live with them, but only if she wanted it, too. She owed the old woman so much, it was her grandmother who had taught her she could do anything she set her mind to. The sacrifices the old woman had made for her were great, but her German heritage would explain it all away as something you just did for family. Family was the most important thing. But her grandmother's will, her spirit, the kick in the pants and the constant nagging that reminded Grace that she could and would do important things—that was something Grace relied on every day.

She found them in the kitchen, devouring the oatmeal chocolate-chunk cookies that Grandma Wenny and Emily had baked earlier at her house. Emily and Grace had talked the old woman into having dinner out, finally settling on the Greek Isles Restaurant, where Grandma Wenny had explained that the Greeks were a people to be admired for all their contributions, unlike the French, who she insisted couldn't be trusted, using their high prices and small portions of food as proof. Grace let her get away with this kind of talk. Sometimes trying to change old ways, old beliefs, old prejudices was a losing battle.

"So is this a bedtime snack?" Grace asked, sitting down at the table across from the two.

"I should stay up later to make sure Grandma Wenny isn't scared," Emily said, avoiding Grace's eyes and concentrating on the cookie she was holding over a glass of milk, half dunked.

"I don't think Grandma Wenny is scared of anything," Grace said. "Nice try, Em."

"Emily tells me about her Mr. McDuff."

"Yeah, I still can't find him, Mom."

"I'm sure he's here somewhere."

"I don't like sleeping without him. I thought maybe I could sleep with Grandma Wenny tonight. You know, just until she gets used to the house."

"I think she'll be fine in her own room," Grace said, but she watched the two exchange a glance as Emily finished the last bite of cookie, and Grace knew the matter had already been discussed. "Emily, go on up and get your pj's on. Grandma Wenny and I will come up and tuck you in."

"Okay." But there was another glance as Emily slid out of the chair. Grace could tell Grandma Wenny was listening and waiting until she heard Emily reach the top of the stairs.

"She said the bad man took her Mr. McDuff."

"She overheard Vince and me talking about a case. She just misunderstood."

"He was here, in the house."

"No one's been in the house." But Grace knew immediately that Grandma Wenny didn't believe her. She had never been able to lie to the old woman. Fact was Grace didn't know if Barnett *had* been in their house. Was he the one who'd left that stupid ceramic gnome? And if he had been here, what did he want besides letting her know that he could come and go as he pleased?

"I can feel it. He was here in the house."

"We've had lots of workers in and out. They've been working on the renovation."

"No, no. This is a bad man. He was here. And he took Emily's Mr. McDuff."

CHAPTER 53

8:50 p.m.
Highway 6

Melanie's eyes begged to close. Even against the oncoming headlights she was unable to keep them open and remain alert. When was the last time she had slept? She honestly didn't remember. The adrenaline had carried her this far, but when the sun went down it seemed her energy went down with it.

Charlie had been asleep in the back for almost an hour, according to the snores. Andrew Kane appeared wide-awake in the seat beside her, though his head leaned against the window. Melanie could see his eyes staring straight ahead. Jared looked wide-awake, too. Every time the oncoming headlights lit up the Taurus's interior, Melanie caught him watching her in the rearview mirror.

Now she heard the rustling of the map from behind her and noticed a stream of light from the Maglite they had found in the glove compartment. There were other things they·had found inside the Taurus, things that bothered Melanie for some reason. Instead of a Jesus picture tacked to the visor, there was a picture of a dark-haired woman hugging a little boy who shared her eyes.

On the floor in the front, Andrew had accidentally kicked a stuffed teddy bear. When he picked it up, Melanie was struck by how carefully he handled it, almost as if it were alive. He had laid it on the seat between them, and as much as Melanie didn't want it there she could also not bring herself to move it. It reminded her too much of Charlie's old stuffed Pooh bear. And the photo reminded her that this was a mother's car they had taken. A mother who worked at that manufacturing plant, probably at a shitty job for shitty pay, just so she could take care of her little boy. And now the little boy wouldn't have his teddy bear tonight.

"The next intersection should be Highway 34," Jared said, startling her when he leaned up against the front seat. "Take a right."

"I don't think I can drive much farther, Jared."

"I know. I've been watching you, Mel." He put his hand on her shoulder and gave it a reassuring squeeze. "You've done a good job, Lil' Sis."

She glanced back at him in the rearview mirror, looking for sarcasm and not able to see a trace. When they were kids he used to call her Lil' Sis whenever he took care of her, comforting her with that same reassuring tone that made her feel like everything would be okay. But sometimes even Jared wasn't able to make things okay. Before she could determine whether or not he was still trying to take care of her, he was pointing over the seat at a billboard.

"We can get a room at that Comfort Inn. Looks like it's just on the other side of Hastings."

She almost asked if they could afford it, but stopped herself. She didn't care if they could afford it. Just the thought of a hot shower and a soft bed perked her up. She pulled her shoulders back, stretching against the tightness, the knots of stress balled up in the middle of her shoulder blades. Yes, a hot shower and a good night's sleep would make things better. And tomorrow? Who the hell cared about tomorrow? She had to take one day at a time, one hour at a time.

Melanie saw the brightly lit Comfort Inn sign and then the inn itself on the left side of the road. She smiled, a sense of relief for the first time since this nightmare began. Maybe this is what people meant by an oasis in the desert.

"Don't pull up to the lobby. Park over there, away from the lights." Jared was back to giving orders. She didn't care. She just kept thinking of the hot shower and the cool sheets.

"When you go into the lobby don't give them your real name. And say there's only two of you."

"But won't they see us all come in to go to our room?"

"It looks like a motel. I think we can get in from our own door. If not, they usually have side doors. Once you have the key card we can get in through them." More lecturing, more telling her what to do. "If you have to fill out any forms with address and stuff, put California and say you're headed to Chicago."

"Where in California?"

"I don't give a fuck, Mel. Make something up. Jesus! I can't think of everything." He counted out eight twenty-dollar bills and handed them to her over the seat. "It shouldn't be more than this."

She looked at the rest of the money he still held in his hand. In the dim light of the parking lot she could tell there was more that four hundred dollars. She wanted to ask if he had taken some cash from the convenience store. She quickly decided she didn't care about that, either.

The lobby was bright and cozy with a small sitting area to the right and a breakfast or snack area off to the side of the reception cubicle. The aroma of freshly brewed coffee accosted her as soon as she entered. She checked over her shoulder to see whether the Taurus was visible from the desk. Nothing. She'd done a good job parking it away and out of sight.

"God! That smells great," she told the young man behind the counter. He actually looked pleased to have someone to talk to. The parking lot was pretty empty.

"Help yourself. I just made a fresh pot. Will you be staying with us this evening?" he asked as he began rounding up the necessary paperwork.

Her mind was on the coffee. It had been so long, *too* long, since she had given it up.

"Ma'am? Are you needing a room for this evening?"

"Yeah. I mean, yes. I will be."

"Single or double?"

"Double. There are just two of us." She checked his face. Just? Why the hell did she say just? But he hadn't noticed.

She saw the small TV he had been watching on the counter behind him. She glanced at the wall clock. Not quite ten. The news would be coming on soon, and she didn't want to see any of it. Not now when she could blow it. She wondered how much he had already seen or heard. Was he supposed to be reporting in to the police if anyone suspicious showed up? And then she wondered what would make someone look suspicious.

"Smoking or non?"

His question interrupted her paranoia. "Non," she said out of habit, suddenly regretting that she hadn't taken that pack out of the farmer's car. She could use a smoke right about now.

"If you could just fill out this information. How will you be paying this evening?" He handed the paperwork to her, placing a pen on top.

"Cash," she said, filling in the blanks on the form,

pretending that the process didn't require as much thought as it did. Melanie knew that the best policy was to let others do the talking. KMS was what she lived by—Keep Mouth Shut. Too much information and people looked at you more closely. She didn't need to be remembered. She knew how to blend in. That's what she needed to do now. Just look the part of a weary traveler.

"That's $74.90. Let me get your change. The coffee is complimentary, twenty-four hours a day. We have a free continental breakfast from six till nine-thirty available over in our breakfast area." He pointed across the lobby, then counted out her change, took the form, looked it over and set it aside.

She almost sighed out loud. Why was this so much harder than blending in with shoppers at the mall, and slipping out of stores with merchandise she hadn't paid for?

"Here are your key cards. Your room number is listed on the inside of this folder. And let me show you where it is." He pulled out a paper and showed her on the diagram of the hotel. "We're here. You just drive around back and the door is the fourth from the north. Any questions?"

"Can I come back for the coffee?"

"Oh, sure. Each room has a door to the hallway inside, too, so you don't have to go outside. I'll be here all night. I'll make sure there's plenty fresh for you." He gave her a genuine smile.

"Okay." She turned to leave. She stopped at the

door and over her shoulder said, "Thanks." It was the first time in a very long time that she truly felt thankful.

CHAPTER 54

9:07 p.m.
South of Nebraska City

"Holy crap!" Pakula said, taking his first look as Sheriff Dawes held open the kitchen door to the farmhouse. The flood of white fluorescent lights inside seemed a harsh contrast to the darkness outside.

The mobile crime techs had beaten him to the scene. Darcy Kennedy and Wes Howard had secured the kitchen, yet Pakula couldn't help wondering how many from the crowd in the front yard had already trampled through. The body was slumped in the hardback chair, the head rolled back, exposing the gaping wound in the neck, a violent slash of red against the blue-gray skin. It was probably exactly as it had been found. He wondered if the guy's wife had walked in this very door.

"What about the car?" he asked the sheriff, who stayed in the doorway. When Dawes didn't answer,

Pakula glanced back at him and realized the sheriff hadn't stayed back in order to give them room to do their work, but because he looked as if he might up-chuck. The man stood well over six feet, tall and skinny, teetering back and forth on the heels of his pointed-toed cowboy boots. "Sheriff Dawes, where's the Saab?"

"Oh, it's still in the garage. Nobody's touched it. Keys are in the ignition." He seemed relieved to have something to concentrate on. "State Patrol told me they'd have roadblocks from here to Kansas City. There's an APB out for the Chevy. We'll get the bastards. Maybe before morning."

Pakula hated to discourage the sheriff's opti-mism. If that Chevy already had an entirely differ-ent set of license plates on it, they might slip through the roadblocks.

"You pulling a double shift, Wes?" Pakula walked a wide circle around the corpse, careful not to inter-rupt the techs' grid.

"I could ask the same about you." The kid smiled but didn't take his eyes from the fingerprint he was making appear on the counter next to the bloody butcher knife that had been bagged.

"Why bother tying the guy up? And why do you suppose he used a knife?" Pakula started asking questions out loud as he sorted the pieces.

"He wasn't out of bullets," Sheriff Dawes said from his sanctuary. "He used one on the gas station clerk up the road."

"And that's where you might think he'd want to keep quiet instead of risking someone hearing the gunshot." Pakula squatted in front of the corpse so he could be eye level with the wound. "Yet out here, where nobody can hear it, he uses a knife."

"Is he making a statement of some kind?" Darcy asked.

"You tell me." He stood up, rubbing his eyes and wishing this kitchen wasn't so fucking bright.

Darcy pointed to the gash that started up under the left earlobe. "He did it from behind, left to right, so he's right-handed. No big surprise there. There was a lot more force than needed, practically decapitated the guy. Definite overkill. The kind of stuff you'd find in a crime of passion. But I'm thinking he didn't know this guy."

"Maybe he reminded him of someone." Pakula looked around the kitchen as if searching for answers. "Anything else taken?"

"Wife's pretty upset," Sheriff Dawes said. "I didn't ask."

"Looks like his wallet is still in his back pocket," Wes pointed out.

From this angle Pakula decided it wasn't possible that the cash and credit cards were removed and the wallet replaced. He had started a credit card check on all of Andrew's cards. By morning he'd have the information. Sometimes they got lucky. Sometimes the kidnappers were stupid enough to charge hotel rooms. Pakula was still hoping these guys were stupid enough.

"When will we have fingerprint results from the Saturn and here?"

"There's too many prints in the car to isolate," Darcy explained. "I can't tell which ones might be the robbers' and which ones are probably the previous occupants'. We did find a thumb and forefinger inside the car's back window. I'm guessing it's got to be one of theirs. Because there's vomit smudges. I'm running it for a match but haven't come up with anything else. Might be someone who's never been in the system."

"How 'bout here? Anything?"

"We should have him right here," Wes said, holding up the plastic bag with the butcher knife. "The son of a bitch didn't bother even wiping it."

CHAPTER 55

9:56 p.m.
Comfort Inn—Hastings, Nebraska

Melanie finished the last of the convenience-store pizza. It was cold, the cheese hard, the pepperoni congealed in its own cold grease, and yet it tasted delicious. After her shower she had curled up in one of the double beds, the cool sheets tucked around her, her head and back propped against the pillows. She had a Snickers bar on the bedside table and control of the TV's remote. For the moment, she needed nothing else.

Jared had disappeared out the door to the hotel's hallways and lobby, saying he'd be back, not indicating when. He left the car keys and his precious gun with Charlie, so she *knew* he'd be back.

Leaving the gun seemed unnecessary. The writer, Andrew Kane, wasn't going anywhere. As soon as

they'd entered the room, Andrew dropped into the recliner in the corner and hadn't moved except once to
go to the bathroom. Now he simply stared at the TV
screen.

Charlie stretched out on the other double bed, not
bothering to pull back any of the covers or take off
his high-tops, despite Melanie telling him twice. It
was probably his way of getting back at her for hog-
ging the remote. He had even pouted at first until he
discovered a couple of comic books in the convenience-store stash.

Melanie considered telling him to put the gun
someplace where she didn't have to look at it. She
hated being in the same car and now in the same room
with it. However, tonight she could pretend that it
didn't exist. Tonight she needed to pretend none of
it—the bank, the car chase, the cornfield, the forced
road trip—none of it existed. At least for tonight.

She flipped the channels, trying to avoid the news,
but finally gave up and left it on the CBS affiliate,
waiting for Jay Leno. She snuggled down farther into
the pillows and closed her eyes, remembering how
much she had wanted to close them less than an hour
ago. She tried to think of something, anything, that
would take her mind off the gun and help relax her.

That's what her walks were for, to relieve stress
and tension. No wonder the knot in the middle of her
shoulder blades only continued to tighten and grow.
She tried to remember when her last walk had been.
Three days ago? Two? It seemed like weeks. And

now she remembered, that morning's walk had been hurried, rushed so she could meet Jared at the Cracker Barrel for breakfast. The walk hadn't relieved her tension at all, only adding to it. Then she remembered the poor storm-battered tree. The one with the strange quote attached to it. She had memorized it: "Hope is the thing with feathers." She hadn't been able to figure it out and it bugged her. Even now thinking about it brought back the tension, the unrest she had felt.

She opened her eyes and looked over at Andrew. He was still staring at the TV as if hypnotized.

"Hey," she called out to him, but stopped. She wasn't sure what to call him. He didn't flinch. "Hey, Andrew Kane," she tried again.

This time he glanced at her, shifted in the recliner then went back to the TV.

"You knew that other poem," she said. "That one Jared asked you about. Do you know any of Emily Dickerson?"

"Dickinson," he mumbled without looking at her.

"What?"

"Her name is Emily Dickinson."

"That's what I said."

"Sure, whatever."

He still didn't look at her. Melanie propped herself up on one elbow and said, "Hope is the thing with feathers."

This time he turned, interested or maybe just curious. Melanie didn't care. She had his attention.

"What does that mean?" she asked.

"Why do you want to know?"

"Hey, if you don't know, just say so."

"Hope is the little bird inside us that won't be silenced," he said, meeting her eyes before he continued. "It's what sustains us. It's the thing that keeps us from giving up, even when everything is looking pretty fucking hopeless. It takes something massive to stop that relentless song. Something like watching a plane fly into your tower or knowing an innocent woman was killed because of something stupid. Hope is the thing that sells lottery tickets and enters the Olympics and gets us through illnesses or deaths. That's what it means."

Then he looked back at the TV, as if he hadn't spoken at all.

She didn't have time to think about what he had said because suddenly a news reporter was talking about them on TV.

"Randy Fulton's body was found by his wife in the kitchen of their farmhouse just south of Nebraska City. Helen Trebak, a clerk at the Auburn Gas N' Shop, was also found murdered this afternoon. Law enforcement officials are certain both murders are the work of the bank robbers who attempted to rob the Nebraska Bank of Commerce yesterday and are on the run. This brings the number of their victims to six. The names of the four victims of the bank robbery were released earlier today. They are—"

Melanie fumbled with the remote. She had heard enough. They were lying now. She knew Jared hadn't killed that farmer. She was with him the whole time. It was impossible. She looked back at the TV and suddenly recognized the picture of one of the victims they were showing. She turned up the volume as she tried to place where she knew the woman from. Or did she simply look familiar because she reminded her of someone? Yes, that was probably it.

"Rita Williams, age thirty-nine, a waitress for seven years at the Cracker Barrel restaurant."

Then she knew—that was where she remembered her from. A waitress. *Their* waitress, the one who Jared had harassed.

Melanie looked over at her son to see if he, too, recognized the woman. Charlie had appeared detached from this entire nightmare, but now he sat with his back up against the bed's headboard, his knees pulled up tight against his chest. He was rocking back and forth as if he was going to be sick to his stomach. And before she could ask, he yelled, "Shut it off. Shut it the fuck off."

CHAPTER 56

10:15 p.m.

Max Kramer sat in his den, the only room in the fucking house that his wife had allowed him to decorate as he wished. He stared out at the night as he sipped the expensive wine from Lucille's collection. She hated it when he dared to open a bottle from the reserve she kept for her stuffy, boring dinner parties. Tonight's selection was an old-style Beaujolais imported by Alain Jugenet, one of a handful of small estates that supposedly still did it the old-style way and were said to even hold the wine for up to ten months before bottling it.

He knew little about wines—almost nothing compared to his wife—however, he remembered reading something about Beaujolais being called "the only white wine that happens to be red." He liked that. It had something to do with the "vivid color and its expressive, thirst-quenching qualities" or some such crap that Max didn't really care about. No, what he liked about it was that the wine was different from what it appeared to be, kind of like him. He held up the glass, swirling the wine around the edges, and he smiled, wondering how much this bottle would set his wife back.

His cell phone started ringing. He glanced at the grandfather clock in the corner. It was too late to be anyone he wanted to talk to. He didn't recognize the caller ID number. He knew he should just shut off the phone and let the voice-messaging service pick it up. He took another sip before setting the glass down and deciding to answer the stupid phone.

"This is Max Kramer."

"Are you alone?"

He recognized the voice but still insisted on making him tell him. "Who is this?"

"Who do you fucking think this is? Can you talk? Is there anyone else there?"

"I'm alone. Go ahead," he said while thinking, yes, go ahead and tell me why the fuck I should even listen to what you have to say?

"We're gonna need some new IDs. Make them driver's licenses." Jared Barnett was taking charge. "And cash. Don't get funny with the cash. Keep it small bills. We'll probably need about twenty-five thousand dollars."

"Hold on. Where the hell do you think I'm going to get three new IDs?" And twenty-five thousand dollars? Max wanted to slam the phone against the wall. How the hell did this get so turned around? He wanted to tell Jared Barnett that *he* owed him. That he *still* owed him.

"You're a resourceful guy, Max. You figure it out."

"I think you should turn yourself in."

"What are you, fucking crazy?"

"No, now listen. I can get you off." Max stood up, staring past his reflection in the window out at the full orange moon. He wondered what a liar's moon looked like as he said, "I did it before, I can do it again."

"Yeah, well, I'm not waiting in prison for five more fucking years while you do it. Besides, I thought you were pissed. You sounded pissed. How can I trust a fucking lawyer who's pissed?"

"I was surprised. That's all." Max kept his cool. This bastard could ruin everything. He needed to convince him he was on his side. "You can't blame me for being surprised. I never expected things to get so screwed up, to go so badly. That's all. What the hell happened?"

There was silence, and for a few seconds Max thought he had lost him.

"One false move," he mumbled.

"What's that?"

"Isn't that what they say? That all it takes is one fucking wrong move to change everything? It doesn't matter. Not now. How soon can you get the IDs and money?"

"How am I supposed to get them to you?"

"Don't worry about that. Just get it. I'll call back tomorrow."

"If you tell me—" But he heard the click.

Max stayed at the window, wondering how the hell he'd take care of this. How the hell he'd fix this. One little favor—that's all he had asked from Barnett to pay off his attorney fee. Who could have predicted it'd get this fucked up.

CHAPTER 57

10:32 p.m.

Andrew leaned against the wall of the shower and let the warm water massage his wounded head. The throbbing wouldn't stop. Nor would the image of that Gas N' Shop clerk, her small body scurrying back and forth from one task to the other. Full of life, and now she was dead because he had tried something stupid. Thanks to Jared, Andrew felt like an accessory to the farmer's murder. But he felt completely responsible for that poor clerk.

There had to be something he could do to get out of this. It was clear Jared wasn't going to ever let him go. Eventually, he'd have to kill him. At first, that realization paralyzed as much as it panicked Andrew. But at the moment, he was too exhausted to be either. Especially after examining the bathroom's contents and being disappointed to find only the miniature shampoo, conditioner, mouthwash and soap. The shower had a Plexiglas door instead of a rod and curtain, not that he had had much success with the rod he had found at the cabin. He had even checked out the insides of the toilet tank, only to find that almost all of the mechanical guts were made of plastic. He wasn't sure what he'd expected. He knew hotel rooms didn't provide razors or nail files. He had spent enough time in the best of them over the course of the last two years, traveling to promote one of his books or do research for the next.

Research. All the research, all the interviews about murder and killers that he had done and yet, what good was it to him now? He had gathered all that knowledge, but without the experience of dealing with the real thing, he wasn't sure what he could do. Although, he wondered if *anything* could have prepared him for this.

He wished he could rip off the harness from his shoulder and arm. He wished he had full use of it. Then he would, at least, be on an equal footing with Jared. But, as it was, he couldn't even wash up under his damn armpit without experiencing a shooting pain. In the beginning, when he hadn't even dared to lift his arm enough to fit a sponge under it because of the pain, he worried about body odor. A Nebraska summer, with its heat and humidity was not a good time to break a collarbone. Now he scrubbed all over, ignoring the pain and practically rubbing his skin raw, feeling a bit like Lady Macbeth.

His father would tell him it served him right. Of this, Andrew was certain. He heard his voice in the back corners of his throbbing head: "All your fucking book learnin' can't get you out of this one, can it?" It reminded him of the reprimands he had endured as a kid when his father found him reading instead of doing some chore like shoveling the crap from the chicken coop, a task that hadn't even been on Andrew's to-do list until he was discovered with a book. It was almost as if his father had hoped to drain him, so that he wouldn't have the energy to read. At the end of the day, Andrew's young body would be physically exhausted and aching, but there was nothing his father could do to turn off his curiosity, his desire to read and learn and dream beyond the borders of his family's farm. And that made his father even more angry. He seemed to be forever disappointing the man. John Kane wanted a son to take over the farm when he was gone and instead he got one who couldn't wait to leave.

That's when he remembered Charlie with the comic books, quiet and innocent. And then he thought about Charlie's explosive reaction when he saw that waitress's face on TV. Andrew had believed that Melanie was the weakest link, but now he realized he might be wrong. His mind started reeling, accessing what he knew about the psychological effects of murder. If Andrew was feeling this responsible and guilty about the gas station clerk when he hadn't even pulled the trigger, what must Charlie be feeling? And suddenly Andrew wondered what it might take to get Charlie on his side.

CHAPTER 58

11:17 p.m.

Melanie couldn't sleep. Charlie, in spite of his outburst, was curled up on the bed and snoring. So much for his guilty conscience, and yet, she was relieved. She didn't like seeing him like that. She didn't like thinking he had anything to feel guilty about.

Andrew Kane had given in and stretched out on the other side of Charlie, but Jared had insisted on tying together the author's feet and wrists, cutting in half and using the cord from the hotel's phone. Of course, he didn't care about the phone. He still had Andrew's cell phone. She wondered if that was why he'd left the room. Did he need to call his outside contact? And who the hell was it? He was being secretive, when they couldn't afford to have any more secrets. It felt like a betrayal.

She watched her brother in the dim light from the

TV. She had convinced him to let her keep it on with the sound off when he was turning out all the lights and pulling the curtains tighter. He sat with his elbow on the small table, his fist bracing up his head. That's how he slept. Every once in a while his head rolled off his clenched hand but without waking himself.

She wished she could sleep so easily. When they were kids, Jared had taught her what to do when she couldn't sleep. How to go away in her mind to a place with all the things she loved. He'd made her list them—cotton candy, the Bee Gees, Ferris wheels and corn dogs. That was the summer he had taken her to the county fair, so all her favorite things were associated with that experience.

His tactic helped her fall asleep many nights. It became her weapon against the obstacles that invaded her sleep, the biggest one, of course, being fear. The fear that her father would come up and wake them, ripping off the covers and pouring ice-cold water on them or yanking them out of bed by grabbing onto their ankles and pulling until there was nothing left to hang on to. Melanie could still feel it, her head bouncing off the mattress, hitting the bed rail and cracking against the floorboards. But that was the easy part. Over the years she had tried to erase from her memory the sting of the whip or the smell of scorched skin, her own skin burning under the flaming red ash of his cigarette.

Melanie shook her head. She didn't need to be remembering all that now. What she needed to remember was that Jared had cleaned up the mess that night. She owed him. That was a debt she'd never be able to repay and he knew it. Even if she had supplied him with an alibi for Rebecca Moore, they still wouldn't be even. They'd never be even. And now here they were in yet another mess. How could Jared have let this happen? Only this time it was worse. This time he had involved her boy, her baby, her poor Charlie. She wondered if she would ever be able to forgive her brother for that.

She got out of bed to go to the bathroom and noticed that Jared had left the cell phone on the dresser. She glanced back at him. His head was down, his breathing heavy with sleep. She snatched the phone and took it with her into the bathroom, carefully closing and locking the door. She flipped it open and started looking over the buttons. Somewhere there had to be one that would tell her what she wanted to know.

She hit Menu and there on the list was Call History. This was easier than she'd thought. She clicked on Call History, bringing up yet another list. She chose Outgoing Calls to see if Jared had, indeed, gone off to call his secret contact. And there it was: the date, the time—only an hour ago—plus, the phone number and the person's name. She clicked back to find the earlier call—the one from this morning in the car—just to check, to make certain. There it was again. The same number, the same name.

Why was Jared keeping in touch with his attorney? Why in the world did her brother trust Max Kramer more than he trusted her?

Part 5
Point of No Return

Friday, September 10

CHAPTER 59

7:45 a.m.
Comfort Inn—Hastings, Nebraska

Melanie awoke to the sound of slamming doors. It took her a while to realize where she was. Sunlight filtered in through the crack between the curtains. Somewhere, not far away, she could smell freshly brewed coffee. The last thing she remembered was being stretched out on top of the bedcovers, watching a late-night horror movie—a giant tarantula invading a desert town—and she remembered thinking about pink cotton candy. Someone had pulled the covers up over her, and she curled into them, hugging a pillow as if for security. Which reminded her of Charlie. She raised herself onto her elbow to see that Charlie was gone. Andrew Kane still lay on the bed tied up, only now he had pushed himself into a sitting position, leaning against the headboard.

"Where's Jared and Charlie?" she asked, rubbing the sleep from her eyes.

"Jared's in the bathroom. I'm not sure where he sent Charlie."

"He sent Charlie somewhere?" Melanie sat up, scanning the room in a panic until she saw Charlie's backpack.

"You love him a lot, don't you?"

She met Kane's eyes, looking for sarcasm and surprised to find none.

"You wouldn't get it," she said. "It's been just the two of us for a very long time. We watch out for each other."

"And Jared?"

"What about Jared?" she asked, glancing at the bathroom door without meaning to.

"Nothing." He shrugged his one shoulder as if it didn't matter. "It just sounds like he's gotten you and Charlie into a real big mess."

"Sometimes things don't go exactly the way you think they will." Her mind flew back to another time, another mess. Why was it so much on her mind? She thought she'd removed it from her memory, gotten past it. And yet, Jared's reappearance less than two weeks ago seemed to bring it all back.

"What is Charlie? Eighteen? Nineteen?"

"He's seventeen," she blurted out as if needing to defend her baby before she could even figure out why Andrew Kane wanted to know.

"Geez! He's still a kid."

Her thoughts exactly. Charlie was too young to be involved in such a mess. What the hell was Jared even thinking? And the guns. She'd never forgive Jared for bringing along guns.

"I could help you and Charlie," she heard Andrew Kane say, but her mind was focused on the image of all that blood on their coveralls when they came running out of the bank. It had reminded her so much of that night with her father, the bloody drag marks, all the blood seeping in between the cracks of the linoleum, the splatters on the white wall. She never knew how Jared cleaned it all up. But he did. He took care of it.

"I know some detectives with the Omaha Police Department," Andrew continued.

Melanie heard only bits and pieces of what Andrew Kane was saying. Something about Charlie being a minor, about Jared having killed before and about her not even being in the bank. She wasn't really listening. Instead, she was back at that nightmarish scene, and only now did she realize Jared had never told her where he'd buried him. And she had never asked. She remembered seeing her brother hosing down his tennis shoes and the muddy shovel, scrubbing down the floor and the wall while she just watched, unable to move, unable to help. She wasn't even sure if Jared had told their mother when she got home later that night. And yet, he must have. Why else would she have told everyone that her husband "just up and left"? Why else would she be so absolutely certain that Jared couldn't have killed Rebecca Moore? Because that was exactly what Corrine Starks told the police, that her son couldn't possibly kill anyone. She had to have known.

The bathroom door opened, startling her back. Jared looked awful. He hadn't showered. His short hair stood up in places like Charlie's, but the difference was Charlie wanted his that way. She was certain Jared did not. His face was unshaven even though Melanie knew he had bought disposable razors at the gas station. And his eyes were red and swollen. He scraped his hand over his face when he noticed her staring at him.

"What's your problem?"

"Where's Charlie?"

"Don't worry about your precious little boy," he said in that tone meant to sting her. "He's getting us some new wheels. He should've been back by now." He checked his wristwatch and headed for the door, stopping at the window first to peek out. "Here he comes."

Melanie found her shoes and followed Jared out, leaving Andrew Kane on the bed and closing the door just enough that no one could see inside the room. Charlie pulled up to the door in a white Ford Explorer, looking out at them with a wide grin. He rolled down the window and said, "I stopped at a gas station up the street and just traded vehicles. It was so easy. The lady left this one running with the keys in the ignition while she went inside to pay. We still need to change license plates, but can you believe how easy it was? I wish I'd thought of this a long time ago."

Melanie smiled at Charlie's enthusiasm even while Jared was holding up his hands to get him to quiet down. Then suddenly, Jared seemed to do a double take, looking into the back seat with his cupped hand and face against the window.

"What the fuck did you do?" Jared said as he

reached for the back door handle. It was locked. "Open the fucking door."

Charlie punched at the buttons until he found the right one and heard the click.

"Did it ever occur to you there might be a reason she left the engine running on a warm, humid morning?" Jared asked as he yanked the door open.

Melanie's heart sank to her stomach. There, in the back seat in a child's car seat, was a baby, its sleepy eyes only now starting to open.

"Oh my God!" Melanie's hands flew to cover her mouth.

Jared slammed the back door and pulled open the driver's door, standing aside while he told Charlie to "get the fuck out."

"Wait a minute," Melanie said. "What are you gonna do?"

"Get out of the fucking car, Charlie." Jared had to tell him again because Charlie was in such a frenzy he couldn't seem to undo the seat belt. "I can't believe you fucking screwed up again. Have you ever heard of the fucking Amber Alert? Jesus, Charlie! I'm tired of cleaning up your fucking messes."

Finally, Charlie half slid, half jumped out, and Jared got in.

Before he could close the door, Melanie grabbed at his arm. "What are you gonna do, Jared?"

He wrenched his arm away, giving her a shove back so he could slam the car door. All he said before he tore away was, "I'll take care of things."

CHAPTER 60

8:20 a.m.
Omaha Police Department

Grace raced into the conference room only to find them all waiting.

"Sorry," she said, taking the chair at the end of the table next to Special Agent Sanchez.

"We're still waiting for Rob Thieson with the State Patrol," Pakula said, "but he sounded like he might be really late. Why don't we get started. I think I know most of what he's going to report, anyway."

"That they haven't found the fucking Chevy with any of their roadblocks?" Detective Ben Hertz complained.

"Actually," Pakula said, pushing aside the file folders in front of him, "it's not a Chevy anymore. The Chevy was found in the parking lot of a manufacturing plant just north of Auburn."

"Wait a minute," Grace said. "I thought you told me the gas station clerk was in Auburn and they were headed south?"

"That's what I thought when I talked to you last night. One of the workers reported her car stolen after she got off work late last night. The Chevy was parked two slots away."

"So what are they in now?" Sanchez wanted to know.

"A cream-colored Taurus. But it could already be something else."

"This is ridiculous," Hertz said. "They're starting to make us look like a bunch of fucking fools."

"Do we even know what direction they're headed?" Grace asked, but before any of them could answer, she added, "Is it possible they've back-tracked?"

"I'm thinking it might be easier to find them if we know who the fuck they are." Pakula looked to Darcy Kennedy. "Please tell us you have something."

Grace could see that Pakula hadn't gotten much sleep. He was guzzling coffee and she knew the OPD's coffee was even worse than over at the Hall of Justice.

"Well, I know you're all waiting for me to say it's Jared Barnett," Darcy said, ignoring her own reports piled in front of her. "The thing is, I can't get a definitive print. Even the ones on the butcher knife were so smudged, I swear it's like he did it intentionally."

"Are you saying we've got nothing?" Sanchez almost came out of his chair.

"I do have a perfect print on the inside of the Saturn, on one of the back windows. There was a smudge of vomit next to it, so there's a very good chance it belongs to the one who threw up."

"Excellent," Sanchez said. "So who is he?"

"I don't know."

"What the fuck?"

"Calm it down," Pakula told Sanchez, and Grace realized they were all running on little sleep. She was probably the most rested one of the bunch.

"He's nobody in the system," Darcy explained. "Chances are he's never been fingerprinted before. I did find a match, though."

"Wait a minute," Pakula said. "I thought you said the print didn't match anyone in the system."

"I said it's not anybody in the system but I do have a match on file. Grace had me go back to one of the convenience stores that was robbed last week."

They were all staring at Grace now. She knew what they were thinking: was she nuts for interrupting the tech's time with a string of piddly robberies when there was a manhunt for killers going on?

"She discovered the same person was in each of the stores right before the robberies took place." Darcy pulled out black-and-white photos, and Grace recognized them as stills from the surveillance cameras, the date and time stamped in the corners. And in each photo there was the same young man.

"Look, I'm sorry, but this is ridiculous," Sanchez was at it again. "What the hell does this have to do with anything?"

"One of the videos shows him opening a door to one of the refrigerated cases," Darcy said, ignoring Sanchez. "He left his fingerprints up high and inside. I went back yesterday and after a week it was still there—no others, not that high."

"I hope you're getting to some point soon."

"He's one of our bank robbers," she said, pointing to the young man in the grainy photo. "The prints inside the refrigerated case's door match the ones on the inside window of the Saturn."

This time even Sanchez was quiet.

"But I can't give you a name because he's not in the system."

"Holy crap!" Pakula said, rubbing a hand over his face then up over his head. "You were right, Grace. It's the convenience-store robbers escalating."

"Or practicing." Grace waited for the idea to sink in. "I still think it's Barnett. You said the gas station clerk was shot. Where?"

Pakula wouldn't meet her eyes and she knew even before he said, "In her face. Her jaw was ripped open."

"Any connection to Jared and the bank teller?" Grace asked.

"None that I can find." Pakula pulled out a file and flipped it open. "She went for much older men than Barnett. The only connection I could make was that

she used Max Kramer last spring to get her out of a
DUI conviction, which he's still calling her about.
She probably stiffed him for the bill. One of her
roommates thinks she had a rich married guy wound
around her little finger, but I have her phone records
for the last several months right here and I haven't
found the mysterious guy named Jay. Oh, and we
have this," Pakula said, tossing a plastic bag contain-
ing a piece of jewelry onto the table. "Wes Howard
found this in the mud next to the Saturn. It was Tina
Cervante's. Given to her by JMK, her supposed mys-
tery man."

"Wait a minute," Grace said. "I've just seen those
initials somewhere." And she started riffling through
the papers she had received yesterday for Carrie Ann
Comstock's drug case. "Here it is." She pulled out a
document and threw it down on the table next to the
locket with the initials JMK. At the bottom of the document was the stamped initials JMK next to the signature—J. Maxwell Kramer. "Is it possible Tina
Cervante was having an affair with her attorney?" she
asked.

CHAPTER 61

8:53 a.m.

Andrew didn't know what was going on. He had heard Jared yelling, car doors slamming and then a car screeching away. Now Charlie sat on the end of the bed, staring at the TV and flipping the channels, though he didn't appear to be watching or looking for anything in particular. Melanie paced the length of the room, taking quick glances when she passed the window. Neither one of them seemed to be aware that he was even in the room.

He had asked Jared earlier to untie him and had gotten, instead, a look of contempt, hollow-eyed with just enough of a smirk to know he was no longer a novelty to the madman. He was no longer the fascinating author who had captured his interest. Not only had he betrayed the psychopath's trust but now he was excess baggage. Andrew didn't need to rely on research to guess—to *know*—his time was limited. He also knew his chances with these two would be better than with Jared.

"What happened?" he tried again. Before when he asked he caught a glimpse of Melanie's eyes, enough to realize it was something bad. There was panic there. And there was panic in her short explosive steps. Her entire body seemed to move with a nervous energy that she didn't quite have complete control over. "Did Jared do something?"

"No, I did," Charlie said without blinking, finally settling on the Cartoon Network and a Road Runner and Wyle E. Coyote episode.

"What did you do, Charlie?" He asked it as softly as he could, keeping his own panic from his voice. He tried to ignore the phone cord digging into his wrists. He tried to avoid shifting to a more comfortable position, though he hadn't found one yet. "Charlie, what is it you think you did?" he asked again, trying to duplicate the tone he imagined his friend Tommy Pakula would use, the one that got drug dealers and wife beaters to confess to him. "I'm sure it couldn't have been anything to deserve the way Jared yelled at you."

"No, I screwed up really, really bad." He sounded like a little boy, more like a seven-year-old than a seventeen-year-old. His eyes never left Wyle E. Coyote who'd just blown himself up with a stack of dynamite. "I screwed up again. It's all my fault."

"Stop it!" Melanie's voice made both Andrew and

Charlie jump, though Charlie's eyes still didn't leave the TV screen. "I don't want to hear it." She didn't miss a stride of her pacing.

"It's not your fault, Charlie." Andrew had nothing to lose. "All along you've only done what Jared told you to do. You did what Jared wanted you to. But you don't have to do everything he says. You're a good kid. I can tell. You want to do the right thing." He noticed that Melanie had stopped and was now watching him. When she didn't try to stop him, he continued, "You don't have it in you to do the kind of stuff Jared does. You're not like him, Charlie." No response. Charlie didn't even flinch. The Road Runner had just whizzed through one of Coyote's barricades without a scratch and Charlie didn't even blink.

Andrew looked up at Melanie, waiting until she met his eyes. He had her attention now. But did he have her anywhere close to being on his side? Was she strong enough to go against her brother? Would she see that she needed to choose between her brother and her son in order to *save* her son, if not herself? Andrew knew there was a bond between her and Charlie. He had witnessed the panic in her eyes earlier when she realized Charlie was gone, and seemed to be comforted only when she noticed his beat-up backpack hadn't left with him. But was the bond between mother and son stronger than the bond between sister and brother?

"You know he's going to kill me," Andrew told

her in that same soft voice, keeping out the emotion despite the lump that threatened to bring it on without warning. She didn't look away and his eyes held hers. "Hasn't there been enough killing already?" He couldn't read her eyes. Couldn't tell whether or not he was getting to her. "I can help you. Both you and Charlie. But it has to stop, Melanie. It has to stop now. Can you make it stop?"

It wasn't Melanie who answered. It was Charlie with his knees up against his chest again, hugging them and rocking back and forth. "I couldn't stop," he said. "I screwed up bad, really bad. Jared said nobody can help me. I did it. I screwed up. I wasn't supposed to do anything. I was supposed to wait. Just scare everybody and hold them up while Jared did what he had to do. I was supposed to just scare them. I screwed up." It was like a floodgate had been opened, the words coming almost without him taking a breath except to wipe at his nose with his shoulder, never stopping his rocking rhythm. "I saw her and I lost it. I lost it. I forgot that she couldn't recognize me. I forgot. And I panicked. I thought she'd tell. I didn't mean to shoot her. I just didn't want her to tell. The gun went off. Just like that. It just went off and there was blood. There was a hole in her and she was bleeding and I knew I did it. I didn't want the others to tell everybody that I did that. They saw it. They saw what I did. So I shot them, too. One, two, three. Just like that. The woman at the front desk. Bam! The guy in the doorway. Bam! The old man. Bam! I screwed up. I fucking screwed up."

And then it was over. Charlie continued rocking, his eyes still staring at the TV, but the flood of words stopped as suddenly as they had started.

Andrew looked from Charlie to Melanie, waiting. His heart pounded as he watched her. She had stood the entire time with her arms crossed, her body finally still. Her face was expressionless. Her eyes, too, seemed void of emotion, even the panic was gone as if silenced by Charlie's confession instead of being intensified by it. She'd have to do something now, wouldn't she?

She walked over to her son until she was standing between him and the TV. "Look at me, Charlie." She waited for him to look up at her. She waited for the rocking to slow. "I want you to listen to me, Charlie."

Andrew held his breath. Here it was. The defining moment. Would they finally decide to rise up and stand up against Jared? Was this the last straw for Melanie?

"Listen to me, Charlie," she repeated, and Andrew heard a strength in her voice that hadn't been there before, a resolve and command. "You didn't kill anybody. Do you hear me, Charlie? You did not kill anyone. And I don't want to hear you ever say that again—do you understand? Don't you ever say that again."

Then she walked away and began pacing again as if there had been no interruption, no confession, no exchange, as if there had been no denial. Even Charlie stopped rocking, his feet back on the floor, TV channels flipping again before his unblinking eyes.

Andrew seemed to be the only one who realized what had taken place, what this silent bond of denial meant. And Andrew Kane felt as if someone had just knocked the wind right out of him.

CHAPTER 62

9:05 a.m.

Max Kramer crushed the paper coffee cup and tossed it at the trash can, missing, not even hitting the rim. Not a good sign. The caffeine had made him shakier than usual. Probably not the caffeine but all the wine he'd managed to down last night. After Barnett's phone call Max started opening wine bottles from his wife's reserve, getting a rush each time he popped a cork. He had left before she got up this morning so he wouldn't have to endure both a hangover and her wrath.

He swiveled his leather chair around to stare out the window and down at the mall. Another fucking beautiful day. A little too warm and humid for him, but the Nebraska sky was cloudless, not a wisp of white to mar the blue. As a young man he used to brag about Nebraska's blue skies when he was traveling back and forth to New York City, working for a huge law firm and flying coach because his bosses cared even less about their attorneys than they did their clients. Back then he did have a passion for the law, for righting wrongs, even for blue skies. He couldn't remember the day it stopped. It wasn't one event in particular, some injustice or a major failing. It wasn't any one thing. Instead, it happened piece by tiny piece. First one exception, one exemption, one small unintentional slip to take advantage of the rule of law. Then another. And another. He couldn't even remember when the unintentional changed to the intentional. It had happened so gradually, so smoothly, so easily.

He checked his Rolex. Less than an hour until he had to be in court. He thought about Grace Wenninghoff turning down his deal. He had Carrie Ann Comstock ready and willing to identify Jared Barnett as the convenience-store robber and the prosecutor hadn't taken the bait. He wondered if he shouldn't have played such hardball. Wenninghoff surely wouldn't have hesitated had she known who he was ready to finger. But he couldn't sound too anxious, too willing to hand over the man he had spent the last year and a half getting out of jail.

And God knows, Carrie Ann wasn't exactly the most reliable witness, let alone liar. Jesus! She couldn't even get down the details of how she was supposed to know Jared Barnett, the simple story he had made up for her. Every time he showed her Barnett's photo she kept saying she had seen him in her apartment building hauling out some huge bag of trash late one night. The stupid crack whore couldn't get anything right. It was just as well that Wenning-hoff had passed.

His cell phone interrupted his thoughts. He pulled it from his jacket's breast pocket and sighed when he recognized the caller ID, the same number from last night.

"Max Kramer."

"You got everything ready?"

"There's no way I can have a new ID made that quickly for one of you, let alone all three of you. You need to give me a couple of days."

"I don't have a couple of fucking days."

Max noticed something different in Barnett's voice. The calm-and-collected, but angry, tone seemed a bit frantic. Could it be that the bastard was feeling a little vulnerable?

"I need at least another twenty-four hours," he said, not able to contain his smile.

"Forget the IDs. Just get me the fucking money."

Max sat up in his chair. The minute he thought he had control, Barnett took it back. It was like a fuck-ing chess match, a chess match with a madman. "Okay," he said. "Where are you? How am I sup-posed to get it to you?"

"There's a truck stop off the interstate. Take this down. Are you getting this down? Because I'm not gonna fucking repeat it."

Max grabbed a pen and started jotting on his desk pad. Yes, the calm-and-collected Jared Barnett was beginning to crumble. He could hear it in the crackling sound as Barnett unfolded and folded some kind of paper, perhaps a map. "Go ahead."

"It's about fifty miles west of Grand Island. I can't remember the name of the fucking truck stop, but the exit is for Normal."

"Normal what?"

"Normal, Nebraska, you stupid bastard. Bet you didn't even know there was a town named Normal in Nebraska, did you?"

Max rolled his eyes. He wanted to tell Barnett that Normal was the last place he'd expect Barnett to be. It was too fucking ironic, and he wondered if Barnett had chosen it on purpose.

"Have the money at the truck stop by two p.m."

"By two?" Max said. "How the hell am I supposed to get the money there, let alone by two?"

"You're a smart guy, Kramer. If you could get me out of jail for murder, surely you can figure this out."

"Okay, I can probably wire it somehow. You'll need ID to pick it up."

"Have it wired in the name of Charlie Starks. And don't screw this up, Kramer. I'm getting fucking tired of screwups."

Max wanted to tell him that he was the one who had a right to be sick and tired of screwups. Barnett was the one who got himself into this mess. If he had stuck to the plan, none of this would have happened. Instead, he told him, "I'll try to have it there by two."

"Don't try. Have it there. You set me up, Kramer, and you go down with me. You get that?"

"Don't worry. It'll be there."

Max waited for the click. He swiveled his chair back around to his desk. He could probably find the name of the truck stop online, and he flipped his laptop computer on. He could probably make the wire transfer online, too. He knew his wife's money market account number by heart. While he waited for the Internet connection he punched in a number on his cell phone.

She answered on the third ring. "Grace Wenninghoff."

"Grace, it's Max Kramer. As an officer of the court I have some information that I feel obligated to tell you."

Yes, obligated, he thought. No one could fault him for turning in a client whom he had helped and sacrificed for. Not when that client was now on a killing spree. Forget about anyone finding fault with him. He'd probably end up being a fucking hero for being the one to turn in Jared Barnett.

CHAPTER 63

9:20 a.m.

Melanie couldn't stand it. Jared had been gone too long. Where the hell was he? And what the hell was he doing? She continued to pace the room, to wipe her sweaty palms on her jeans until her hands felt raw. She didn't want to think about that baby, those sleepy eyes, those chubby cheeks. No, Jared couldn't. He *wouldn't*.

She heard a car door, and instead of racing to the window, she froze. Charlie heard it, too, only he was watching her, waiting to read her. So was Andrew Kane. What did they expect of her? What the hell did they want her to do? She didn't get them into this mess. This wasn't her fault.

The door swung open and now everyone stared at Jared. Melanie examined his eyes, his mouth and then his hands, looking for signs. Would she be able to tell? What was she supposed to look for? Was she expecting to see blood? *More* fucking blood?

"We need to get out of here," Jared said. When no one moved or responded, he picked up Charlie's backpack and tossed it at him. "Let's move. Now."

"What did you do, Jared?" Melanie asked, not able to include "baby" in her question, almost as if she didn't want to know, but still giving him a chance to make things okay again. She ran her fingers through her hair and noticed her hands were shaking. Would things ever be okay again?

"I took care of things," he said as if he had simply completed an everyday task like taking out the garbage. "I got us another fucking car. Even switched the plates already. But we've got to get the hell out of here."

When still no one moved, Jared took on his careful voice, even allowing himself a smile when he said, "I picked up some McDonald's for us. It's all in the car, so come on. Let's go. I want to get to Colorado before nightfall."

Charlie shut off the TV and slung the backpack over his shoulder. Melanie couldn't help thinking the boy's stomach would override his brain each and every time. But instead of being angry she wanted to smile at his innocence, his simplicity. She checked the bathroom before following Charlie out. She stopped again at the door when she noticed Jared wasn't helping Andrew. Her brother stood at the foot of the bed, waiting, and then she realized he wasn't

waiting to help Andrew up. Jared was waiting for
Charlie and Melanie to leave. He wasn't planning on
taking Andrew Kane with them. That's when she noticed the white nylon cord he was pulling out of his
pocket and wrapping around his fists. And suddenly
her stomach fell to her knees again, just as it had
when she saw that baby in the back seat.

"Keep his hands tied up," Melanie told Jared, pretending that's what he intended to use the cord for.
"I'll drive."

"Go get in the car, Mel," Jared instructed, his
voice now distant and cold. "I'll be right there."

She caught the author's eyes when he glanced up
at her, and she realized there was something different in them. Maybe resolve. Certainly not panic. It
was almost as if he knew exactly what Jared had in
mind, as if he had expected it. In his desperation he
had promised to help her and Charlie. She knew he
probably only said it in the hopes of saving himself.
He probably would have found a way to trick her, to
set her up, to hurt Charlie. She'd hurt herself before
she'd let Charlie get hurt.

"What's the holdup?" Charlie was suddenly in
the doorway behind her, looking over her shoulder.
"I thought we were in a hurry."

She didn't turn around, but already smelled the
sausage and knew he had started breakfast without
them.

"Jared was just getting Andrew up," she said,
avoiding Jared's eyes. "Charlie, why don't you help

him, so that we can keep him tied up in the back seat. I'm driving."

Charlie scooted in around her, and she could feel Jared's anger. Still, she avoided looking at him. Before he could protest, Charlie had Andrew on his feet and shuffling out the door.

CHAPTER 64

10:33 a.m.

Pakula asked for the third time, "You think Kramer's fucking with us?"

"If he's involved," Grace said as calmly as she had both times before. "And we know he has to be somehow involved because he wants us to catch Barnett."

Pakula let out another sigh. He pulled his tie loose, hoping that would help him breathe. It didn't. "I don't know. It feels too easy. Tell me exactly what he said." He expected Grace to get impatient with him, but instead she started at the beginning.

"He said he got a call from Barnett, asking for help. Barnett told him that he only meant to rob the bank but things went wrong. He wasn't about to turn himself in. He didn't want—"

"He said Barnett said that exactly? That he wasn't gonna turn himself in?"

"Yes, and that he didn't want to go back to jail."

Pakula couldn't believe how calm she was, when he felt like a wet rag. Why the fuck was it so hot again?

"He said he knew Kramer would never be able to get him off this time," she continued, the details the same as the last time she told him. She didn't even need her notes. "That all he needed was some money. And then he told Kramer to wire the money to the Triple J Truck Stop on Interstate 80, west of Grand Island, just off the exit for Normal, Nebraska."

"How much money?"

"He asked for twenty-five thousand dollars. Kramer said he has it ready to be wired if and when we tell him to."

"And this morning was the first time he heard from him?"

"That's what he said."

"But he has to know we can check that out." Pakula didn't trust this asshole any more than he trusted Barnett. Were the two of them setting up something? A distraction, perhaps, while Barnett headed in the opposite direction? "You think he's on the level?"

Grace filled her arms with the stack of files from his extra chair, looking for a place to set them so she could sit down. He grabbed them from her, a little embarrassed that he hadn't thought to do it himself. He put them in the corner and let them slide into a mess. Then he sat in his own chair so he wouldn't tower over her, even though he wanted—needed—to be up and moving.

"At first I was skeptical. But Max Kramer has no idea we have the locket. He can't possibly know that we suspect him of anything." She shook her head as if she couldn't believe how slimy the guy might be. "There was something in his tone, and I can't even explain what it was, but he almost sounded self-righteous about this, like, of course, he had no choice but to do the right thing. I mean, give me a break."

"So he probably thinks he'll be able to milk this, too?"

"Maybe."

The phone rang and Pakula stood to answer it even though it was right at his elbow.

"Pakula."

"I've got a SWAT team assembled and ready to meet us there." It was Sanchez—he didn't need an introduction. "The Black Hawk will be ready for us in about twenty minutes."

"Twenty minutes? You've got to be kidding."

"We don't have much time. Are you ready to go or not?"

"I'll be ready," Pakula said and Sanchez was gone.

He looked down at Grace and wiped the sweat from his head as he grabbed his jacket off the back of his chair. "God! I hate helicopters."

CHAPTER 65

10:40 a.m.
Highway 281N

Andrew knew from watching the road signs that they were headed in the wrong direction again. They were on Highway 281N. Colorado was west, not north. Jared kept the map laid out in his lap. He gave Melanie directions, left or right, but not much more. And neither she nor Charlie asked. Neither of them seemed to mind letting Jared be in complete control again.

He leaned his head against the back seat. How stupid he had been, thinking either of them were strong enough to take on Jared. Back at the hotel, the way she manipulated the situation, the way she got Jared to take him along, made Andrew think Melanie had grown a backbone. Now he realized he was wrong. She had eased back into her role as accomplice as if everything was back to normal.

She had the radio turned up, listening to Rush Limbaugh after fiddling with the dial, preferring talk radio to the morning's livestock and grain prices. It was already turned up when the news brief began, and yet she reached for the dial to turn it up even more.

"We have new information on the Amber Alert that was issued this morning. At around seven-thirty a white Ford Explorer was taken from a Texaco gas station north of Hastings, off Interstate 80. The young mother had left the engine and air conditioner running for her fourteen-month-old baby while she went inside to pay for her gas. Someone drove off with the SUV and the baby. Now, law enforcement officials are saying that the alleged car thief may not have realized there was a baby in the vehicle when it was stolen. We've just been alerted—and this is just coming in as I'm reading it off the wire, so bear with me—that the Ford Explorer has been found. An anonymous tip was phoned in after the Amber Alert was issued. It's uncertain who called in and told law enforcement officials where they could find the vehicle. The SUV was found in a retail-shopping parking lot with the engine and air conditioner running and the baby…"

The announcer hesitated as if not prepared to read the rest on air, and Andrew expected the worst. He could see from Melanie's face that she did, too.

"The baby is fine. She appears to be just fine. She was found still strapped into her car seat and fast asleep. Again, I repeat, the SUV that was reported stolen earlier this morning has been found. The Amber Alert has been—"

Melanie snapped the radio off. But before she moved her hands to the bottom of the steering wheel, Andrew could see that they were shaking.

CHAPTER 66

12:22 p.m.

Melanie was tired of Jared bossing her around again. This way and then that way. Right then left. They were backtracking and still headed in the wrong fucking direction, and she knew it. And it wasn't about keeping off the interstate or confusing law enforcement officials. No, Jared had something else planned. She could feel it. And he wasn't telling her again. Just like he wouldn't tell her about the baby. How hard would it have been to tell her the baby was okay, instead of simply saying he had taken care of things?

She glanced over at Charlie, sitting next to her reading another comic book. He was quiet and content, no sign of this morning's outburst. She didn't want to think about that again. It only made her angry, angry that Jared would involve Charlie in this.

It was Jared's fault. All of it. The entire mess. She knew she should be relieved that Jared hadn't killed that little baby. Only a monster would do something like that, a monster like her father. And, no matter how angry she was with Jared, she knew he wasn't any more a monster than she was.

She looked up in the rearview mirror and Andrew Kane's eyes were there to meet hers. He was watching her, studying her as if trying to figure her out. Maybe he was grateful she hadn't let Jared kill him back at the hotel. Maybe he simply wondered what would happen next. She ignored him and looked, instead, for patrol cars. Most of them would have been busy this morning looking for a white SUV and not a black Toyota Camry. They were sticking to the two-lane highways, although from the signs she knew they were approaching the interstate again. After driving north and away from it, here they were again driving south toward it.

"We have to make a stop," Jared said suddenly. "I want you to get on the interstate and head west."

"I thought we were avoiding Interstate 80."

"There's a truck stop. It shouldn't be too far."

"You're hungry again?" It couldn't be much after noon yet.

"No, we're not eating there. I need to pick something up."

"What can you possibly pick up at a truck stop?"

"Just do what I fucking tell you to do, Mel."

Her face burned. Her hands balled into fists

around the steering wheel. She kept her mouth shut and her eyes ahead. Sometimes he reminded her of her father, and this was one of those times.

CHAPTER 67

1:40 p.m.
Triple J Truck Stop—East of Normal, Nebraska

Pakula watched from the tinted windows of the TV-repair van. His knees still felt a little unsteady but he was glad to be back on the ground. And he was glad he wasn't in charge. All this firepower made him nervous.

He was used to Omaha—a river valley with lots of hills and trees and buildings. Out here, where the landscape couldn't be much flatter and there were wide-open spaces where you could see for miles, there wasn't anywhere to hide. He thought for sure Barnett would be able to spot something: the reflection of a rifle scope or even a black boot on the rooftop of the deserted gas station across the road. There weren't any fucking trees. Just the parking lot, a long expanse of concrete surrounded by flat pastures of grass.

They didn't even know what kind of vehicle Barnett was driving now. Although they did know from Kramer who was with him—his sister and seventeen-year-old nephew. And hopefully—Pakula prayed—Andrew. He had reminded Sanchez several times about Andrew and asked what precautions were being taken. Did the SWAT team know they had a hostage? Had they seen pictures of Andrew as well as Jared? How would they know the difference between the two? How could they guarantee they wouldn't make a mistake?

Sanchez only shrugged and told him there were no guarantees with anything. Pakula knew he himself was sounding more like a civilian than a law enforcement officer. He knew the risks and had always been willing to take them, but in the past it had always been a matter of taking the risks for himself, not for a friend. Not for a friend he already felt responsible for.

"Almost two," Sanchez announced into his headset, and Pakula braced himself, his body stiffening just as it had earlier right before the Black Hawk had taken off. In retrospect, that part had been a cakewalk.

CHAPTER 68

1:56 p.m.

Melanie parked in the last slot in the corner, exactly where Jared instructed, away from the door of the truck stop. She cut the engine, but he made no attempt to leave the car. Instead, he sat back in the seat, looking out the rear windows, looking up as if expecting something to come out of the sky.

"Didn't you say you had to pick something up here?" she asked.

"Yeah, wait a minute. Something's not right." He slouched down in the seat. "I left the gun in the glove compartment," he said. "Charlie, get it for me."

Melanie reached for the compartment before Charlie could. She opened it, hesitated, took a deep breath and wrapped her fingers around the gun. It felt so odd and yet familiar and not quite as heavy as she remembered.

"Tell me what's going on, Jared," she said, pulling the gun out and holding it in her lap.

"Give me the gun," Jared told her, but he stayed slouched down instead of reaching over the seat for it.

"Not until you tell me, Jared. No more secrets. What are we picking up?"

"Just some money. I had Max Kramer wire some money for us."

"Max Kramer?" She remembered the phone calls he had made to his attorney. Was it possible he was simply asking Kramer for help? "What makes you think you can trust him?"

"He got me off before, didn't he?"

"I thought he got you off because you weren't guilty."

"Yeah. That's what I meant." Jared's head and eyes kept darting around but he stayed low, which only made Melanie more nervous. "Don't worry about Kramer, Mel. I've got some insurance back in my room."

"What do you mean, insurance?"

"Melanie, give me the fucking gun. You know that I'm just trying to take care of you and me."

"What about Charlie?"

Melanie looked over at Charlie. He was sitting perfectly still, half slouched in his seat, following his uncle's example. He was always following Jared, doing exactly what Jared asked without question, without thought.

"Of course, Charlie, too. But you know, Mel, Charlie's been screwing up a lot. He's the reason we're in this fucking mess. Isn't that right, Charlie?"

She could see the boy cower from Jared's words and she was startled by the image of another boy, cowering, bracing himself, not for words, but for blows. Charlie reminded her exactly of Jared as a boy. And when she looked back at Jared she could see how much he now reminded her of her father. Why hadn't she seen it before? Jared's quick temper, his outbursts of rage. No, it wasn't possible.

"Charlie, I'm giving you a chance to make it all up," Jared told him, smoothing his voice into a tone Melanie used to believe was genuine. "I want you to go inside the truck stop. There'll be an envelope waiting. It's in your name. Just ask for it at the counter, okay? Can you do that, buddy?"

Charlie was nodding, and he reached for the car door, but Melanie stopped him.

"Don't, Charlie. You stay put."

"Melanie, stay the fuck out of this." Jared had already forgotten about his soft voice. His eyes were even more frantic now. What did they see? What was he expecting? Were there snipers waiting? Is that what he expected? Is that what he would let happen to Charlie?

She glanced over at Andrew Kane and he must have taken it as an invitation.

"Make a choice, Melanie," Andrew told her, softly, quietly. "This is the end of the road."

"Shut the fuck up." Jared punched the author in his wounded shoulder, then he crouched back down. "Charlie, go on in. And hurry the fuck up. We need to get the hell out of here."

"Charlie, stay put," Melanie told him, and that's when she understood what she needed to do, just like all those years ago. In a brief moment everything became so clear. She raised the gun and pointed it at Jared over the seat. He looked as if he wanted to laugh at her, until his eyes met hers.

"I choose Charlie," she said, and she pulled the trigger.

Monday, September 13

CHAPTER 69

10:30 a.m.

Grace wasn't sure why they were even humoring Melanie Starks; maybe she wanted to get Max Kramer more than she realized. Right now they had nothing concrete to connect him to the bank robbery. He had confessed to an affair with Tina Cervante and to giving her the locket with their initials. But that was all. He insisted he had no idea why Jared Barnett would target her in such a violent way.

Pakula led the way through the house. Corrine Starks had to let them in because of the search warrant, but she didn't have to be happy about it. One of the young officers Pakula brought along stayed downstairs with Ms. Starks, keeping her from interrupting their search, but the poor guy couldn't shut her up. However, her profanity seemed focused on her daughter, Melanie, calling her a murdering whore. Grace couldn't imagine being put in that position as a mother, choosing a son over a daughter, but then she couldn't imagine having a son like Jared Barnett.

The other officer stayed beside Melanie, keeping a close watch and leading her by the elbow, despite her hands being cuffed in front of her.

"Is this it?" Pakula asked Melanie when they came to the closed door at the end of the hallway.

"Yes," she said.

Pakula opened the door and went in first. He pulled a pair of latex gloves out of his pocket and started to put them on while he looked around the room.

"He said he had some kind of insurance," Melanie said. "I know it'll connect Jared and Max Kramer. I just know it."

It was a small room cluttered with piles of dirty clothes, magazines and boyhood things: a dartboard on the closet door, a baseball trophy and an autographed baseball amongst the empty take-out containers and wrappers. Grace couldn't help wondering if there was really something here or if Melanie Starks was conning them. She and her son, Charlie, were looking at a stack of felony charges that, if convicted, could mean the death penalty for both of them. They kept insisting—though Charlie Starks wasn't quite as convincing as his mother—that Jared Barnett had killed everyone in the bank, but the ballistics report showed two different guns had been used. The second gun, however, had never been found. As much as Grace believed Jared to be a cold-blooded killer, she couldn't see him going into the bank with two guns blazing like some Wild West bank robber.

"He used to hide things," Melanie was telling Pakula, "by stuffing them inside an ordinary object. You know, like a football or maybe a pillow."

Once again, Grace found herself wondering what made someone like Melanie Starks stand by while her brother killed six innocent people. Seven if they counted Danny Ramerez. His body had been discovered late Saturday in a Dumpster behind the Logan Hotel after residents complained of the smell. Ironically, he had been stuffed inside a black garbage bag not unlike the one Rebecca Moore's body had been found in seven years ago. Max Kramer's crack whore—who couldn't seem to get her story right about the convenience store robberies—was able to make a positive ID of Jared Barnett as the man she had seen hauling a black bag out of the Logan Hotel the night Danny Ramerez supposedly disappeared.

As for the convenience store robberies, Charlie Starks admitted—surprising even his mother—that Jared had used them only as practice runs. Charlie had scoped out each store then reported back to Jared who was waiting outside. The boy talked about it as if it were some game the two had played.

Grace crossed her arms and leaned against the doorway, watching Pakula search through Jared Barnett's closet, emptying shoeboxes of baseball cards and tossing out a couple of footballs, neither of which seemed to have any hidden compartments.

She glanced at Melanie Starks, trying to determine if she was, indeed, conning them, hoping to cut a deal for both her and her son. Life with the possibility of parole for Charlie and less time for her. Grace and her boss had agreed that, if Melanie Starks could, in fact, implicate Max Kramer as the mastermind of the bank robbery as well as the murder of Tina Cervante, it would be worth the deal. What an odd twist of fate it would be if Max Kramer, the defender of death row inmates, ended up on death row himself.

"I don't think there's anything here," Pakula said as he dug through the dresser drawers and looked under the bed. He shoved aside the piles of clothing and pulled back the bedcovers and suddenly there it was.

Grace knew as soon as she saw it. Underneath Jared Barnett's bedspread was Emily's stuffed white dog.

"It's Mr. McDuff," she said without realizing how ridiculous it probably sounded.

"Excuse me?" Pakula said.

Grace went over to the bed and picked up the stuffed animal. "Emily's been missing this since Wednesday. She kept telling me that the shadow man took it."

"The shadow man?" Pakula was looking at her

now as if she were nuts. Even Melanie looked confused.

"I think your brother must have taken it from my house."

"Why would he do that?"

Then Grace felt it. She found the slot cut into Mr. McDuff's back and, without pulling it out and contaminating it, she could see Jared Barnett had inserted an audiocassette. She held it up to show Pakula and Melanie.

"He must have known that I might be the one looking through his things, and of course, I wouldn't miss this. I think we have our evidence." And she looked to Melanie. "If this is what I think it is, you might have your deal."

Two years later
Manhattan, New York

Andrew Kane smiled up at Erin Cartlan as she handed him a bottled water.

"They're lined up out the front door," she said, pleased, referring to the line of people outside the door of her bookstore waiting to meet him and get an autographed copy of his new book.

"I hear it's your best yet," the brunette in front of him said, waiting for him to finish her inscription. "*East of Normal?* Wherever did you come up with that title?"

"You'll figure it out when you read the book," he answered.

"Is it true it's based on something that really happened to you?"

"You know book publicists," he said, keeping his

eyes down and scratching his name on the page. "They'll say anything to sell tons of books."

He handed her the book and that's when he saw her. She was in line, not ten feet away. He almost didn't recognize her. She was dressed in a tailored brown suit and her hair was cut short. She was actually very pretty. If he didn't know better he'd think she was a professional businesswoman and not an ex-convict out on parole. She waved when she saw him notice her. He waved her to the front of the line.

"Do you mind?" he asked the gentleman who was next and, of course, what could he say but no he didn't mind.

Andrew stood to greet her, not knowing what was appropriate. She saved him by offering her hand.

"God, Melanie, you look great. How long have you been…" He stopped himself before saying "out of jail," but he could see she knew the rest of the question.

"Only a couple of months."

"And how's Charlie?"

"Good. Really good. Three more years and he has his first parole hearing." She turned back to the long line, distracted and smiling when she said, "Look at you." Then she turned over the copy of his novel she had already picked up. "It's good. I like how you did it."

"Well, there are some things I used creative license with."

"I know." She smiled. She'd obviously already read the book and was pleased with her portrayal.

"How did you find out about…" and she leaned in, lowering her voice, "my father and, well, you know?"

"Mostly your mom and some newspaper articles. I suspected Jared had to kill him to end the abuse and that's partly why Jared was the way he was. Did I do okay?"

"Oh, yes, I loved the book," she said, hugging it to her. "Even if you did get a few things wrong or rather used creative…what was it?"

"Creative license. You know," and he pulled her aside, indicating to Erin and the waiting line of people that he'd only be another minute or two, "I never would have believed you were capable of doing what you ended up having to do."

"Really?" She leaned in close again. "What you didn't realize was that it wasn't the first time for me."

"Excuse me?" He wasn't sure what she meant.

"My father?" She looked around to make sure there was enough chatter behind her that she couldn't be overheard. "It wasn't Jared that night. He just cleaned up the mess."

Andrew stared at her, only now realizing what she was saying, that she had killed her father and not Jared.

"So can you autograph my copy to me and Charlie?"

AUTHOR'S NOTE

Like many other suspense writers I use bits and pieces about real-life crimes and killers in my novels. Through research and interviews I often discover fascinating details that inspire a plot twist of a killer's M.O. or an unusual piece of evidence. And always I hope it's these small details that add authenticity to my novels.

One False Move, however, came about in an entirely different way. In March of 2001 I retreated to my favorite cabin at Platte River State Park, isolating myself to finish my second novel, *Split Second.* My dogs and I were the only occupants out of the thirteen cabins that surround the lake. During our second evening I heard a helicopter flying low over the park. In a matter of minutes I learned that two men had robbed a bank in nearby Lincoln, Nebraska. By the time I heard the news they had already shot a farm couple in order to steal their pickup and were on the run. The state park was in the middle of the manhunt, and so was I.

The experience sparked the idea for *One False Move,* and that summer I scratched out pages of notes even though I knew I'd have to put them aside while I wrote two more Maggie O'Dell novels. In the fall of 2002 I pulled out the notes again in order to finally start writing. That same fall three men walked into a bank in Norfolk, Nebraska, with the intention of robbing it. Forty seconds later they left without any money, leaving five innocent people dead and triggering a state-wide manhunt. It was the deadliest bank robbery in Nebraska's history.

Although my idea for *One False Move* came a year and half before and was based on an entirely different bank robbery and manhunt, I was struck by some of the similarities. I talked to law enforcement officials and reporters who had been personally involved in the Norfolk case. Their experiences and stories gave me a greater appreciation for what I was writing about and most definitely enriched my novel.

Most of them were asking the same questions I had already been asking—why and how could anyone do something like this? What pushes some of us to do evil while others will never cross that line? If it's human nature to fight for survival, to what extremes are we willing to go? These are the same questions I seem to ask in every one of my novels. However, this time I realized the questions were not simply rhetorical. Both crimes had hit a bit too close to home. This time I was using bits and pieces of two separate crimes that had affected either me personally or people I knew.

It was one more reminder that truth is stranger than fiction. And although I write fiction, I now realize with the help of my readers that what I write might not be only for entertainment but can sometimes touch people in ways I never imagined or intended. This has definitely been an experience that has given me a new level of sensitivity to the crimes and characters I portray in my novels.

I want to thank all of those who shared their experiences with me concerning that fatal day in Norfolk in September 2002. And to the victims' families, I extend my deepest sympathy.

New York Times **Bestselling Author**

SUSAN WIGGS

Before an estranged couple is killed in an unthinkable tragedy, they designate two guardians for their children—Lily Robinson and Sean McGuire. Brought together by tragedy, the two strangers are joined in grief and their mutual love for these orphaned children. Sean and Lily are about to embark on the journey of ups and downs, and love and hope that makes a family.

"Wiggs has done an excellent job of depicting what lies beneath the surface of relationships…"
—*Booklist*

*Available April 2005,
wherever books are sold!*

*table
for
five*

MSW2167

ALEX KAVA

32055 AT THE STROKE OF MADNESS	___ $6.99 U.S.	___ $8.50 CAN.
66915 SPLIT SECOND	___ $6.99 U.S.	___ $8.50 CAN.
66824 A PERFECT EVIL	___ $6.99 U.S.	___ $8.50 CAN.
66701 THE SOUL CATCHER	___ $6.99 U.S.	___ $8.50 CAN.

(limited quantities available)

TOTAL AMOUNT	$ _____
POSTAGE & HANDLING	$ _____
($1.00 FOR 1 BOOK, 50¢ for each additional)	
APPLICABLE TAXES*	$ _____
TOTAL PAYABLE	$ _____

(check or money order—please do not send cash)

To order, complete this form and send it, along with a check or money order for the total above, payable to MIRA Books, to: **In the U.S.:** 3010 Walden Avenue, P.O. Box 9077, Buffalo, NY 14269-9077; **In Canada:** P.O. Box 636, Fort Erie, Ontario, L2A 5X3.

Name: _____
Address: _____ City: _____
State/Prov.: _____ Zip/Postal Code: _____
Account Number (if applicable): _____

075 CSAS

*New York residents remit applicable sales taxes.
*Canadian residents remit applicable GST and provincial taxes.

MIRA®

www.MIRABooks.com

MAK0405BL